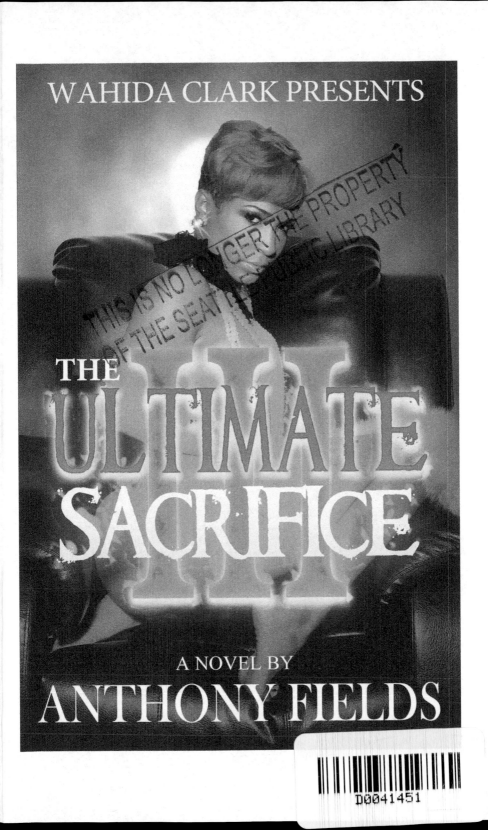

WAHIDA CLARK PRESENTS

# THE
# ULTIMATE
# SACRIFICE
III

A NOVEL BY
# ANTHONY FIELDS

This is a work of fiction. Names, characters, places, and incidents either are the product of the author's imagination or are used fictitiously, and any resemblance to actual persons, living or dead, business establishments, events, or locales are entirely coincidental.

Wahida Clark Presents Publishing
60 Evergreen Place
Suite 904
East Orange, New Jersey 07018
973-678-9982
www.wclarkpublishing.com

Library of Congress Cataloging-In-Publication Data:
Anthony Fields
The Ultimate Sacrifice III/ by Anthony Fields
ISBN 13-digit 978-19366493-5-8 (paper)
ISBN 10-digit 19366493-5-7 (paper)
LCCN 2012913559

1. Urban- 2. DC- 3. Drug Trafficking- 4. African American-
    Fiction-

Cover design and layout by Nuance_*Art*
Book design by Nuance_*Art*
Edited by Linda Wilson
Proofreader Rosalind Hamilton


Printed in USA

# ACKNOWLEDGEMENTS

As always my first acknowledgement is to the creator of all the worlds. All praise is due to Allah... To both my parents, Thomas Fields and Deborah Wiseman, who passed away before they could see their baby boy make it, you both shaped me into the man that I am. I love yall and rest in peace.

To my oldest sister Toi Wiseman, your support has been overwhelming and I truly appreciate it. Your love and generosity will one day be reciprocated. Give my love to Ashley, Danesha and Lil Dave. Give my respects to your other half, David Tucker. I appreciate you too, slim. Keep on keeping it 100 with the good men. To my nephews who are coming up in the game now, Asa and Abdul, this prison life is not for you two, but if you play the game, always play by the rules. To my nephews, Trayvon, Lil Buck and Lil Rob. Be careful in finding yall's way, the world is full of illusion. Learn to get out of your own way and be the men that you need to be. To my nieces, Chasity and Imani, I love ya'll. To my younger brothers, Dee and Dre, I'm sorry that we are not as close as we should be.

To Poochie, Rinda, Ebony, Lil Pat and Ashley, thanks for the support over the years. To Mrs. And Mr. Tucker, I really respect how you two have adopted me as your own. Thank you for all the love and support. A special shout out goes out to my son Kevin Grover. Youngin, you are my heart and now that you've ended up behind the wall, find yourself and struggle to become better. I love you. To my daughters, Aniyah and Destinee, I love you two with all my heart.

To all the good men in Canaan USP, hold me down. My success ids one for the whole team. To Mike Boone, Joseph "J-Rock" Gray, Reggie Quiller, Chuck (52$^{nd}$ St. NE), Hasan Givens, Derrick Taylor, Blue Black, Moody, Whop (B-More), Dee, Corn, Big Shaq, Cedar Gardens Omar, Boo, Face, Al Jeter, Dee (18$^{th}$ & M). Jay (58$^{th}$ Street), Fat Cat, Champ-Bey, Jugg, Taha, Fila Rob, Tony Hammond, Uconn Ron, Wayne Wayne, Black Junior, Eddie, Asay, Lou Medley, Scrap, Tim Tim, Big Shaq (Hobart), Tywan, Jay, Rob Barton, Donzell McCauley, Stinka, Chew (15$^{th}$ & Death Row), Lil Mike, Kevin, Que, P.J., Hubcap, Trey Manning, Goody Bey, Ed, Face, Ced, Cat eye Kay Kay, Black Drew from the old Barry Farms, Fats, Football, Ball, Black Pete, Bam, Khalid, Butch, Red Peete, Shaggy Dog, Ugg, Shorty Black, and others. To all my Baltimore homies – Bobby Steele, Mel, Terry, Cakes, Que and E. To my Crip homies who read all my books and support me --- To Hoover Rell, Hoover Love, Crook and Day Day. To Big Kiko from the East Coast Block Crips, to all my Blood homies – S.I. (Garland Tyree), Head, Boo and others.

To Khalif Mujahid, Nick, Tone, Erick Hicks, Luke, Smiley, Toe, Butch Woods, Itchy, Fat Koola, Tonio Jones, Jerry McCullough, Tinyman, Cadoza, Steve, Bone, Randy Shaw, Marvin, Fat Bug, Moe Styles, Joe Joe Green, Andy, Scoop Hagans, Cortez Carroll, Playboy, Pork (Moe Johnson), Lil Eric Weaver, Chin, Draper, Jazz, Coo Wop, Twan, B.F. Simpson, Youngboy Tay (Dante Allen), Spree, Sconey, Dontay Steward, Jihad, Ronzell, Ki-Whop, C-Rock, Cortez Gaitlin, Money, Jontay, Pinball, Crank, Lil Kamau, Chez, Big Dawg, Pretty B, Lil Carl Meade, Wellin Wayne (B.F.), Tyrone Carter, La La, Lil Dave Burris, Marquise, Lonnie(the one that Veron 'Boo' Dammons told on), Cartoon.

To my fellow authors that represent the genre --- to Jason Poole, Eyone Williams, Nate Welch, Cash and Victor L. Martin. To Ne Ne Capri and Tiphani Montgomery --- keep doing what yall do. To Michael Rozelle (I hope you get on. Ock.)

To all the book clubs that support Anthony Fields --- thank you. To ARC BOOK CLUB, READERS IN MOTION, BOSS READERS BOOK CLUB, URBAN REVIEWS, COAST 2 COAST READERS. APOO BOOK CLUB AND OOSA. Without you and the fans that hold me down, I'd be nothing. So here's my chance to say thank you to --- Ms. Janice X, Vanessa Meadows, Melanie West, Abrienne M. Suggs, Katherine Riasco, Tambudzai Blake, Yvette Williams (ATL), Shante Harris- Hannon, Michelle Lawson (B-More), Magdelina Williams, Locksie, Melody Kearney, Toy Smith, Crystal Gamble-Noble, Ms. Toni Doe, Nina Marie, A. Bracey, Passion 814, Keisha Z. Noel, Cutelady 113, Michelle Renee Rawls, Sunshine 123, Rosemarie Phipps, Andre White, Cassandra D. Summers, Kenya L. Oneal, Khadijah Kemp, Kim Robinson, Tami Orr-Brisco, Selena Eleby, Tiffany "Diva Divine" Simpson, Sheba Morris, Rita King, Kim Cosby, Shirley Crawford, Victoria Gibson-Bivins Canaday, Shonda Devaugh, Gmerice Riddick, Minah, Drren Lowery, Lisa Tyrell-Perry, Larissa Robinson, Nate Nati Holmes, Kathy Jackson Adams, M. Diggins (Virgin Islands), Ms. Pitts, Mocha "Kia", Mo Betta, Reda, Shantay N. Riley, Bookfiend 77, Rita Smith King, Leona Romich, Latasha Hall, The Ice Queen, Rhonda Thomas, Victorious Woman (Highpoint, N.C.), Lady T., MLC "Ns. Mimi", Ms. Toy (Dallas, TX), Julia A. Miller, Tazzy T2 Bossy E, Laquita Adams, The Literary Book Joint, Lakisha Benson, Sistar Tea, S. Colbert, Hotchklate, Tekesha King, Tammy "Meme" Herbert, Tiah Short and DC Book Diva Publications, Maxine Smith (Aurora, ll), Rebecca O' Connell, and Ulah Batchelor, Darlene Parks, T. Davis aka Chyna Dahl.

To my special friend Dolita Wilhike --- thank you for all of your letters, and support. Keep striving to be a better you. Hold me down when you touch down. Be safe and sweet and sexy. New Orleans in the house, but how about them Redskins and RGlll?!

To Wahida Clark and WCP, thanks for the opportunity to bring my stories to the people. The reader are what matter most and I try to give them the best of me everytime. To all my fans and supporters that I didn't mention, thank you and get at me so that I wont forget to mention you again.

To everybody in the DMV and beyond, hold me down. To Randall Bagley, you are my partna, hold me down. To the dude that made all this possible Michael "BX Cue" Williams, thank you for all the typing and editing and ideas you gave me. We gotta get ready for the next one. To all the aspiring authors behind the fence, keep striving to become published. Let no one stand in your way.

To everybody everywhere --- One Love.
I can be reached at:
Anthony Fields #16945016
USP Canaan
PO Box 300
Waymart, Pa. 1847
D.C. stand up!!!
Buckey Fields

# The Ultimate Sacrifice III: No Regrets

## A Novel

### By

# Anthony Fields

# DEDICATION

This book is dedicated to all the good men locked down in Supermaxes everywhere, And to all the good men on death row. To David Jackson, T. Hager, Joseph Ebron, Khalifa A. Mujahid, Henry James, Delmant Player, Pat Beamon, Pat Andrews, Kevin Bellinger and countless others. This one's for you. Hold your head!

This book is also dedicated to Toni McDaniels, who told me that readers don't want sequels and trilogies anymore. Had I listened to that advice, there would be no Ultimate Sacrifice III. You motivated me to go all out on this one. Bottoms up

# CHAPTER ONE

## Shawnay

My eyes had to be deceiving me. They couldn't be seeing that smile. That smile attached to that face. And that face hadn't changed much in years. It was still one of the most handsome faces I had ever seen. At 5'11" he still seemed to tower over me although I stood on my elevated front porch, and he stood on the sidewalk. His skin appeared to be kissed by the sun itself. His once 'spinning until dizzy' head full of waves was gone, replaced by a smooth baldhead. His goatee was freshly trimmed. The silver Hugo Boss drawstring sweatshirt was baggy, but his physique underneath could not be hidden.

"Better late than never . . . "he said as his eyes stared straight through me.

"Huh?"

"Better late than never. Before you opened the door, you said, 'You're early, aren't you?' Evidently you weren't talking to me because you didn't know it was me. So in all actuality, I'm late. Eleven years late, but I'm here. That's why I said 'Better late than never.' Were you expecting someone?"

"No . . . Yes, but how? How did . . . you . . ." Suddenly, emotion overwhelmed me and my knees buckled. His last message to me from the bearded man crossed my mind. Is he here to kill me?

"How did I what? How . . . did I get out of prison, or how did I get your address? Which one?" Antonio asked. That smile never left his face.

"Uh . . . both . . . I guess. I mean . . . I can't believe it . . ."

"I'm here. Standing in your doorway. A person from your past that has come back to change your future. Don't look so shocked, Shawnay. Aren't you happy to see me? I'm still standing after you crossed me and hurt me so bad it knocked me to my knees. You never thought you'd have to answer to me, huh? You thought that by moving to Virginia and severing all ties with me that I'd never find you. You never thought I'd face you in this lifetime and see the stain of betrayal on you. How can I not see it when you wear it like a scarlet letter on your clothes, in your eyes. You didn't think that I'd ever find out about you and Khadafi? Did you? About your son Kashon?"

My heart stopped and time froze. I became afraid. Antonio knew everything. I couldn't even try to lie. "Antonio . . . please . . ."

He took a step forward and put a finger to my lips. Then he kept coming forward until I backed up into the foyer of my house. Paralyzed with fear, I watched his every move. Antonio reached behind him and shut my front door. Then he locked it without even looking back.

"Where are my daughters?" he asked. "Your son?"

"They are at my grandmother's house. I have to pick them up soon. They will come here . . . please don't hurt me."

"Hurt you? Why would I do that? Because you let Khadafi fuck you? Because you probably sucked his dick and gave him some ass. Did you give him some ass?"

"Antonio . . . please . . ."

5

# THE ULTIMATE SACRIFICE III: NO REGRETS

"Okay, I won't ask questions that I can't stomach the answers to. But I would never hurt you. How could I hurt the one person that I love so much?"

"The man with the beard . . . you sent him," I muttered, "to kill me."

Without saying another word, Antonio pulled me close. He hugged me tight and whispered in my ear, "I would never do that." Then his lips found my neck. Antonio kissed my face and my lips and sparks began to fly. All those old feelings I thought were long gone resurfaced and intensified. My whole body caught fire for the man that I once loved more than life itself. My arms moved on their own as I embraced him. My hands probed his rock-solid body. Under his sweatshirt I rubbed his chiseled stomach and his chest. Our tongues explored each other's mouth, and in the background I could've sworn that R. Kelly was somewhere singing "I Believe I Can Fly." I felt as if I could levitate. His touch, his tongue, his smell had me above the seven heavens. Antonio's fingers skillfully undid the button on my pants and unzipped my zipper. I couldn't stop him even if I wanted to. He was a man possessed, and who was I to deny him this moment? His moment. I opened up and invited him to my love, my nectar, my sex. I felt his fingers slide into my panties and enter me while his thumb slowly massaged my clit. A sudden climax came down on me and gripped me tighter than the embrace his powerful arms had just held me in.

Seconds later, my hips gyrated and then my love slipped out of me and onto Antonio's fingers. I felt as if I would suffocate. "Breathe . . . Breathe . . ." I reminded myself. Wanting to return the favor, my fingers found his zipper. Then my palm was full of him. I gripped the dick that I had fallen in love with as a teenager and caressed it, rubbed its head, and spread pre cum all over it. My stomach growled and my body

6

told me that I was hungry. But not for food. I wanted to taste him and then feel him deep inside me. It had been eleven years since I'd seen it, touched it, kissed it, sucked on it or rode it.

I wiggled myself out of Antonio's one arm embrace and pulled his hand from my pants. Dropping to my knees, I gripped the two fingers he had just used to make me cum and put them in my mouth. I sucked on them for a while and then licked every finger on that hand. Then I reached into his pants and pulled his dick free. My mouth found him, and I sucked that man's dick as if his cum was my life's blood. I sucked him as if he was the oxygen I needed to breathe. Greedily, I ate him. I had to remember to breathe . . . Eleven years . . . breathe . . . Eleven years had passed since I'd last tasted him . . . breathe . . . I needed to bridge that gap in time. I wanted to beg for his forgiveness, but for the moment, forgiveness would come in the form of his essence, his seed, and his semen. Antonio's moans filled the hallowed halls of my foyer, and they turned me on more and more. The more I got turned on, the bolder I became.

I slurped and gagged and gagged and slurped until most of his dick was in my throat. "Shawnay . . . oooh baby, suck that dick!" It didn't take long before Antonio came in gushes that flowed right down my throat.

I kept right on sucking him . . . breathe . . . breathe . . . and sucking him until he rose again. I was fully caught up in the moment. I wanted to stay on my knees, but he pulled me up. Antonio looked me in the eyes and then kissed me full on the mouth. He led me to the stairs that led up to my living room, and then he pushed me gently until I was sitting on the fourth step. Antonio pulled my pants down and off. Then my panties were next. He dropped to his knees on the bottom step and spread my legs. I sat back and leaned on my elbows, giving myself over to him completely. Breathe . . . Breathe . . .

Breathe . . . All I could do was throw my head back and grip his baldhead as his tongue found my center. My heart swelled as my toes curled. Antonio resurrected feelings inside me that were long ago buried. His signature moves on and around my pussy were patented inside me. I knew them well, my body knew them well, and we both screamed for more. Every inch of my womanhood was licked, kissed, and nibbled.

It didn't take long for me to cum again. My juices glistened all over his moustache. But that wasn't enough. I pressed his face firmly into me and let his nose, lips, and tongue bring me to another body rattling orgasm. I felt epileptic, so completely closed off in a box of pleasure that I never realized Antonio had stopped licking me until he entered me. My eyes clenched tightly as my legs opened wider to accommodate him. All I could do was bite down on my bottom lip as he pushed himself deeper and deeper into me, stretching me, filling me.

Breathe . . . breathe . . . "Oooowww! An . . . tonio! It hurts—baby—please—" I moaned through clenched teeth.

Antonio hooked one of my legs in the crook of his arm and leaned it all the way back to where my foot was on his shoulder, and my toes were damn near touching the step above me. He was gentle at first, but then without warning or provocation, he pounded into me with angry strokes. I hollered out in pain and ecstasy.

Antonio's frustration showed itself while being released upon me . . . breathe . . . breathe . . .

"Did Khadafi fuck you like this? Did you scream out his name? Was his dick as good as mine? Can he go deep like me? Did I ever cross your mind as you fucked him? How could you let him shoot his seed into you?"

The pressure built up inside of me, and I felt myself about to cum again. I heard the questions that Antonio riffed off in rapid succession, but I didn't dare answer. How could I answer those questions and not tell the truth? I wanted to tell him to just shut the fuck up and keep long-dicking me. I wanted to let him know that I was about to cum all over his dick. I wanted to tell him that his dick was inside my stomach, and it hurt so good. I wanted to beg him to never stop fucking me, but the only words that came out my mouth was, "Antonio, damn I love you! I never stopped and I never will."

Without saying another word, Antonio continued to pound into me. Then suddenly he lifted me off the steps. His rock-hard dick remained inside me as he carried me up about four stairs and into the living room. Both of my legs were now hooked into his arms as he stood in the middle of the floor and fucked me. My arms were wrapped around his neck as my head rolled backward. Antonio's stand-up fuck game was one in a million, and I loved every minute of it.

"Did you love me while you was fucking my man?" Antonio asked. "Did you love me when you was sucking his dick? Cummin' on his dick? Swallowing his cum? Did you give him some of that phat ass?"

Again I remained silent. Antonio must have figured that my silence was incriminating because he stopped with the questions and dropped me down onto my La-Z-Boy recliner. "Then again, forget that I asked you any of that shit. Maybe it's best if you don't answer. Just show me what I been missing out on. Make me cum again."

As I gripped Antonio's dick and got my best rendition of Vanessa Del Rio on, I felt a vibration under my leg. At first I thought it was my body tingling all over, but as the feeling persisted, I realized that I was sitting on my cell phone. I wanted to ignore the caller, but remembered my house phone was forwarded to my cell phone, and the caller might be one of my kids or my grandmother. Without breaking my stride, I used my free hand to reach under me and get my cell phone. I opened my eyes and focused on the caller ID. Khadafi. I had totally forgotten about our date for seven o'clock. Shaking my head to clear the cobwebs from between my ears, I held the cell phone in front of me and knew that I had to answer it. "Hello?"

I listened to every word Khadafi said and responded accordingly. Then I ended the call. Looking up from the phone, I noticed that Antonio had disappeared. Automatically I looked down and noticed I was fully clothed, but my pants were open and my hand was inside my panties. The clock on my phone read 7:03 p.m. Realization set in, and I had no choice but to laugh at myself. The last fifty minutes or so I had been asleep. My sexcapade with Antonio had been a dream, a wet dream, an interactive wet dream. I remembered exactly when I first sat down exhausted and closed my eyes.

I pulled my soaking wet fingers out of my panties, dropped my cell phone, and stood up. Khadafi had called and cancelled our date. He begged me to reschedule, and I agreed. Heading up the stairs, I disrobed as I went. I needed a shower, wanted a shower badly. It would be my only chance to use my rabbit and play with my pussy before I picked up my kids.

# CHAPTER TWO

## Khadafi

As bad as I wanted to see Shawnay, I accepted the fact that it wasn't meant to be. I was halfway to her house when I got the call from Kemie's mother telling me to come to the hospital. So I turned off of I-66 West at the next exit and headed the other way to Prince George's hospital. All kinds of terrible thoughts filled my mind as I struggled to digest what was hidden behind the few words that Brenda Bryant had said. "It's Kemie! Come to the hospital right now."

I feared the worst, but hoped for the best as I cautiously did the speed limit on the interstate. To calm myself, I thought about Shawnay and my son. My son Kashon. For the life of me, I still couldn't believe I fathered a child, a child by Shawnay of all people. Ameen's baby mother, Shawnay, was now my baby mother. Our kids were siblings, and that meant Ameen and I were forever bound together by blood and sacrifice. I couldn't believe how things had turned out. If somebody would've told me three and a half years ago that everything would be as it was now, I wouldn't have believed it. Never. Not in a million years. My mind took me back to that time . . .

In 2007, before going to Beaumont USP, I was in Atlanta Pen with a childhood buddy named Mousey. Every day that Mousey and I walked the track in Atlanta, all he talked about was his codefendant Keith, whom he had grown up with. They were like brothers from the same mother, different fathers.

11

THE ULTIMATE SACRIFICE III: NO REGRETS

They went on a caper to rob a dude from Florida who had come to DC and set up shop. The robbery turned into a double homicide, and Mousey and Keith got away clean. After running his mouth to a couple niggas in the hood, cops got wind of the culprits and vamped down on Keith. Keith turned on Mousey and testified against him in court. I, more than anybody, knew the pain that lived in his heart every day. Keith was somebody that he loved. Love is pain. Having been betrayed by a friend before and being in prison for killing him, I vowed to Mousey that if I ever crossed paths with Keith I'd kill him.

Being a man of my word, when I heard that Keith Barnett was on his way to Beaumont Pen, I plotted his death. And then carried it out with the assistance of four friends—Ameen, Umar, Boo, and Lil Cee. I chopped Keith's bitch ass up into pieces and left his remains in a green duffle bag in the shower room.

The institution was placed on lock down, and all my men and I were rounded up and put in SHU. All except one of us, Lil Cee. For some reason, Lil Cee was separated from us. Where he went, we had no clue. Under the shadow of a murder charge, and with the death penalty looming, we assumed that Lil Cee had snitched. After about ninety days in the hole, the reality of the four of us being stuck on the murder charge that I and only I was guilty of, dawned on everyone. Ameen decided that he would cop to the body.

He figured that since he already had almost fifty years to do, he could do whatever number the Feds wanted to give out for the murder. His rationale was that since Umar, Boo, and I were all going home in the next eight to twelve months, it made no sense that all of us would be stuck in ADX on lock down. So after a lot of discussion and tears, Ameen made the

Ultimate Sacrifice for us. All he asked for in return was that we take care of his family.

Eight months later, I went home on a mission. I killed Lil Cee's mother and three-year-old sister as soon as I got off the plane and made it to Southeast, DC. With my ride or die bitch, Kemie by my side, I put on for my city and terrorized it at the same time. In four months' time, I was responsible for the deaths of fifteen people.

In the midst of all that, I started fucking Ameen's baby mother, Shawnay. I was wrong and I knew it, but she was a temptation that I couldn't resist. She was my yin to Kemie's yang. The exact opposite of a ride or die chick, and I fell in love. Somehow, someway, Ameen found out I was fucking Shawnay. But I never knew that he knew.

In December of 2008, I had a fight with Kemie at home that caused the neighbors to call the police. That night I was arrested for domestic violence and taken to Upper Marlboro Detention Center. Four and a half months later, I was sent back to Beaumont Pen for violating my parole. Not even twenty-four hours later, Ameen pulled out a homemade shank and stabbed me seven times. As blood leaked out of me and onto the pavement, I thought I was gonna die. For some reason known only to Allah, I survived. But the damage was done. The man that I loved, the one who had freely taken a murder charge for me so that I could be free, had tried to kill me because I fucked his woman.

Early 2010, I went back to the streets, scarred, hurt, and vengeful. I allowed myself about a half a year to get situated and healed, mentally and emotionally. Then I went back on the prowl. I became death all over again and everybody that crossed me felt my wrath.

My first victim was Tony Coleman's baby mother, Shayla. At a little after 12 a.m., I caught her closing up the restaurant where she worked. I ran up on her and crushed her ass, point blank range. My partner TJ was with me.

With no other visible targets left to kill, I started to focus on my money again. My stash was getting low, and I hated a low stash. The first person that came to mind was Lijah Smith, my uncle Marquette's girlfriend at the time of his death. Too consumed with grief and vengeance, I totally forgot about Lijah having all of his money until then. I made it my business to pay Lijah a visit at the house that she shared with my uncle. I surprised her and some nigga she had in the house, and after getting the money that she had left, I killed them both. My stash was a little better, but not like I wanted it to be. So I hooked up with my partner TJ, who had a zest for money and killing just like me and went on a caper. An old head, LaLa, another known killer rounded out our trio. We went into a house on Canal Street in Southwest, DC and killed muthafuckas. The take for that caper was 100 pounds of weed, 19 keys of cocaine, 350 thousand dollars and a rack of guns. We divided all that shit equally.

Along the way, I ended up killing the rat piece of shit that put us down with the caper. This nigga Mark Johnson was a gangster rat. The worse kind of rat. So I left his ass down the wharf with the foul-smelling ass fish.

Then a rack of strange shit started happening. Both of Ameen's brothers got killed on the same day, and a few other bodies fell. I knew something was going on, but I couldn't figure out what until one day down Capers, two niggas tried to ambush me and kill me.

We had a shootout in the middle of the street, but no one was hit. That day I realized my attacker was no one other than Lil Cee. He looked different, but it was him. I hadn't seen his hot ass since 2007, and there he was tryna kill me. I shut down shop and started hunting for his ass, but I couldn't find him. A few weeks later, he found me.

We were at an all white party. TJ, LaLa, and I had gone to chill and party with the bitches. It was our night off. No gangsta shit intended. At the bar, Lil Cee bumped into me. We had a verbal confrontation and then shit got physical. Him and his man, a black baldheaded nigga jumped me, and that night I tried to kill him, but his bitch ass ran and got away. But the baldheaded nigga wasn't so lucky. I opened his head up on the parking lot, along with a few innocent muthafuckas. That night turned out to be a wild night. That same night, the old head LaLa took the cops on a high-speed chase and then leapt off the bridge and into the river. His body never surfaced, and he was never seen again. Helluva way for a gangsta to go out. If he did in fact go out.

Then came the drama. I found out from Marnie (Kemie's friend that I had been fucking off and on for the last couple of years), that she was pregnant with my child.

I knew exactly what would happen if Kemie found out about that, so I left her ass. Had I not, Kemie would've had two bodies under her belt instead of one. But just as things started to calm down and go back to normal, Kemie rushed out of the house one day only saying that something had happened to her cousin Reesie. That day she discovered that her cousin was dead and then somebody tried to kill Kemie.

# CHAPTER THREE

## Khadafi

Rain drops pelting the windshield of my Escalade snapped my reverie, and I focused on the road. I hit the button to activate the windshield wipers. It didn't take long for the rhythmic sounds of the wipers to lull me back into a reflective state. My son came to mind, and the day I bumped into Shawnay in the cafeteria. That's what changed my life forever. The day I laid eyes on my son. Kashon Tariq Dickerson's face and his curly hair lit up the HDTV screen in my mind. I knew without a doubt that he was an eight month old version of me. I navigated my way to the hospital as if I were programmed to autopilot. All the while thinking a child, a son, could possibly tamper with my cloak of invincibility and make me vulnerable. The way Money's father William Smith had been. I remembered telling him that as a father he could create more sons, but if I killed him, his son could not replace his father. That night a father chose to die for his son.

Thoughts of Kashon led to other thoughts of the child that Marnie now carried, and the one that Kemie had lost. Who had Kemie been pregnant by? And why didn't she ever tell me that she was pregnant? Was that a sign of her guilt? Had she known that Phil was that baby's father? Silently, I prayed that Kemie would wake up from her coma so that I could ask her these questions and then kill her myself if she gave the wrong answers. When one life ends, a new life begins . . . I quickly flashed back to the night Marnie told me that she was pregnant. I grabbed my cell phone from my lap and dialed Marnie's number. Her voicemail picked up after three rings. I was about to leave a message, but then decided against it. I needed to talk to her or better yet, I needed to see her. A visit to her house was now a part of my plans for later.

Thinking of Kemie and Marnie made me think about Reesie. Kemie's cousin was dead and nobody knew why. I dialed another phone number and listened to it ring. Again, I got no answer on TJ's phone. Where the hell is cuz? And why ain't he answering his phone? I hadn't spoken to TJ since the day we kidnapped Phil.

I figured that he had to know about Kemie getting shot and Reesie's death. Was he distraught and mourning in his own private way? He had to be. That was all I could think of to explain his silence. When TJ's voicemail picked up, I left a message. "Get at me, cuz. No matter what you going through, get at me. One love."

By the time I turned into the parking lot of Prince George's County Hospital, the rain had lightened up, and it was almost pitch black outside, but the parking lot was well lit.

Shawnay crossed my mind one last time as I climbed out the truck and tucked two 9 milli's in the waist of my jeans. I zipped my black and red Prada jacket up and covered the guns. Throwing my hood up and on to keep my braids from getting wet and frizzy, I headed for the entrance to the hospital.

On the fourth floor, the smell of sanitizer and hospital food assaulted my nostrils. There was another smell as well, and I tried not to focus on it. But the smell of blood and death were unmistakable and unrelenting.

Several of Kemie's relatives, who had been camped out at the hospital even longer than me congregated in the chairs outside her room. Suddenly, my heart rate quickened as I approached the room. Why were her relatives crying and being consoled? Upon seeing Kemie as I entered the room, I was relieved to see that her condition hadn't changed since I'd left earlier that day. Kemie's face was still bloated, and her head was bandaged. Some of her gold tipped dread locks hung loosely and surrounded her face. A tube extended from a respirator and into her mouth. Another tube filled both her nostrils, and an IV drip flowed into her right arm at the wrist. Her breathing was calm, and according to the machines beside her bed, her heart rate and blood pressure were normal.

Glancing over to the chair by the window, I saw Brenda Bryant, whose eyes were glued to the TV. The evening news was on.

" . . . Russell Lambert sentenced two Southeast men to prison time today. Antwan Ball and David 'CooWop' Wilson were sentenced to eighteen years and fifty years. Ball and Wilson were alleged co-leaders of the notorious Congress Park Crew. Supporters of Antwan Ball gathered outside the US District Court to decry what they feel is an obvious war on young black men in the Southeast area."

Brenda Bryant looked up and saw me standing there. She clicked the TV off and stood up to face me. Her eyes were red from crying. "Did you know that Kemie was pregnant?"

"Not until the doctor told me they aborted the baby the other day. Right after her first surgery."

"That would've been my first grandbaby," she responded and stared off into a space behind me somewhere.

"Kemie found out she was pregnant about a month ago. I believe it was around the time when she couldn't find you, and you ended up being in the hospital. She was happy as hell initially, but then she became very afraid. She wouldn't say much, but I knew why. I've never been the type to get in y'all relationship, but obviously I knew about her love for you and what she felt for Phil. I was the one there for her when he broke Kemie's heart while you were in prison. That was a rough time for her, and she went through a lot. Eventually, she got over him, and she promised me that she'd never go down that road again.

"I believed her, but I also know my daughter. I knew how fickle she could be when it comes to matters of the heart. I couldn't blame her for it, though, because it's the Bryant curse. All the Bryant women have inherited the same disease of the heart. I went through it with Kemie's father, my sister with Reesie's father and now Tera's father. Reesie and TJ. Kemie and you. Kemie and Phil. We always love the wrong men. The men that are no good for us. Even our mother had the disease." A tear fell from her eye and she swiped at it with her backhand.

"My daughter and I were a lot alike. We shared a bond that went beyond the mother and daughter thing. I guess that was because I was practically a child myself when I had Kemie. When I learned that Kemie had picked up with Phil after you went back to prison on that violation, I was livid. I told her she was playing with fire for believing she could have both of you, even after you came back home. DC is too small is what I told her. Somebody's gonna tell Khadafi. He's gonna find out and someone is gonna get hurt. But you know Kemie, she wouldn't listen to me. That girl has always been too headstrong. Just like her no good ass daddy. No matter what I did or said, it didn't matter. Phil had his hooks back into Kemie, and as sure as her last name is Bryant, I knew that she wouldn't let go. Kemie came by the house one day and told me that she was pregnant. She had missed a period and did two home pregnancy tests. For some reason she wanted to give you a child. 'It will slow him down. May change his attitude about the way he lives in the streets.' That's what she said to me.

Always the visionary, but she couldn't see the forest for all the leaves on the trees.

"Then the reality of the baby not being yours crossed her mind. That's when she became afraid. She knew you'd kill her, the baby, and Phil. She cried a lot that day. Being the voice of reason, I begged her to abort the baby, stop seeing Phil, and start anew.

"You know what she said? 'I can't take a life, Ma.' That's what my baby said to me. She said the baby had a right to live just like everybody else. She couldn't take a life. So she decided to keep the baby, stay quiet about paternity, and deal with the consequences later. After all, there was a possibility that the baby was yours.

"So imagine my state of mind a couple of weeks later when my daughter comes to the house and breaks down again. I thought the pregnancy was making the girl go crazy, ya know? Fuckin' with her emotions. So naturally I was floored when Kemie told me that she had killed Phil. I didn't believe her until she told me the whole story. Something that she had weeks before, so adamantly told me that she couldn't do, she'd done. She'd taken a human life. That pill was hard enough to swallow, but what she said next chilled me to the bone. I asked her why she was crying. Her reply was 'I'm crying, Ma, but not one of my tears is for Phil. Phil didn't love me. He never loved me. Today I realized that. My tears are tears of joy because I cut loose the shackles of Phillip Bowman off my ankles. I cry because today I solidified my bond with Khadafi and proved to him that my love for him is the only real love I know.' Being with you was her preordained position in life, she said." Silence filled the space for a few seconds.

"Do you know what a DNR is, Khadafi?" Brenda asked me.

By now I had tears in my eyes threatening to fall. I shook my head.

"A few minutes before I called you. I spoke to Kemie's doctor. He asked me to sign a DNR. DNR means 'Do Not Resuscitate.' He said it would be easier on everybody to not resuscitate my baby if her heart was to fail. He said her body is taking a beating, and it might be best to let her go if that happened. It took all of my strength inside me not to curse his ass out. I refused to sign the DNR. Why should I? My baby is gonna make it. She's gonna wake up from all this and get back to her old self. Kemie is a fighter and nobody knows that better than me and you. The reason I called you here is because I know firsthand the type of pain you feel. It's written all over your face and mine too.

"And as bad as I want to kill whoever did this to my baby, I refuse to. I have done a lot of wrong in my life, and I believe that past sins are sometimes revisited on the kids. I feel that it's my fault that my daughter is—"

"But how can you—"

"How can I what? Feel that it's my fault? Because I can and I do. I have never asked you for anything ever. As long as I been knowing you—I saw the way that you threw money around. I know how you live, but I never asked you for anything. Well, today I'm asking you to honor and respect my wishes."

"Your wishes? What wishes?" I asked, looking vexed.

"I want this continuing cycle of violence to stop. Today. With Kemie. My wish is that you let it go. Let God deal with whoever did this to Kemie. Vengeance is mine saith the Lord. Whoever shot Kemie will get theirs. Let God handle it. I want you to stop killing, Khadafi. Stop it now."

I was floored by what Kemie's mother was saying to me. She wanted me to let the person responsible for shooting

Kemie go unpunished, all in the name of her sudden Christian conversion. It never fails. In times of true adversity, people always turn to religion. Thoughts of Italian mobsters and old movies came instantly to mind. I remembered a scene where a favor was asked of the godfather and his reply was, "This thing you ask of me, this I cannot do." It was the way I felt at the moment. But instead of replying, I simply turned my back on Kemie's mother and walked out the room.

********

My thoughts were still cluttered with all kinds of things as I rode the elevator down to the bottom floor. Including everything that Brenda Bryant had just said. Then I remembered something that an old head had told me while I was still in prison. "Always beware of the three crosses. The double cross, the triple cross, and the holy cross." I smiled as I stepped off the elevator. Kemie had confessed her sins to her mother as if she were a Catholic priest who could absolve all sins. It was a revelation, but one that meant nothing because Brenda Bryant could be trusted.

But who else had she run her mouth to? I reached the exit doors in the hospital lobby. The rain was now coming down harder than ever. I ran a hand over my freshly done braids and sighed. Then I threw my hood up over my head. The two guns in my waistband shifted as if to remind me of their presence as I stepped through the automatic exit doors. I got maybe ten steps into the parking lot, when suddenly thunder struck.

*Bok. Bok. Bok. Bok. Bok. Bok. Bok.*

What I thought was thunder turned out to be gunshots, and my instincts kicked in. I dropped to the ground and rolled over to the nearest car. Quickly, I pulled both burners and got to my feet. With rain in my eyes, I blindly fired in the direction I believed the shots to be coming from. The car I used as my shield was under fire by at least two guns now. Not knowing how heavy the artillery was that was coming my way, I made the quick decision to make a break back to the hospital. My soaking wet clothes seemed to weigh a ton as I ran. Gunshots shattered the glass on the hospital door as I zigzagged my way through the doors and slipped on broken glass.

Hopping up, I scurried toward the back of the hospital lobby in the direction that everybody was running in. People were screaming and running as bullets continued to rain down on the hospital lobby. At some point, the shots stopped. I came out from behind a counter with both guns in my hands. I had to get out of there. In minutes the hospital would be crawling with cops. My anger was at its boiling point, and I was about to explode. My clothes were wet and messed up, and that contributed to my bad mood. Somebody faceless had just tried to take me out. I laughed to myself as I sprinted to the exit doors and stepped through them where the glass had been earlier. I waited to see if shots would ring out as I appeared, but they didn't. "Bitch ass niggas," I muttered as I jogged to my truck. Tucking both guns back in my waist, I found my keys and hopped in the truck. In seconds I was barreling out of the parking lot and onto the Baltimore Washington Parkway. My breathing regulated as my adrenaline subsided. Questions filled my mind, but no answers came. For some reason, Lil Cee's face appeared in my head and wouldn't leave. The only thing that saved my life was the rain and Allah. Again, my life had been spared, and again I couldn't figure out why.

# CHAPTER FOUR

## Detective Tolliver

I spread a stack of photos all over my desk and studied them. The Nomeka Fisher and Teresa Bryant crime scenes stood out the most in my head. I had combed both apartments personally, and the lack of physical evidence at both scenes baffled me. Prints were pulled from both scenes, and the only thing I had was TJ's prints at Teresa Bryant's place, but according to her family, he was her boyfriend. I had expected to find TJ's prints at the Nomeka Fisher crime scene, but hadn't. I thought about the last conversation I had with Nomeka before her death.

"Don't be out there trying to conduct no investigation on your own. I'm paid to find the people who killed your brother and cousin. Ms. Fisher, I want you to promise."

"Detective, I'm not gonna do anything but ask questions. This dude TJ's name keeps coming up, and I believe he killed my brother up Capers, even if he didn't kill my cousin in that house on Canal Street. My brother didn't deserve to be gunned down like that. He was executed."

"You are preaching to the choir on this one. Leave the question asking to me. Things can get dangerous out there, and I don't want you to get caught in the middle of something that can get you hurt."

24

"Detective, I was born and raised in the projects. Danger is my middle name. Whoever killed my brother is gonna pay for it."

I slapped my right hand onto my forehead and dragged it down my face. Why did people always have to be so stubborn? Nomeka Fisher did what I asked her not to do, and all it got her was dead. Ms. Danger is my middle name.

"Benny, would you mind fetching me a cup of coffee on your way back in."

Detective Benjamin Alvarez gave me the head nod on his way out the door, but seconds later he stuck his head back into the room. "John Wayne style or sugar and cream?"

"Three sugars and one creamer, Benny. Thank you."

Nomeka Fisher had been a beautiful girl. Skin the color of mocha latte and a body made for hip-hop videos. She had been beaten and shot. Her naked body was left exposed for the world to see. A medical examiner's report suggested that she had just recently had sex. The questions were whether or not she was killed by the perp she'd allegedly had sex with? Or another person? And was her death connected to her brother? I'd definitely wager and say the answer to that question was yes. One thing that I knew with certainty was that somebody went through great pains to clean up after themselves inside of Nomeka's apartment. Was her killer TJ? Khadafi? Or somebody else?

Now on the flipside of that coin, Teresa Bryant was found in her bed partially nude, but basically dressed as most women did for bed. Her body showed no visible signs of trauma. She had appeared to simply have died in her sleep, but modern science knew better. Teresa Bryant was smothered, thereby making her death a homicide. Her apartment was also cleaned either before or after her death. The most powerful common bond in both cases was one man, Tyrone "TJ" Carter.

# The Ultimate Sacrifice III: No Regrets

I opened the file on Teresa Bryant and read all the reports inside. There was no sign of forced entry at Teresa's apartment. Since she lived on the sixth floor of the Malbury Plaza high rise, it was logical to deduce that her killer hadn't entered her apartment through any window or balcony. Her killer had to come in via the front door. And her killer was somebody that she knew. TJ? I reread the reports that I'd gathered after talking to Teresa's family and friends. According to them, Teresa and TJ were in love and had been for years. He had no reason to kill her. No one even knew when TJ had last been to Teresa's house. The neighbors hadn't heard a sound in apartment 610 for days. Nobody at Nomeka's apartment building remembered seeing a man fitting TJ's description on the day she allegedly died. So essentially, I had nothing. Nothing at all.

"Here's your coffee, Moe," Benny said and handed me a Styrofoam cup with coffee in it.

"Thanks, Benny. I owe you one." I sipped the lukewarm acrid tasting coffee.

"You owe me more than one, Moe, but who's counting?" Benny replied before disappearing behind the walls of his cubicle.

"This shit tastes terrible," I muttered and put the cup down. Leaning back in my chair, I gripped both my temples and massaged them. Then my stomach growled, reminding me that I hadn't eaten all day since breakfast with Dollicia. I picked up the phone and called Domino's pizza.

After ordering my pizza, I shifted all the crime scene photos around and searched for anything. Again, I came up empty. I had nothing. Nothing but seven different crime scenes with over twenty-five people murdered, and so far two names. Tyrone Carter and Luther Fuller. TJ and Khadafi.

Slowly, I read over the list of seven people who'd been killed inside the house on Canal Street in Southwest.

Then I carefully reviewed the list of the six people killed at the Arthur Capers Recreation Center. The name that stood out most was Thomas 'Woozie' Fields. He was connected to the one man found down at the Harbor Marina, Mark Johnson, and the two people found shot to death in a parking lot adjacent to the beauty salon and barbershop owned by Mark Johnson. The victims were Mark's wife and a man identified as her lover. The next two names were also connected to Woozie Fields, Nomeka Fisher and Sheree Tate, his sister and the mother of his children. I closed that file and opened another marked with the word's Omni Shoreham Hotel. My eyes read the reports of the officers who first arrived at the scene of the massacre. Five innocent people were killed. I read over those names again. The last file on my desk contained two names and additional paperwork. The two latest victims connected to Khadafi and TJ were related. Teresa Bryant and Rakemie Bryant were cousins.

One dead of unnatural causes, and the other shot on a desolate stretch of road and left to die. If nothing else, they were simply guilty of association. Teresa to TJ and Rakemie to Khadafi. I downed the last dregs of my terrible tasting coffee just as my cell phone vibrated. I recognized the number. "What's up, Rio?"

"Somebody shot up the lobby of PG hospital about an hour ago, that's what's up!" Detective Rio Jefferson said.

"PG hospital? That's a crying shame, Rio, but PG hospital is in Mary, and in case you failed geography class. Not our jurisdiction."

"I know that, smart ass. I got a buddy that works the violent crimes unit in PG, and he called me about the shooting. We always coordinate and exchange info when certain crimes might be DC-Maryland related. Witnesses say that a man walked out of the hospital doors moments before the gunshots erupted. Seconds later, as the glass partitions of the doors were shot out, that same man ran back into the hospital lobby as if he was being pursued. Two sets of gunfire followed him into the lobby as everybody present ran and sought shelter. The man who ran back in the hospital was the intended target."

"I'm kinda busy, Rio, and I'm hungry as hell. Now, what exactly does this have to do with me?"

"I'ma pretend like I didn't just hear that, Moe. I'm trying to help you if you'd just listen!"

"Okay. My bad. Go ahead."

"Which one of our victims happens to be at PG hospital right now?" he asked. That's when the light bulb in my head came on.

"Rakemie Bryant."

"And who do we know has been at her bedside since she was admitted?" I sat up and forward in my chair, now very attentive.

"Luther Fuller."

"Now you're thinking. Since your boy has been around the hospital so much, several nurses have become familiar with him. And one of those nurses just happened to be working the admittance station in the lobby during the shooting. And for the prize behind curtain number three, who do you think she identified as the man who left the hospital but returned seconds later with a gun in each hand?"

"Khadafi."

"This muthafucka leaves a crime scene behind wherever he goes," Rio added.

"Nobody was killed, right?" I asked.

"That's the only good thing about it. No one was injured. The rain was pretty heavy outside, so maybe that threw off the trajectory of the bullets. So now your case against Fuller gets that much wider. Now you have somebody trying to kill him and not the other way around. We gotta try and get him and Carter off the streets sooner than later."

"Easier said than done, Rio, easier said than done. I gotta walk through with Pete Rozelle in the morning at the Canal Street crime scene. Then I'm going back up to the rec center in Capers, have a look around, see if I missed anything. The Omni Shoreham Hotel massacre hasn't yielded any evidence that will stick against these pieces of shit. I'm gonna attend Teresa Bryant's funeral in a few days and see who all shows up there. I wanna see if TJ shows his face. Then I got Bryant's apartment to go over again and Nomeka Fisher's. I gotta full plate for the next five to seven days, but I'm not gonna rest until I bring down both TJ and Khadafi. Speaking of which, have you heard anything about the guy that leapt off the bridge?"

"Lafayette Dotson, also known as LaLa. Almost forgot about him. But naw, haven't heard a thing. He's presumed dead. A search of the Nissan he'd been driving right before he took a leap, turned up a sandwich bag full of heroin. There were traces of that heroin all over the car, which tells us that Dotson must've snorted some before jumping off the bridge. So that would make him under the influence. Multiply that by the depth of that water, the raging undercurrents at that time of year, and the height from which he leapt, and I'd say that Lafayette Dotson is definitely sleeping with the fishes as the mafia would say. But until a body officially turns up, he's a fugitive."

"Did Khadafi fire back at his attackers?"

"I'll check, but I don't think so. According to Rick, that's my buddy at PG. He was dodging bullets, and then he dashed out the door minutes later. Let me talk to Rick and I'll call you back."

"You do that, and thanks again, Rio. When this is all over, dinner and a comedy club is on me and Dollicia."

"I'll hold you to that, Moe. Later."

"Tolliver!" a voice called out.

"Yeah?" I responded.

"A pizza guy is out here!" Detective Marty Green shouted from the front of the squad room.

"I'm on my way, Marty. Thanks."

********

Early the next morning at 8 a.m. on the nose, I pulled into the 1000 block of Canal Street in Southwest behind Pete Rozelle's SUV. Pete Rozelle worked as a crime scene investigator for the Bureau, but was on liaison duties with the DC police. He was the closest thing to one of the CSI guys on TV that we had. The man was born for the shit. A smaller man with an enormous amount of wisdom and intelligence was hidden somewhere inside of Pete's body. Literally, the man was close to 6'4" and over 300 pounds of what used to be muscle. It was definitely possible to house another person inside of him. Dressed casually in khakis, a black leather jacket that was a size too small and brown hiking boots, Pete met me at the stairs that led to the front door of our crime scene and shook my hand.

"Moe Tolliver, how's it hanging?" Pete asked, squeezing my hand a little too tightly.

"I'm not going to be able to feel and see how it's hanging if you break the bones in my hand, Pete," I replied, dislodging my hand from his grip.

"My bad, Moe. I been training for a strong man competition coming up in Brandywine, Maryland soon. I been tryna loosen up all day." Reaching into his pocket, Pete pulled out a packet, opened it, and threw back its contents. "Amino acids and vitamins. Gotta do something besides work these crime scenes, Moe, or I'd go crazy tryna figure out why God allows these shit bags to kill people the way they do. I'm Catholic, you know? Almost twenty years of this shit and all I got to show for it is premature gray hairs, a divorce, two kids that I never get to fuckin' see, and a couple strong man trophies. How's that for the American Dream, partna?"

Not really knowing how to respond to the big man, I said the first thing that came to mind. "Over thirty-eight million Americans who couldn't afford health care are now eligible under the new 'Health Care Reform Act.'"

Pete stared at me with a quizzical look for a few seconds, and then a big smile crossed his face. "And I'm Barack Obama's long lost Kenyan cousin. C'mon, let's get to work."

"This Canal Street murder scene has got a bug up your ass, huh?"

"Yeah. I believe that everything started here with the robbery and murders. They set off a chain of events that not only have a bug up my ass. I got the chief breathing fire up my ass. I gotta invest in fire resistant pants nowadays. Over thirty-five murders in the last sixty days isn't good for business."

"Gotcha. Say no more. I'ma make this one come alive for you. I can be the soothing salve for your aching ass. No homo."

Pete led me through the scene again, pointing out the locking mechanisms on both entrances to the house being undisturbed. Inside job was the conclusion that we all reached.

"One of the witnesses said they saw a U-Haul truck parked on the side of the house that night, right?" Pete asked.

I nodded.

"Well, no U-Haul was parked outside that night once the cops showed up. We checked."

"It was found torched two days later in Northeast. A witness also saw the U-Haul truck leave, and it was accompanied by another vehicle. Make and model unknown. It makes sense though. The perps knew to drive something big enough to clean out the house. And the other car was probably driven by the inside man."

"I'll come back to that later," Pete said and went on to point out every detail and discrepancy that he found. I listened attentively and wrote everything down.

"The house was searched and ransacked. The perps were smart enough to wear gloves because no other prints were found here other than the eight victims."

"Hold it, Pete. You just said eight victims. There were only seven people—"

"My bad, Moe. I just got this info yesterday. A set of prints that we couldn't identify just came back to the guy found at the Harbor Marina the day after our vics were found here. Mark Johnson's prints were all over this house.

That's why I told you earlier I'd come back to your inside man being in that second car that accompanied the U-Haul truck. Mark Johnson's Benz was found parked outside this house the night the murders happened. That means that he rode in a car with one of the perps. He was driven to the Harbor Marina and killed there. Probably double crossed. Our perps didn't want to share the take with him."

"That makes sense, Pete, but then my question is, why not kill Johnson here with everybody else? Why take him to the Harbor Marina and kill him?"

Pete Rozelle scratched his head with his large hands. "Honestly, Moe, I have no clue. I thought about that myself. Johnson being killed down by the water—"

"The guns!" I blurted out. "The fucking guns! They went to the marina to dump the guns in the water!"

Like a proud father, Pete Rozelle smiled at me and nodded. "That was the primary reason. Killing Johnson there must've been secondary. Get some divers out there and put one in the water, and if you're right, which I'd bet you are, you've got your murder weapons."

# CHAPTER FIVE

## Khadafi

How many times can one man escape death? I asked myself this question over and over again as I methodically rolled hydro into a Swisher Sweet cigar. I vibed off some old DMX music as I lit and puffed on the trees to calm my nerves. My life was a movie, and I lived it in 3D every day. Leaning my seat all the way back in the DTS, I stared out the window and puffed on a blunt. I thought about my life, my thirst for blood, and my desire to kill. Most niggas talked that killing shit. Me, I lived it. And I'ma die by it.

When Allah calls for my soul, and I have to answer for my sins, what will I say to the creator? I could always cite situations like last night and say, "See . . . Allah, they were tryna kill me, too." After leaving the hospital with nothing but my pride scarred, I immediately went home and showered. Calmly, I ate a turkey and cheese sandwich and then dressed in warm black clothes, preparing myself to send the murder rate sky high if I caught the people I needed to see. I laughed as I found myself out in Maryland, still trying to see if I could run into the dude, Poo, who I'd mistakenly left alive after robbing him and killing his girl. Then I made my way to two different neighborhoods to see if I could run into Lil Cee. And it was raining hard as shit. After a couple hours, I gave up and went back home. All the while thinking about Chris Bowman.

The early bird catches the worm they say, so there I sat on 'V' Street in front of Phil and Chris Bowman's mother's house.

34

# ANTHONY FIELDS

The sun wasn't quite yet at its zenith in the sky, but for a December morning it wasn't that cold. And sitting in my car with the windows rolled up, it was actually warm. Periodically, I'd glance to my left at the three-story red-brick house with the black wooden shutters and black cast iron gate around it. As of yet, no one had entered or exited. I eased out of my North Face jacket and tossed it into the backseat.

How many times can one man escape death? There goes that question again. It didn't seem to want to leave my mind. Did it really need an answer? Well, I had none. All I knew was that I'd been the greatest escape artist since Harry Houdini when it came to cheating death. I cheated death as a seven-year-old kid when I hid in the closet as two men beat my mother to death. The fact that I sat terrified in that closet and watched through a small crack as she was being killed, transformed me and made me into the man that I am today.

There's no doubt in my mind that had those men spotted me in that closet, they would've killed me because I'd witnessed my mother's murder. I later avenged my mother's death. By now I was sure everybody knew that I escaped a possible death by lethal injection when Ameen decided to take the murder beef for me down in Beaumont. After coming home in 2008, I escaped certain death while sitting in my Range Rover on MLK at a traffic light. A dude with long braids tried to rip my head from my body with a choppa. The same dude tried to kill me again weeks later as I left the Masjid on Benning Road. A lot of innocent people died that day, but not me. A dude I eventually killed was after my life and kept me on the run, but I always seemed to avoid my own demise. All I know is that through it all I'm still standing, relatively unscathed. A little scarred, but nonetheless, I'm here. Even after the attempt on my life last night. I glanced again at the house on 'V' Street and then closed my eyes.

# THE ULTIMATE SACRIFICE III: NO REGRETS

********

The next time I opened my eyes, people were all over 'V' Street. I glanced at the clock on the dashboard. It was seventeen minutes after 11 a.m. "Fuck! How in the hell had I allowed myself to fall asleep while on a mission?" I was mad as shit at myself. Not knowing what or who I had missed in the three hours that I'd been sleep, I glanced at 219 one more time and then pulled off. I hit Florida Avenue and just drove with no particular destination. I needed to think, to understand, to plan. Grabbing my cell phone, I dialed Kemie's mother. She answered on the third ring.

"Hello?"

"Ms. Brenda, it's me. How's Kemie doing?"

"Nothing's changed, Khadafi. We're in the cafeteria eating right now."

"I thought about what you said to me last night," I blurted out.

"What part?" Brenda Bryant asked.

"The stopping the violence part—about letting God deal with whoever shot Kemie—"

"And?"

"I can't do it. Peace is for the Peaceaholics, not me."

I could hear the wind leave Brenda Bryant's chest as she exhaled.

"Speaking of last night," she said, "did you—never mind—take care of yourself out there, Khadafi. I'll call you if Kemie wakes up. Tomorrow is Reesie's—we'll be at the cemetery for most of the day. And stay away from this hospital for a while. It's crawling with cops." With that said, Brenda Bryant hung up.

One day, she'd understand the decision I made. Turning the other cheek is for Christians, politics is for politicians, and killing is for killers. I have to kill people. It's the natural order of things. I turned on the radio and then headed down Capers.

********

"Boy, what the fuck is going on with y'all?" Esha asked me as soon as I stepped through her door.

"Going on with who?" I asked curiously.

"Every gotdamn body. Reesie is dead, and now we just heard from her little sister that the police say she was killed in her bed. Ain't nobody seen or heard nothing about LaLa's geek ass since he jumped off the fucking Fourteenth Street Bridge. Muthafuckas running around talking about Worm hot. He done told on some niggas out Maryland. Fat Rat is out Upper Marlboro locked up for killing a muthafucka at a nightclub a few nights ago. Kemie got shot and don't nobody know why. Ain't nobody seen or heard nothing from TJ in about a week. Somebody shot up the hospital where Kemie is, and the word is that whoever did it was shooting at you. And bitches is running around saying that Devon telling people that you killed Bean and his brother Omar. So again, I ask—"

"What did you just say, cuz?"

"I asked you what's going on—"

"Not that part." I cut Esha off. The part about Devon."

"See, that's what the fuck I'm talkin' 'bout. All y'all muthafuckas are crazy. Lil Keisha and nem' told me that Devon is running around saying that you killed Omar and Bean."

I couldn't believe my ears. How in the hell had Devon found out my biggest secret? And if he knew it, who else knew? Suddenly my mind focused on TJ. Where was he? Did he know about Reesie? If so, was he taking her death hard? Or was he the one that killed her? Had Devon ran his mouth to TJ about what he knew?

Knowing Devon Harris all my life, I knew that he was a pussy. He didn't want it with me in no shape, form, or fashion, so him trying to move on me never crossed my mind. But still, his mouth was vicious, and I needed to close it for him. "Where he at, Esh?"

"Where who at?" Esha asked.

"Devon. Cuz gon' fuck around and get somebody killed out here if he keep running his mouth about that Bean shit. That was my fuckin' man. Why would I kill him? Omar, too. Them were my partnas that I came up with. I don't know where Devon got that bullshit, but cuz need to chill out. That's what I need to tell him. Where he at? You seen him?"

"Khadafi, don't do nothing to that boy. You know how he is. He just talking like he always do." She paused for a minute and then said, "He's with Tubby. They down Third Street. Tub got a spot down there and Devon be hustling for him."

I left Esha's house and jumped back in my car. Then I rode straight to Third Street. It didn't take me long to spot my homie Devon standing with Tubby and Pee-Wee. I double parked my car, hopped out, and approached Devon. All eyes were on me. I ignored Tubby and Pee-Wee.

"Ay, cuz," I said to Devon as I stepped right in his face. "If I hear that you said my name one more muthafuckin' time in connection with Bean and Omar getting killed, I'ma crush your bitch ass. Fuck I'ma kill Bean for? Omar and Bean were my fucking men. I'd never betray them or the hood like that. I loved both of them niggas. On my mother, cuz—"

"Redds. What's up, slim? What—" Tubby started.

"It's Khadafi, cuz. Khadafi. I told your ass before. That Redds shit is dead."

"My bad, slim. Khadafi. What's going on?"

"This skirt ass nigga running around telling bitches that I killed Bean and Omar." Tubby and Pee-Wee both looked at Devon incredulously.

"You said that, slim?" Pee-Wee asked Devon.

Devon looked at me and then at Pee-Wee and rolled his eyes like a bitch. "I said that."

"Where you get that from?" Tubby asked him.

"Muthafuckas talk," Devon said and then got quiet.

"Well, let me tell you this, nigga. I don't give a fuck where you heard that, who said it, and why. All I'm saying is stop saying it before your mouth get you in a situation that you can't talk your way out of. Or are you tryna see me about what a muthafucka told you?" I slid all the way up on Devon and put my nose to his. I could smell his breath and the fear emanating from his body. "Huh? You wanna see me? Omar was your brother. If you think I killed him, then you should be tryna see me, right? What's up? You tryna see me?"

After about two minutes that seemed like an eternity, Devon spoke. "Naw, dawg, I ain't tryna see you. You got that."

"I know I got it. Stop running your muthafuckin' mouth, cuz. Or next time be ready to kill something." I looked at Pee-Wee and Tubby. "Y'all be safe out here." I turned and walked back to my car. Before getting inside, I turned back around.

"Ay, Pee-Wee. You ain't heard nothing from TJ, huh?"

"Not a word, slim. Not a word."

Since I was in the area, I ended up at James Creek Dwellings at Marnie's front door. I spotted her car outside, so I knew she was home. I wanted to see her. Needed to see her. Walking up to her front door, I knocked.

# CHAPTER SIX

## Marnie

I just happened to be standing beside the window when I saw the gold Cadillac DTS pull into a parking space. I knew it was Khadafi, even before I saw him get out of the car. At the sight of him my heart fluttered. I couldn't deny the fact that I loved his thugged out, red-headed ass. Muthafucka. I couldn't stand his ass, but I loved him more than anybody alive. I loved the way he wore his clothes. At 5'10", about 175 pounds, cinnamon brownish skin and reddish-brown hair that he kept immaculately braided in cornrows that hung down his back, Khadafi was the sexiest man alive. I stood at my window and watched him knock on my door. Acting like I wasn't home, I let him knock for a while. Finally, I walked over to the door and opened it.

"What?" I asked, feigning an attitude.

"Fuck you mean 'what'?" Khadafi said, looking at me like I had three heads and then pushed his way past me and into my house.

"What part of what I said didn't you understand, nigga? Last time I checked, you heard real good and you comprehend well. And ain't nobody tell your ass to come in, did they?"

Khadafi pulled off a black North Face ski vest and then unzipped an all black Versace jacket with the white Medusa head emblem on the back. The stretch Versace headband around his head kept his braids in place. I was glad to see him.

"Where the hell you been?" Khadafi asked.

"Working. Why?" I replied.

"I been calling you almost every day. You heard about Reesie and Kemie?"

Instead of answering the question, I walked past Khadafi into my kitchen and tried to find something to eat. The baby had me craving all kinds of goofy stuff and I ate all the time.

"Did you hear what I said?"

"I heard you. Of course I heard about them. That's why you haven't heard anything from me. I been fucked up about Reesie since I heard about her." Fishing around the fridge, I found some leftover Ms. Debbie's crab cakes, greens, and rice and gravy. "I'm sorry that I can't say that I'm broken up about your girl. I wouldn't wish that on anybody, but I'm more fucked up about my girl Reesie." Sticking the food in the microwave, I leaned on my kitchen counter and waited.

Suddenly, Khadafi appeared in the kitchen across from where I stood. "I knew how you and Kemie felt about each other and why. That's between y'all. But I was hoping that you and I can come to some type of understanding about the baby. I don't want you and Kemie beefing forever."

"Is this what you came here for? Huh? To preach some togetherness shit to me about me and Kemie getting along? Who the fuck do I look like? One of Rodney King's daughters? Because I'm not. I'm Monica Curry, and all I care about is me, my unborn child, and you. So if you did come here to preach that all in the family shit, you can miss me with that and let the door hit you where the good Lord split you."

*Beep. Beep. Beep.*

I went to the microwave and extracted my food. While opening the Styrofoam tray, I turned my back on Khadafi, placed the food on the counter and ate. I was sincerely broken up about Reesie being dead, and I didn't know what to do or say. A tear escaped my eye. Then suddenly I felt Khadafi's body on mine. His arms wrapped around my waist and his lips found my neck. His smell, his warmth, his touch, sent my already crazy hormones into overdrive. "Kha—dafi—stop—it! Get . . . get—off—me!" My protest sounded so weak that even I didn't believe myself. I tried to keep my guard up and resist my greatest weakness, but knew that it was a losing effort. Before I knew what was happening, my pants were at my ankles along with my panties. All I could do was moan with a mouthful of crab cake as Khadafi reached under me and gently massaged my soaking wet pussy and clit. His lips and tongue were all over the back of my neck. He moved my hair and gently kissed me there. The man seemed to have three hands because he massaged my nipples through my shirt with one hand, played with my pussy with one and somehow was able to unzip his jeans and pull out his dick. All I could do was let go. Let go and grab the edge of the countertop as he entered me. He felt so good inside me that I wanted to scream. I wanted to holler and never stop. I wanted to be fucked roughly and told Khadafi just that. I told him I wanted him so deep in me that it hurt. I needed to hurt sexually to match the pain in my heart. For him and for my girl Reesie. I backed my ass up further onto his dick and worked my body like I was part centipede. Slithering and sliding. Wiggling and fighting. I bit down, swallowed the food in my mouth, and begged for more. It didn't take me long to orgasm all over Khadafi. After the first one though, I hungered for more.

Grinding my full weight back into Khadafi, I forced him to step back a few steps. When I had enough room, I bent completely over and grabbed my ankles. Instead of closing my eyes, I focused on the peach colored polish on my toenails and enjoyed his every deep thrust.

"Oooh, it hurt—but don't . . . Don't stop!"

My hot, wet, pregnant pussy had Khadafi saying shit that I couldn't understand. I wanted to cry out, "Speak English, nigga, so I can understand what you're saying." But instead I kept quiet. Well, not quiet, I just hit a few high notes when my spot got hit. Then finally he came deep inside me with a shudder and an exhale.

"Damn! What the fuck you got in there? A tiny fireplace? It felt like I stuck my dick in an oven. Your pussy hot and wet as shit," Khadafi exclaimed as he let himself slide out of me. Standing up after pulling my clothes up, I smiled.

Yeah, nigga, take that. Aloud I said, "Glad you liked it, but your ass ain't getting no more."

"Is that right?"

"Yeah, that's right. We don't fuck with each other like that. The last time we saw each other you told me that you loved me but couldn't be with me. Then you left and went home to your bitch—"

"Come on with that shit, cuz. You can't disrespect that woman like that."

I couldn't believe that Khadafi was in my house taking up for Kemie again. I was livid. "Why? Because she's on her deathbed? Nigga, you love her, not me. Fuck her and fuck you. I can't believe I just fucked your ass again. Stupid ass me." I tried to leave the kitchen, but Khadafi stepped in my path. "Move, nigga." I tried to push past him, but he was having none of it.

"Marnie, calm your feisty ass down. I fucks with you to the fullest, and I've decided that I want you to keep the baby."

"I heard that Kemie might not make it. Is that true?" I asked.

"Her condition is still listed as grave. She's in a coma, but it can go either way. Whoever shot her put a bullet in her head, and it's still there. If it moves wrong, it'll kill her. If not, she's good. I been with her since I was like seven years old. She's a fighter. She's gonna pull through."

"I wish Reesie would've pulled through. I can't believe she's gone." I teared up instantly and got real emotional. Khadafi hugged me close. I felt surrounded by strength. I felt secure, comfortable. "I miss her already. Why did somebody have to kill her?" I pulled back a little and looked up into Khadafi's eyes. The main question that had been on my mind for days came out. "Do you think TJ killed Reesie?"

Khadafi's eyes clouded over, and he turned his head away. The silence in the kitchen was deafening. After a while, he answered, "I ain't gon' lie to you and say that that question never crossed my mind. But it doesn't make any sense to me. Why would TJ kill Reesie? He loved her. They been fuckin' with each other for the longest. I don't believe he'd do no shit like that. There's no reason to."

"So where the fuck is he, so we can ask him? Nobody knows where he is. That makes him look guilty to me. Where is he?"

"I have no idea. I been wondering the same thing."

********

Khadafi and I ended up making love three more times, and then we showered together. When he fell asleep in my bed, I lay beside him and gently stroked his face, played in his hair, and whispered sweet nothings in his ear. My heart was smiling, and my soul was content. The way I felt, I never wanted the feelings to end. So I did what I knew best. I prayed for Kemie to die. Closing my eyes, I asked God to take Kemie's soul. She was wicked anyway. There was no good in her. Images of the night she was shot came rushing to mind. No matter what I did, those images wouldn't go away. I remembered driving to their house in Tacoma Park and parking outside. For hours I sat there before Kemie came rushing outside to her truck. Following her to Southeast, she ended up at Reesie's apartment building. I remembered seeing

44

Reesie's family outside and everybody flicking off about something. Kemie got emotional as well, and I figured something bad had happened to Reesie. However, I couldn't let that come in between my plan to kill Kemie. I had to carry the hit out. It was the only way for Khadafi, the baby, and me to be a family. So when Kemie hysterically ran to her truck and pulled off, I was right behind her. I followed her to the top of Southern Avenue and Alabama. She parked the truck in an empty lot. Apparently, she had stopped to cry and mourn for Reesie. I drove past her truck to the Maryland side of town. There I parked and ran across Southern Avenue until I reached the Land Rover. Pulling the gun from my waist, I walked up to the truck and tapped on the driver's side window. Kemie's head lay on the steering wheel. She popped up at the sound of my taps on the window. I still remembered the look on Kemie's face as I mouthed the word 'good-bye' and then lifted the gun. And as bad as I wanted to pull that trigger, my pain screamed, "Yeah, go ahead and do it. It's the only way!" My heart second my pain's motion, but my soul told me no. And I didn't do it. I couldn't do it. I had never killed anybody before, and my soul wouldn't let me become a murderer. Not like that. Not for the reasons that I had. So I lowered the gun and ran back across the street to my car. A gunshot startled me. I looked back in the direction of Kemie's Land Rover. I never saw the Buick Roadmaster following me. I never even saw it pull up. But I did see its driver stand at the Land Rover and fire into the truck. Sparks flew from the barrel of the gun. Then I stood riveted to my spot and watched TJ, Khadafi's best friend, run back to the Roadmaster and pull off. Whether TJ saw me or not, I'd never know. Another thing I'd probably never know was why he wanted to kill Kemie. But one thing I did know. If Khadafi ever found out that TJ shot Kemie, he'd definitely kill TJ. What I also came to know is that I was glad

TJ did shoot Kemie. Again, I closed my eyes and prayed that Kemie died. Then I wrapped my arms around my man and fell asleep.

********

Khadafi, up and getting dressed caused me to stir, look up, and then sit up. "Where are you going?" I asked, hoping that I'd see him again later.

"I gotta do what I gotta do, and the less you know the better," Khadafi replied and smiled. "Why? What you gonna do for the rest of the day?"

The sun beaming through the window reminded me that it was still afternoon outside. "I gotta get ready for the funeral tomorrow, but I'ma go and see my cousin Reggie who just came home."

"Reggie? What Reggie? Just came home from where?"

"My uncle Lump's son, Reggie. He just came home from a penitentiary in Pollock, wherever the fuck that is."

Khadafi sat down and tied up his Versace boots. "I know you ain't talkin' 'bout Champ. Reginald Yelverton, Lil Reggie?"

"Yeah. You know my cousin? Don't tell me y'all beefing neither, boy."

Khadafi smiled that Kodak smile that warmed my heart.

"Naw. Champ is my man. We was down Beaumont together. He was my celly for about three years. We lost contact when I went to the hole, and he went to Leavenworth. I fucks with Champ. Where he at?"

"He's up Hope Village. I promised Lump I'd go up there today."

"Cool. I'm going with you. I gotta little money on me I'ma give him."

"A'ight. Let me get up and get dressed. You riding with me or you going to follow me there?" I asked, hoping he'd ride with me.

"I'ma follow you there. I told your ass that muthafuckas is after my head. I'd never forgive myself if something happens to you. I'ma go in the kitchen and make me a sandwich. I'm ready when you are."

I got up just as Khadafi walked out of my bedroom. I stared at the door a minute longer than I should have. Again, I thought about TJ shooting Kemie and asked myself was I wrong for not telling Khadafi what I saw. As quickly as the thought came, it left. Stepping into my walk-in closet to get dressed, I decided that I'd only be wrong if things came back to haunt me. Other than that, fuck it.

# CHAPTER SEVEN

## Khadafi

H ope Village was notorious for being a death trap because several newly freed men had met their death on its front steps. That's why I never let the Feds send me to a halfway house. I always maxed out to avoid being sent to Hope Village. It sat smack dab in the middle of one of the most dangerous projects in Southeast, DC.

Against my better judgment, I pulled both my 9-millimeters off my person and slid them under the driver's seat of my Cadillac. Getting out of the car, I followed Marnie to the entrance of the main building. We had to be buzzed in. Inside an office, Marnie told the COs that we were there to see Reginald Yelverton. The CO in the office made a call, and ten minutes later, Champ walked down the hall. Marnie ran up to Champ and jumped in his arms. He spun her around and then put her down. He stared her up and down. "Damn, lil cuz, you done got big as shit. How old are you now?" Champ asked. "The last time you came down Lorton to see me, you was about seven, I think."

"I was nine, thank you, and I remember that day. And I'm now 28, boy." Marnie moved out the way.

Champ looked past her and spotted me. "Dirty Redds?" A big smile spread on Champ's face.

"What's up, cuz? You finally made it out, huh?" I replied, returning the smile. I walked up to Champ and embraced him. Champ looked like he was about twenty-five years old, but his appearance was misleading. He was actually forty-two years old and had been locked up for twenty-four straight calendars.

"Slim, what are you doing up here?"

"Came to see you. Your cousin Marnie is my heart. She told me you were up here. I told her I wanted to come and see you. As a matter of fact, here you go." I pulled a couple thousand dollars out of my jeans pocket and handed it to Champ.

Champ shook his head and said, "Naw, slim, I'm good. You know E Goody came up here and hit me off. Slim hit me heavy, I'm straight."

"Nigga, just because Eric Goodall married your sister, doesn't mean that he's the only good man that can hit you off with loot. Here slim, take that for your pocket. I'ma be offended if you don't."

"A'ight, slim. I ain't tryna have you messed up at me. Niggas die when you get mad. How the fuck you end up with my lil cousin?"

"I picked him. This the 2000's, Reggie. Women do the choosing now," Marnie said and smiled.

"I already know. I got like twenty numbers in my cell phone already, and I ain't been on the bricks but a week. They got a little visiting room over there," Champ said while pointing. "Let's go in there."

I had no intention of staying in no halfway house unarmed with potential enemies lurking everywhere. "Naw cuz, I can't stay. I'ma let you and Marnie get caught up without me being an interruption. I just came to rise up and salute a good man, plus give you my number and some bread. I know Goodall gon' take care of you, but I'm here if you need me."

"I appreciate that, slim. You always kept it real, even in— damn, I forgot. You just missed that hot ass nigga, Lil Cee by about a week or two." The mention of Lil Cee's name had me suddenly all ears.

"What you mean, cuz? I just missed Lil Cee?"

"My bad. We just missed his rat ass. I got here about a week after he left this joint. My man Black Junior—"

I couldn't believe it. I had the chance to kill Lil Cee and had missed it. It never crossed my mind for a second that Lil Cee would accept going to a halfway house. Him living in Hope Village never dawned on me at all. I felt like a grade A dummy. The man was sitting right under my nose, and I didn't know it.

"—he was in the next building. Junior said he stayed here about forty-five to sixty days before they released him on home confinement. That's how these people do a nigga, I hear. You do sixty days—"

"I don't mean to cut you off, but look, cuz, I need to holler at you for a minute." I turned to Marnie and said, "Boo, let me holla at Champ alone for a minute, and then I'ma bounce. I'ma call you later on and slide back through. I'ma go to Reesie's funeral from your house, a'ight?"

Marnie's face lit up like a Christmas tree and I knew why.

"A'ight, boy. Be careful out there. I'ma be waiting for your call." Marnie walked across the hall to the room that Champ pointed out.

Once she was inside, I pulled Champ to the side. "Cuz, a lot of shit done went down behind that Keith Barnett shit down Beaumont. I—"

"I heard about Boo, Umar, and what happened with you and Ameen," Champ interjected.

"Well, listen. Lil Cee told me that he went back to court to help Ameen."

"He did. My partner Buck told me that Ameen beat that shit."

"Okay, cool. But here's the thing. We thought Lil Cee had ratted us out, but he never did."

"But how—?"

"I already know what you're thinking. It's the same shit we thought, but we never had no paperwork on slim. We just assumed he was tellin' because they separated him from us. Armed with that assumption, Ameen made the Ultimate Sacrifice for me, Boo, and Umar. To show my appreciation and to send Lil Cee a message, I came home and killed his mother and little sister. He got that message. About a month ago, Lil Cee and another dude tried to bring me a move down Capers. I peeped the move and shot my way out of the jam. Me and a couple of my men. I searched high and low for his ass but couldn't find him. And all the muthafuckin' time, he was right here at Hope Village. Listen, we bumped heads again about three weeks ago at a book release party. Him and his man jumped me. Me and my men killed a rack of people outside that night."

"We heard about that shit before I left Pollock."

"Right, five people died in the parking lot. One of the victims was the dude who jumped me with Lil Cee. I chased Lil Cee, but he got away. That bitch nigga is faster than Usain Bolt. Anyway, now slim is gunning for my head, and I can't find his ass. Last night somebody brought me a move while I was leaving PG hospital visiting my girl. I think it might have been Lil Cee, might not. But the point is, I need to find him, cuz. I made a mistake by killing his people without any proof that he was wicked, but I can't bring them back.

"And Lil Cee ain't tryna hear that 'I'm sorry' shit, feel me? He wants blood. Mine. So I need you to try and find out where his home confinement is. Throw some money around to one of these hot ass CO bitches and get an address for me. If it wasn't life and death, cuz, I wouldn't involve you. But I don't have no other way of getting at him. I need to kill him before he kills me."

Champ leaned on the wall, taking in everything that I said. After a minute or two, he looked up and smiled. "You know it take me a little longer than others to process information, because I'm punch drunk, but you my man. I got you, slim. Say no more."

"Thanks, cuz. I appreciate it."

# CHAPTER EIGHT

## TJ

"Just the other day/taking life for granted, passing time away/I was there for you, you were there for me/we would be together for eternity/I never knew there'd be sorrow/ ..."

Sitting in the back of the Greater Tabernacle Baptist Church, I listened to Reesie's cousin Derrick sing the classic Men At Large song and cried. Every now and again I'd glance around at all the grieving faces in the packed church and catch them staring at me. Could they see through my tears? Was I that transparent? Did somebody present know, instead of just suspecting, that I was the one who put Reesie in that casket up there? Ever since the night I smothered her, I have lived with that one nagging regret. I never realized how much she complemented me and balanced me until it was too late. I panicked and let my emotions get the best of me. When Reesie told me about Khadafi killing Bean and Omar, the hurt and pain of that betrayal fueled my desire to never be betrayed again. My mind played tricks on me and told me that Reesie was no different, and that given the opportunity she'd betray me, too. So I did what I thought best. My tough facade was now crumbling, and I truly wished I could undo what I did. Life is funny. Reesie's soul left her body, but Kemie retained hers. My first instinct after hearing that she wasn't dead was to go up to PG and kill her.

Especially since she'd seen my face before I shot her. I still see her face and the look of utter shock as I appeared. I had been in the parking lot of Reesie's apartment building the whole time watching her family mourn outside. When I saw Kemie's truck pull into the parking lot, I smiled. It was exactly what I wanted.

But I also spotted a black Chrysler 300 that followed her. Instantly, I recognized it and knew the driver was Marnie. I was curious as to why Marnie would be following Kemie, but knowing the situation between them two, I assumed a simple confrontation. From my spot in the parking lot, I watched Kemie run to her truck and pull off. Then I watched Marnie pull in behind her.

I pulled out a few cars behind Marnie and followed her. We all ended up on Southern Avenue. Parking my car, I sat and watched Marnie run across Marlboro Pike and stop at Kemie's truck. My eyes got as big as candy apples when she pulled the gun. "Kill her!" I mumbled as my knuckles gripped the steering wheel. Mentally, I willed Marnie to do the job for me. But it wasn't meant to be. Shaking my head, I watched Marnie back up and then walk away. I got mad and leapt from the Roadmaster. I ran up to Kemie's Land Rover and did what Marnie couldn't. I tried to nail Kemie's ass to the passenger side door of her truck. Then I ran. I never looked in Marnie's direction again because I was consumed with getting away, and I didn't know if she saw me or not. That's the only reason she's still alive. Because maybe she didn't see me. But if I get an inkling of an idea that she did, I'ma punish her ass, too.

". . . life goes on, and it's not the same/'cause I can't help sometimes, calling out your name/but then I realize that you won't come around/oh what I wouldn't give to see your smile/'"

The cries, the screams, the palpable tension inside the church was starting to get to me. I knew that I wouldn't stay

54

much longer. At that exact moment, my home girls Esha, Keisha, and Dawn, all surrounded me and hugged and kissed me.

"TJ, I'm sorry about Reesie," Dawn said in my ear. "Whatever I can do to ease your pain, and I mean whatever, just let me know and I got you."

I looked Dawn in her eyes and saw the sparkle that she wanted me to see. Scandalous bitch, I thought.

"Are you going to the repast?" Esha asked me. I shook my head. "Well, I'll see you when you come around the way then."

The three women walked away and went to view Reesie's body. That was my cue to leave. As I was leaving out, I ran into the person that I least expected to see. Khadafi. At first sight, my blood started to boil. Especially every time I saw him smile at me in my mind. A smiling face that never hesitated to tell a lie. Deep inside I wanted to punish him, torture him, kill him slowly. I wanted to pull my gun and shoot him once every hour for as long as it took him to die slowly. But this was not the time or place. So I thought about something I learned while in prison out Maryland. Khadafi was a man who had lived amongst animals his whole life. It was his nature to be deceptive and predatory. Any man who lived in a wolves den long enough would learn how to howl. I understood that and accepted that. Dealing with a dude like Khadafi, I had to become something else.

I had to transform and do things that I normally wouldn't. The more I thought about it, the more I wanted to become like the snake. Always be aware of the snake with no rattle or no hiss. It would strike with no warning or clues. Yeah, that's me. The snake.

"Cuz, what the fuck? Where you been?" Khadafi whispered to me as we embraced.

"Long story," I replied.

"Listen, let me go in and pay my respects to Reesie, and then you and I need to rap."

"That's a bet. I'ma be outside standing by my car." I turned and exited the church. My Roadmaster was parked about a block down. I leaned on my car and gutted a Swisher Sweet cigar. Then I filled it with weed and placed the blunt behind my ear. I reached into my backseat and pulled out a gallon of Remy VSOP. Popping the top, I swigged straight out of the bottle. Although I was already a little buzzed, I planned to get twisted. Pouring out a little liquor, I said, "That's for you, Reesie."

For the last seven days or so, I had been strategically putting all the pieces in place to do what I needed to do. As soon as I sparked the blunt, I spotted Khadafi walking toward me. I pulled on the blunt, inhaled the acrid smoke of the purple haze, and exhaled.

"Pass that shit, cuz," Khadafi said as soon as he was within arm distance. I passed him the blunt. After a few pulls, he passed the purple back. "Cuz, these last few weeks been wild as shit, huh?"

I nodded, but kept quiet.

"I been tryna get at you since I last saw you. The time we snatched the dude Phil up."

"My bad, slim. You know this is the anniversary of the week my people's got killed in their house," I lied. "I always chill out to get my thoughts together on that. I heard they found the dude Phil in one of the abandoned spots down Capers."

"Yeah. I went on and crushed him after I got all the info I could out of him."

"He was somebody you thought brought you a move in the joint, huh?"

56

"Yeah. That bitch ass nigga was with some niggas that I wanted to crush. I figured that he'd know where they rested at."

This nigga was standing right in my face lying to me like it was nothing. I couldn't believe how easily he did it. The evening we snatched the dude Phil, he told me that dude had something to do with the shit that happened at the Omni Shoreham Hotel that night. His bitch ass didn't even keep track of his lies. I played it off as if I didn't know that he was lying.

"Other than that I been fucked up about my baby. When I find out who did this shit, I'ma kill their kids and everything. I just been laid up by myself tryna figure all this shit out."

"I heard about Kemie, slim. I'm sorry to hear that she might not make it. What the fuck happened?"

Khadafi leaned back on the car beside me and said, "Cuz, I'm still baffled by all this shit. A rack of shit done happened since I last saw you. I found out that Marnie is pregnant. Then a couple of days later, Kemie's mother calls and tells Kemie that something happened to Reesie. Kemie jumps up and breaks out the house. About an hour later, I get a call saying that she's been shot. Somebody shot my baby three times, once in the head. I swear to God, cuz, I'ma smash a nigga's ass as soon as word gets back about who was behind it. In the meantime, I've narrowed it down to two people, the dude Phil has a brother named Chris that's supposed to be getting a rack of money. Maybe he put two and two together and came up with Kemie about his brother's death."

"But why would he come up with Kemie, slim? What does Kemie have to do with Phil?"

Khadafi fumbled for the right words, recovered nicely and said, "See, the beef in the pen started over Kemie. The dude went in my phone book and got her address and wrote her.

Somehow Phil got involved. I figured his brother Chris got hip to the whole beef. So I'ma crush Chris, too. And the second person is Lil Cee, the dude that brought me a move on Seventh Street and at the hotel."

Puffing on the almost finished blunt, I digested everything Khadafi said and wanted to laugh in his face. His slip of the tongue created the need to compile lies on top of lies, and that shit was weak as hell.

"Well, if you need me, slim you know how I get down. If they violate you, they violate me."

"When it's time and I need you, I'ma holla. But on another note, when you go around the way, cuz, don't pay no attention to them rumors they out there throwing around."

"What rumors?" I asked, already knowing exactly what Khadafi was talking about.

"That shit ain't even worth repeating. All I'm saying is keep your sucka radar on point and always remember who loves you."

"And who might that be?"

"Me, nigga. We are all we got, you and me. Till death do us part."

"No doubt, slim. No doubt."

"Look, I got some other shit I need to handle, but in a few days, you and I are gonna get together and chop it up, then make a little blood spill in these streets. Keep your phone nearby so I can get at you. You heard anything else about that Black Woozie shit or LaLa?"

"I told you I been on some incognito shit. I ain't heard nothin'. I think La dead though, slim. He would've got at us now if he was alive. Remember the bitch Nomeka that I was fuckin'?"

"The bad, brown-skinned bitch with the Infiniti?"

58

"Yeah, that's her. That bitch turned out to be Black Woozie's sister. She tried to kill me, but as you can see, she failed. I didn't."

"Damn. This shit is some wild shit, ain't it? We got muthafuckas tryna kill us damn near every day. This ain't livin', cuz. This is just waitin' to die."

"It's the life we live, slim. Life ain't promised to us. Every day brings us closer to an early death. Are you ready to die, slim?"

Khadafi gave me a funny look, and then said, "I don't even know, cuz. I guess ain't no man ever really ready to die. That's a helluva question though. What about you?"

"I guess so. I don't think about it much. I don't plan on going anytime soon. If a muthafucka trick me out of my life, he deserve it. Because I wasn't man enough to keep it. That's how I feel about it. But look, fuck all that. I'm about to bounce. Get at me when you need me. I'm out."

"Hold on, cuz. One more question . . ."

# CHAPTER NINE
## Detective Tolliver

That definitely ain't no cigar they're out there smoking," Josh Devereaux exclaimed as he looked over at me. He put his eyes back on the Nikon camera mounted on the harness that sat on his forehead. "You could just jump out and arrest them for possession of marijuana. Last time I checked, you need a medical permit to smoke marijuana in America."

"They'd both be out on personal recognizance before the ink dries on the paperwork. No way, Josh. When I get these two, it'll be for multiple counts of murder, held without bond, the whole shebang. I need them interrogated, deprived of legal representation, and ready to break."

Adjusting the binoculars glued to my eyes, I studied the two men that I believed were responsible for over twenty-five murders combined in the last fifty days. TJ and Khadafi were both leaning on a black Buick Roadmaster.

"The guy with the dreads, watch him. Every time he moves, you can see a slight shifting of something beneath his shirt about the waistline. I'll bet you a fish platter from Daddy Grace's that your boy is packing. And the last time I—"

"—checked, it's illegal to carry a concealed firearm in the District." I finished Josh's sentence, and we both laughed. I looked at TJ dressed in dark jeans, black loafers, a black button down shirt, and a black wool peacoat. His dreads were pulled back on his head into a ponytail. I could see exactly

60

what Josh was referring to. "That fish platter sounds good, Josh, and I think you'd win, but he might be packing a cell phone, an iPod, a blackjack, a flashlight, who knows. If I go out there and check—what if I'm right about the cell phone? Then he's on to us, and him and Khadafi clean up and disappear. Not gonna happen.

"As it stands, these two guys have no idea how close I am to bringing them down. I don't want to tip my hand if I don't have to. CPWL is one year in jail. Murders are forever."

I continued to observe the two killers in their natural habitat. TJ's body language came across to me as defensive. He gesticulated with his hands as he talked to Khadafi, as if trying to get a point across.

Silently, I cursed under my breath. The academy had offered a class at Galludet University that taught officers to use sign language and read lips. I was kicking myself in the ass at the moment for not taking that class. I wanted to know what Khadafi and TJ were talking about.

Khadafi listened attentively to whatever TJ was saying. His body language screamed passive-aggressive, although he looked completely harmless leaning on the Roadmaster. He was dressed in denim jeans, black designer boots that looked expensive, a black, thick turtleneck sweater, and a black pullover cap over his braids. "Do you read lips, Josh?"

"I wish," my CSI photographer replied.

I cursed again as I realized that my favorite lady had finally left me. Lady luck had been with me all morning. I was able to cut through the bureaucratic red tape and get the District Cable Vision to loan me a van to stake out Teresa Bryant's funeral. Then I'd been able to pry Josh away from another case to tag along with me and snap a few photos. I had a gut feeling that TJ would show up at Teresa's funeral. He had to, or look suspect in the eyes of the world in her death. But it was pure lady luck on my side that I got to see TJ and Khadafi together. Now suddenly, lady luck was gone.

"Josh, I think they're—Khadafi is walking away. Make sure you get the license plate on that Roadmaster. And get a couple shots of that Caddy that Khadafi's driving and its plate, too." As I watched the two killers pull off, I decided the case might be a little bigger than I'd originally thought. I'd have to enlist some help.

********

Three hours later, I addressed an assembled group of patrolmen that worked out of the First District Station. They were familiar with the Arthur Capers projects, its reputation as a hot spot, and all the people who made it so.

"Listen up, men—excuse me—and woman." I smiled at the lone woman sitting in the room. "We are at war. It's us against two domestic terrorists. These guys are responsible for over twenty-five murders or more in the last two months." I paused to let the numbers sink in. Somebody present whistled.

"That's why I say we're at war. And when I say we, I'm talking about you and me. We have to become homeland security." I walked over to the large bulletin board. Two enhanced photos were stuck to the board.

"This man right here . . ." I stated, pointing at TJ's picture, "is Tyrone Carter. But the streets call him—"

"TJ," the lone woman said venomously, and then introduced herself as Emily Perez.

"Correct. You know him?"

"Everybody that patrols the blocks down at Capers projects knows him," Emily Perez said. "I've personally chased him a few times. He's a fast muthafucka."

"You're familiar with him. Good. Detective Salisbury selected the right group for me. TJ is a suspect in several homicides committed in Forestville, Maryland, but they have zero evidence to prove it. Score two homeruns for the bad guys because we have the same problem. That's where you all come in. I need to bring him down.

"Tyrone Carter was arrested twice for murder as a juvenile, but was found not guilty in trial both times. No witnesses. The second photo here is of another man you should all know. Luther Fuller. Mr. Fuller now goes by the name Khadafi, as in the Libyan dictator. Some of you may remember his uncle Marquette Henderson, who pillaged and plundered Arthur Capers for years. All those who know these two, raise your hand." Every hand in the room went up.

"Okay, good. I believe that these two terrorists are responsible for the seven murders at the house on Canal Street, a murder at the Harbor Marina, the six murders at the rec center down Capers, the five people killed in a parking lot at the Omni Shoreham Hotel, and about five to eight other murders in and around Washington, DC. I need to get them off the streets. To do that, I need your help. I need to get as many edges as possible in conjunction with evidence that will stick. I need you to be extra vigilant out there—down Capers. Watch Khadafi and TJ's every move.

"I need you to harass their friends—within policy of course. I need information that I can use. When you bust anybody from that area, talk to them about these guys and see what you get. Consult your snitches on the streets, get whatever info you can on these two guys. If you stop either one of them, look for guns. If you find any, take them and let these two go. We're looking for murder weapons. Find some credible people that will testify against TJ and Khadafi about any crimes they've witnessed. Make deals with guys or girls that you arrest in exchange for something concrete on TJ and Khadafi. And I say all this not of my own authority, but by direct order of Captain Dunlap. So you've got protection and deniability. Every one of you will be given a card with my contact info on it. Call me anytime. And if there is anyone here who lacks motivation, let me say this before we close. The Mayor is all over our Lady Dragon police chief, and in turn, she's all over Captain Dunlap. If we don't get TJ and Khadafi off the streets before they kill again, the captain is gonna be pissed because he'll be knee-deep in shit. And I don't have to remind you all that when the shit rolls, it rolls downhill. Meeting adjourned. Let's get to work."

# CHAPTER TEN

## Ameen & DC Jail

Assalamu Alaikum Wa Rahmatullah," I said, turning and looking at my right shoulder, and then repeated it over my left shoulder. After ending my noon prayer, I said a du'a to Allah and prayed for guidance and freedom. But not particularly in that order.

Rising from my knees, I slipped on my shoes and walked to the bars on my cell. Sticking my arm between the bars, I hit the top of the metal connected to the wall. "Sarge, pop me out," I shouted and suddenly my cell door opened.

Since I was still locked down in the Special Management Unit called South One, I had limited mobility. Lieutenant Worthy put me on detail, but during the day I had to stay on my tier, which was closed off by a thick, steel fiberglass door. I could stop by all the other cells on my tier and assist the men, but the tier door separated me from the rest of the unit. That separation was a deterrent, but it also worked in my favor. It separated the police from me and alerted me to their presence when I was up to no good.

My partner, Mark Robinson-Bey had just got in from the SMU unit at Talladega, Alabama. I went and stood in front of my man Mark's cell. "You know the drill, slim. Shake the bars if you see the cops coming."

Mark gave me the 'my head just shrunk' look and replied, "I got you, moe. Been doing this shit for too long."

"My bad, slim. I ain't mean to cuss at you." I smiled and walked to the mop closet that sat at the end of the tier.

# THE ULTIMATE SACRIFICE III: NO REGRETS

Glancing over my shoulder one last time at the police bubble in the middle of the unit, I slid into the mop closet and stepped up onto the deep sink. I reached up to the ceiling and pushed a piece of cement with all my might. The cement block shifted and lifted away from its base. I kept pushing and directing the cement over. Once a large crack appeared, with one hand I reached into the crevice and felt around for a minute. My fingers finally felt what I was looking for. Grabbing the small bundle, I jumped off the sink and peeped out of the mop closet. "How it look up there?"

"Ay, moe, you good. Stop being all nick nervous. Geeking ass nigga," I heard Mark say. "I ain't gon' get you cracked."

I extracted two pieces of steel from the strips of blanket and dropped to my knees. Finding the concrete spot that I wanted, I put a sock over my right hand, placed one piece of steel on the floor under my knee, and kept the other in my hand. Pressing the steel on the concrete with full force, I moved it back and forth on the cement. Slowly, but surely, the piece of steel was starting to sharpen.

Working as if I was on a grinder, I sharpened the steel until it was time to give my hands a break. I put both pieces of steel back in the piece of blanket and placed the whole bundle, along with the sock, into the empty mop bucket. Then I pushed the mop bucket out onto the tier.

"How that joint lookin'?" Mark asked me once I reached his cell.

"I'm almost done. I figure I got about another day's worth of work on the first and then I'll start on the next one." I flashed the almost finished weapon at Mark.

Mark's eyes got big as shit. "Kill my mother. . . . That joint wicked already, and you talkin' 'bout you got another day's work to put in on it. Ameen, you tryna kill something around here, huh?"

"Naw," I lied. "All I deal with is murder one shit. Wait until you see both joints when I finish with 'em. They gon' have ridges and all that shit in 'em. Street shit."

"And you gon' take both of them joints to open pop' with you?"

"You better believe it. If one of them hot niggas jump out there, I'ma nail their ass to the everlasting concrete. Whoever tryna get it, can get it."

"And you keep saying that you tryna go home. You ain't tryna go home. You go and see the housing board next week, right?"

"Yeah. I go the twenty-third."

"This lock down shit ain't nothin'. I need to stretch my legs a little."

"No bullshit, moe. No bullshit."

Later on that night, I lay in my bunk listening to songs on my iPod Touch that I had smuggled in. Although I'd been gone eleven years, I still had a friend or two on the streets that came through in the clutch. A Musiq Soulchild song made my mind wander.

"—you say I don't know how to love you, baby/well I say show me the way/I keep my feelings deep inside I/shadow them with my pride eye/I'm trying desperately baby just work with me/teach me how to love/ . . ."

Did I really know how to love? That question plagued my thoughts. Had I been taught how to love? Did I even really know what love was? Had I ever loved anybody in my life? My parents? My brothers? Shawnay? My friends, Umar and Boo? Khadafi? I really didn't know. The love I have for my daughters is a natural parental love that is deep inside of a person that doesn't have to be taught. So outside of them, what did I really have to go home to? My life had changed drastically. I wasn't close to anyone in my family and financially I had nothing.

The woman that I had convinced myself I loved had moved on with her life and even had a toddler son.

No matter what I did every day, no matter how much working out I did or how many knives I made, I could never shake the pain that I inherited the day that my daughter Kenya told me that she had a little brother named Kashon. I was devastated then and I still am. That pain won't leave me. But I still stand. I continue to keep my head up and survive. Shaken but not stirred.

My daughter never mentioned to me who her brother's father was, but it didn't matter. I already knew.

"The address was Shawnay's, ock. Khadafi has been staying with your baby mother," Umar had said over the phone before he was killed.

Luther Fuller. Khadafi. Although I was deeply hurt and disappointed in Shawnay, I lay in my bunk and allowed myself to empathize with her. That was something that I never allowed myself to do before. Hadn't she almost died twice because of me? Slowly, I put all the blame where it belonged. With me. I was the one to blame for breaking up my family. Had I been thinking about Shawnay and my two daughters more, and less about my so-called friend, Eric, I wouldn't be in the situation I was in now. Had I not been too loyal and partially blind, I would have never sent another man to my woman's house bearing gifts. Everything that had happened thus far was my fault.

"Girl I know I lack affection and expressing my feelings/it took me a minute to come and admit this /but see I'm really tryna change now/wanna love you better, show me how/I'm trying desperately baby please work with me/ teach me how to love—"

Coming to grips with that fact, I decided to forgive Shawnay for her transgressions. It was time for reconciliation between her and me. In my heart I believed that I owed her that much. I just hoped that she felt the same way. In the meantime, there was one more murder that I needed to commit, and then I could start laying the foundation that led to change. Change and reconciliation. I needed to commit the perfect murder so that I didn't kill my shot at freedom.

This murder would be well thought out, planned, and executed properly. Cochise Shakur, the dude that had killed Boo, his family, and probably Umar, was living on the second floor of DC jail in SW2 housing unit. He was also the person responsible for killing a number of Muslims at the Masjid on Benning Road. There was no way in the world I could let him get away with all that. I already had Lieutenant Worthy set up my eventual release from South One. All I had to do was maneuver my way to SW2. On SW2, my two homemade knives would be put to good use. I planned to always keep one knife on my person for emergencies, and the other was strictly for Cochise Shakur.

# CHAPTER ELEVEN

## TJ

Sometimes I wondered whether heaven and hell were real. I wondered if all that stuff wasn't created in somebody's mind to keep children in line. And then it passed down from generation to generation like an old wives tale. I sat up and took another sip of Remy VSOP straight from the bottle. Then I laid back down in the grass behind my father's grave and stared up into the sky. The cold December air got through the layers of my clothes and gave me the chills, but the Remy warmed my soul. Lying in the grass, I watched the clouds in the afternoon sky move at a slow moving pace. But I knew how deceptive that was. To the naked eye, clouds moved at a slow pace, but in all actuality, they were fast-moving as the earth revolved. Thoughts of heaven and hell always brought up thoughts of God. Like I'd done many times before, I'd asked myself could there really be a Supreme Being sitting high above the heavens overseeing and manipulating all actions and events on earth like a great puppeteer with every living soul on strings.

The thought of a benevolent, higher power didn't coincide with my life, my pain, my reality. It was hard for me to believe a forgiving power would allow earthquakes to kill thousands of people, tsunamis, hurricanes, storms, tornadoes, wars, terrorist attacks and all that shit. Why would a God allow that? Why would he allow serial killers to kill young girls and kids? Pedophiles, rapists, and muthafuckas like me to kill without compunction? Why would he let some thirsty niggas kill my father, his wife, and their ten-year-old son? What had they done to deserve that?

"What did you do to God, Pop?" I asked aloud. "Huh? All my life you been on your born again Christian shit hard. Church, saying grace at the table, reading the Bible. You did all that shit and what did it get you but dead at an early age? Where was God when them niggas was killing you, Serita, and Antoine? What was Serita's sin? What did Antoine do at ten years old to deserve to never grow up. All because of me and the life I lived on the streets.

Muthafuckas killed you—killed you because of some money I made selling drugs. If God was beefing with me for my sins, then why are y'all dead and I'm still here?" Suddenly, I stood up.

"Can somebody fuckin' riddle me that?" I shouted with tears in my eyes at the sky. "I'm listening. Tell me that, why don't you, God? If you're up there. If you're listening, answer that for me. Why the fuck am I still here? Why haven't you allowed me to die yet? Haven't I killed enough people yet? Or are you really sadistic and wanna see me kill more? Huh?" Swaying to and fro, I waited for answers that I knew would never come.

"Yeah, that's what I thought. We talk to you, but you don't talk back." I lowered my voice, stared down at my father, stepmother, and little brother's graves and said, "Or just like I figured, it ain't nobody up there to answer. You're an old wives tale."

I wiped the tears from my eyes, put the bottle of Remy down on my father's grave, adjusted the fresh bouquet of roses I'd put there earlier to mark the seventh anniversary of their deaths, and said my good-byes to my family. As I made the long trek back to my car, I reminisced about the days after my family was killed. Bean and I dressed up in war gear and painted the town red, literally. We went from neighborhood to neighborhood and punished all enemies and potential adversaries.

We even killed a few niggas just for the fuck of it. I simply killed until I satisfied my thirst for destruction and revenge. As I hopped into my car, I picked up my cell phone from the driver's seat and checked my missed calls. I stared at the phone numbers for Devon and Dawn and wondered what they wanted.

Even though I was a little tipsy, I was sober enough to drive without drawing attention to myself. Thinking about my dead family and Bean made me think about another possible dead comrade, LaLa. After driving around aimlessly for a while, I ended up on Fifteenth Street, at the very top of Montana Avenue in the projects.

Images of the last time I'd come to Montana popped up in my head, and I surreptitiously looked around to see if I spotted the dude, Malik, and any of the youngins' that he was with that day. If there was anybody out there present that day when we all pulled guns on one another, I didn't recognize any of them. I drove down Fifteenth Street until I spotted a few friendly faces. Ten dudes stood on a porch in front of a tenement. About four of them I knew growing up in the juvenile joints and other prisons.

"Youngblood, what's up, slim?" I called out. Derrick Aull stepped away from the crowd and walked down the walkway.

"Who dat?"

"TJ, slim," I replied and cut off the car. I stepped out the car.

"Ay, big boy," Derrick said as he met me in the street. "What's up with you, huh?"

Before I could respond, my men Moe Best and Eric Hileigh came down the walk, too. I embraced Moe and Eric. We kicked it about the old days for a while, and then I got around to what brought me to their hood.

"Have y'all heard anything from LaLa?"

"Not at all," Eric said.

Moe just shook his head and stared at the ground.

"Cuz, that shit crazy. It's been what? A month or so since that book release party. I don't even believe LaLa jumped off no fuckin' bridge. Who the fuck would do some geekin' ass shit like that? In the wintertime at that. I think the police killed La and covered it up," Derrick said.

Ignoring the goofy shit that Derrick was saying, I asked, "His family ain't hear nothing from him either?"

"I talked to his brother, and slim said that they ain't heard shit," Eric replied. "He said their mother is going crazy, but holding on to hope that LaLa is alive."

"Muthafuckas talkin' 'bout they seen LaLa here and there. They out here having straight LaLa sightings like he Tupac or something," Moe Best stated and laughed.

"Well, look, I'm 'bout to bounce, but y'all men be cool out here, and holla at me if anybody hear anything about LaLa." I said my goodbyes and left.

********

I was walking through the hood when one of the little homies walked up and asked me what my dice was hitting for. Jim-Jim was a good young dude that always wanted to gamble. That was his hustle. I liked him because he was a thorough youngin' who was known to nut up and pull his pistol when he got mad. He reminded me of myself at his age. "I ain't got no dice."

The youngin' smiled a toothy smile and said, "Don't even trip. I got some. Let's go in the hallway over there."

Jim-Jim pulled out a pair of red dice and a wad of money. I pulled out a couple hundred, got on my knees and got busy. Being as though I was still buzzed off all the Remy I'd drunk earlier, it had me talkin' a rack of shit and hitting numbers left and right. About thirty minutes later, I threw the red dice and laughed. In the end, Jim-Jim had won all his money back and most of mine. "I can't let you break me, youngin'. I gotta keep food and drink money."

"Nigga, everybody know you rich. All the muthafuckin' work you put in out here. How a gangsta gon' be working with short money?" Jim-Jim asked.

"Don't believe everything you hear, youngin'. What's been up out here?"

"The same old shit, moe. The police been on some different shit out here. They out here snatching niggas, literally. You heard me?"

"I hear you, youngin'. It's hot out here, huh?"

"Five hundred degrees. They setting up road blocks on Seventh Street and all that shit. Got me scared to carry my heat with me. They gone have a nigga over the jail in the juvenile block forever for one hammer. I ain't goin' out like that."

I lifted my shirt to reveal my pistol gripped chrome Glock 18, fully automatic handgun. "I don't give a fuck how many cops out here. I ain't traveling three feet without my heat. I do too much dirt out here for that shit."

"I feel you, moe. As a matter of fact, I'm about to bounce and get right. I feel naked out here without my girl."

"Your girl?" I repeated.

"Yeah, my four-fifth is my bitch, and I love her with all my heart. I'ma holla back."

I stood on the porch of 701 and watched Jim-Jim walk up the block before pulling out my cell phone. I called Dawn's

74

number. She answered on the first ring. We talked for about ten minutes and then I ended the call. I still remembered what she'd told me at Reesie's funeral. ". . . whatever I can do to ease your pain, and I mean whatever, just let me know and I got you . . ."

We had a date set up for later, and I planned to take her up on her offer. Just as I put my cell phone back, it vibrated. I thought the caller might've been Dawn calling me back to cancel, but the caller ended up being Devon. "Yeah, what's up?"

"TJ, I need to holla at you about some important shit."

"A'ight, I'm around the way. Where you at?" I replied.

"I'm standing in front of Esha's house. Me and Bay One out here. Where you at?"

"I'm standing in front of Wayne-Wayne nem' court. Come over here."

"I'm on my way," Devon replied.

# CHAPTER TWELVE

## TJ

Huddled up in the hallway, Devon animatedly recounted how Khadafi pulled up on him while he was with Pee-Wee and Tubby and disrespected him.

"Somebody told him about him killing my brother and the fact that I said it. This nigga walks right up on me and gon' tell me 'if he hear that I said his name one more time in connection with Bean and my brother's deaths, he gon' crush me.' He called me a bitch and everything . . ."

"You are a bitch," I thought and continued to listen to Devon vent.

"Fake ass nigga gon' tell me that Omar and Bean were his men, and why would he kill them? He popped all that fake ass 'I'll never betray my men' shit. I love the hood,' he said."

"Did you tell him where you got your info from?" I asked calmly.

"Hell naw, dawg. When he—naw. Pee-Wee—no—Tubby asked me where I heard that Khadafi killed Bean and Omar from. I told him that I just heard it around the hood. I didn't give no names. I ain't tryna get y'all to beef. I wanna kill that nigga, Tee. No bullshit! That nigga disrespected me in front of everybody. Talkin' about my mouth gon' get me in a situation I can't get out of. Fuck that nigga think he is?"

Looking down at my fingernails while I cleaned under them, I couldn't help thinking, He's a killer and you're a bitch. That's who he is.

I knew in my heart that Devon was biting off way more than he could chew by fucking with Khadafi. It took an official killer to kill another killer and Devon wasn't it. A part of me wanted to be real with him and tell him to stay in his lane and get money, but another part of me said, "Let his ass jump out there. It's a win-win situation for you. If he succeeds and kills Khadafi, then he did you and himself a favor. His brother Omar and your man Bean would be avenged. If he failed and Khadafi killed him that would eliminate a loose end on your end."

I nodded and agreed with everything my inner voice had just said. Devon took my head nod as a sign of approval and continued his hate-filled spiel. "—talkin' about, 'do you wanna see me'. But I knew he was strapped and I wasn't, so I played it smart and told him that I didn't wanna see him. But I'ma do more than see him. I'ma murk that nigga, dawg. Watch my work. Niggas think Devon pussy, but I'ma show niggas how I get down in the new millennium. I'ma push all that nigga's shit back."

"Didn't I tell you not to repeat what I told you about Khadafi killing Bean and Omar? I could've sworn I told you that," I replied as I pocketed my fingernail clipper.

"Dawg, fuck I'm supposed to do? Huh? Keep a secret like that? Fuck naw. Muthafuckas in the hood need to know how sheisty that nigga is. He running around reppin' the hood and screaming 'hood love' this and 'homies over everything' that, and all the time that nigga been killing niggas that loved him and grew up with him. I got toasted off the Moet and told some bitches about it. That shit ain't nothing though. I don't give a fuck who say what. I'ma kill that nigga, dawg."

The more I tried to talk to Devon, the dumber I felt. If he wanted to roam around the jungle and collide with the lions, who was I to stop him?

77

"So you needed to tell me all this for what?"

"You are the closest person to him. You know what he did was some cruddy ass shit, but you don't wanna finish what you started because you got a soft spot for that nigga. I don't. He killed my brother and for that he gotta go. I need you to direct my path on how to get at him and I need a hammer."

Suddenly conscious of where we were, and the fact that everywhere you went, the walls had ears, I told Devon, "Let's go for a walk."

We walked around the neighborhood for the next forty minutes talking. I gave Devon everything I knew about Khadafi, except his home address. And that was only because I didn't know it. I never had any reason to go to his house. "You have to catch him off guard and that's gonna be tough, but he can be got. No man is untouchable. Here's what you do." I ran a whole plan down to Devon, and he bit the hook like Bubba the fish.

Once the bar was understood with Devon and me, we went our separate ways. I walked slowly back to my car and parked down by Vaness Elementary School. As I kicked everything that I'd just done and said around in my head, I realized that I had just manipulated a situation and orchestrated the demise of one of two men and all of a sudden I felt Godlike.

********

"What are you gonna give me for Christmas?"

I looked down into the face of a woman who was on her knees with her head in my lap. "Christmas! What the fuck is that?"

"You know what the fuck Christmas is, boy. Don't play stupid with me," Dawn said.

"I got you. Right now, you need to concentrate on what you're doing," I said while pushing Dawn's head back down onto my dick. Eyes closed, it felt like I was getting my dick rode. Dawn's mouth felt like a tight, warm pussy. Smiling to myself, I thought about what my homies down Capers said about Dawn's head. They called her 'Grandmama'. Why? Because she gave that good old fashion head like she didn't have teeth at all. 'It feels like she gums the dick', they said. And guess what? They were right. I heard a gagging sound and then felt Dawn slide the length of my dick into her throat.

"Aww . . . sh—sh—shit!" I moaned.

Dawn's head was so good I wanted her to have not only some Christmas gifts, but a couple of birthday gifts too. After swallowing my cum, she stood up, wiped her mouth with the back of her hand and said, "That was good as shit."

Dawn was a pretty chick. She was only like two pennies short of being a complete dime. Her golden complexion seemed to glow. Her long curly hair accented her complexion. I tried to count all the tattoos visible on Dawn's body, but there were too many. I spotted one tattoo that said 'Jo-Jo' on her neck as she slid her jeans off.

"Who's Jo-Jo?" I asked.

"Huh? What? Oh. This?" Dawn said, pointing at her neck.

I nodded.

"That's my old boyfriend. That nigga was my heart. He broke it and took it with him.

"What Jo-Jo is that?"

"Joe Green. He's from Wellington Park. Be with Lil Greg and Fat Bug and nem'."

"I know Jo-Jo. That's my man. Slim back locked up, I heard."

"Yeah, his geekin' ass came home on that same 'back in the day' wild shit, got shot, and then got back locked up. They gave his ass twenty-four years. I can't do no more bids. That shit is played out."

# THE ULTIMATE SACRIFICE III: NO REGRETS

There's something about bitches with tattoos that turn me on, and Dawn had them everywhere. My dick got rock when I saw the cat's paws that led a trail down to her pussy. One paw stopped right at the top of her clit. From my seat on the couch, I spotted a sparkling piercing in Dawn's clit and another one hanging from her pussy lip. I pulled a rubber out of my pocket and handed it to Dawn. She ripped the packaging with her teeth and then pulled the rubber out.

She placed the rubber in her mouth and got low to where she was bending over, face to dick. Dawn placed both hands flat on both my thighs, and bobbed her head until she gagged a little. When she stood up erect, the rubber was on my dick all the way down to the base. That trick was a classic. Dawn then pulled my jeans all the way down to my ankles. She stepped up onto the couch and stood over me. My face was parallel to her pussy. I stared at the two piercings up close and wanted to taste them, but Dawn was a roller and I knew so, so eating her pussy was out of the question. Slowly, she lowered herself onto my dick and made my toes curl. I knew I was in for a long night.

# CHAPTER THIRTEEN
## Khadafi

*Christmas Day 2010*
*3:39 p.m.*

He's in there!" the crackhead said and held out her hand. I pulled out a wad of money with my left hand and my silenced 9-millimeter with my right. The woman's eyes got as big as bifocal glasses when she saw the gun. I shot her twice. Once, right over her left eye and once in the throat, and then I watched her body drop. Grabbing her by the feet, I pulled her body over behind the big green dumpster in the alley on 'W' Street.

"What son doesn't come to see his mother on Christmas day?" I asked myself as I woke up this morning. So basically acting on a wish and a prayer, I went to the Sunny Surplus costume shop on 'F' Street and bought everything needed to commit the perfect broad day home invasion/murder.

I ditched my Escalade and secured a stolen Mazda MPV minivan from the nearby shopping center. When I pulled onto 'V' Street, I spotted a beautiful, mint green Aston Martin Vanquish parked outside of 219. The exotic sports car screamed money, and Chris Bowman was rumored to have lots of it. But I had to be certain that Chris Bowman was inside the house at 219 'V' Street. That's how the crackhead came into play. Having seen my face condemned her to death the moment she accepted my proposition to knock on the door at 219 'V' Street.

Quickly, I drove the MPV over about two streets near one of the dormitories for Howard University and parked. I pulled out the costume and put it on. The costume came with a synthetic rubber strap on a big stomach attachment. It was awkward at first, but my body adjusted to it after a few minutes of walking in it. I put the big beard on and the red floppy hat and pronounced myself ready. I put my gun in a box and dropped it into the big red sack with the rest of the presents. It took me about seven minutes to drive back to 'V' Street, all the while singing along to Christmas songs on the radio.

"—Merry Christmas from the Temptations," I repeated as I stepped from the MPV, grabbed the sack, and walked through the gate of 219 'V' Street. I rang the doorbell and then knocked on the door. A lady dressed in stylish jeans and knee-high leather boots answered the door. She was probably in her mid-30s and very pretty. She resembled the dude Phil, so I figured she was a Bowman, too.

"Yes."

"Ho-Ho-Ho," I said and laughed so my fake belly would shake. "I have a singing telegram for Christopher Bowman. It's a surprise."

"Oh—is that right? Ain't that special. Chris? Chris? Somebody want you at the door! You sure are popular today, boy, with your big head ass!"

"Take a message for me, Cheryl! You good at that," a male voice called out from the back somewhere. "With your good secretary, twenty thousand a year making ass."

"That shit ain't funny, nigga. You need to come to the door."

To me the woman said, "Here he comes, Santa." The woman left the door and a few minutes later, a dude appeared in the doorframe. He was the spitting image of his brother Phil. Only a little bigger and darker.

"Who the? What's up—"

"I got a gift for you, cuz. Special delivery," I told Chris Bowman.

"A gift? Special delivery? From who? I know that lunchin' ass chick, Rochelle ain't —"

"Naw, cuz. This one here is from your brother. He says he can't wait to see you."

The dude's lips curled into a sneer. "My brother? Nigga, who—"

I reached into the bag for the gun. "Your brother wants to see you"—I pulled the 9-millimeter from the sack and fired it into his face. "In hell." I heard a scream inside the house as Chris Bowman's body fell backward. Stepping up into the house, I shot the woman who had just been at the door.

"Ho-Ho-Ho! Merry Christmas!" I yelled as I walked through the house toward the kitchen, stepping over the body of the woman.

"What you in there hollering about, girl!" a lady said loudly as I followed her voice. I appeared in the doorway of the kitchen and saw an older lady with gray hair, wearing a dress, apron, and flip flops, cooking over a stove. "And who are you?" she asked.

Pointing the gun at her, I said, "Saint Nick. Merry Christmas. Ho-Ho-Ho"—and fired, killing her instantly.

********

"—Tuning into City Under Siege Fox News, I am Maria Wilson, and the top story of the evening is a gruesome discovery of a murdered family on Christmas Day. We now go

**83**

to correspondent Aniyah Fields, who is standing live at the scene of the crime . . . Aniyah."

"Good evening, Maria."

"Aniyah, please fill the viewers in on what's happened there."

"Sad, sad news and an even sadder scene here, Maria. Police were called to the 200 block of 'V' Street in the Ledroit Park neighborhood, after reports of people shot. Apparently, a neighbor came to the house behind me here and discovered the front door open. After closer inspection, a body was discovered in the foyer. The neighbor immediately called police. Although I have not been inside the house here, sources closest to the scene told CUS Fox News that there were as many as three people found dead inside. No names have been released, and authorities are locating and notifying the next of kin. DC police has told Fox News that witnesses reported seeing a man dressed as Santa Claus approach the house here on 'V' Street and then leave minutes later. Santa was allegedly driving a dark colored minivan. Authorities are still investigating as we speak, and when more details into this massacre become available, you'll be the first to know, Maria. Back to you—"

"Thank you, Aniyah . . . In other news today, DC Mayor Vincent Gray has been accused by the City Council of nepotism and cronyism . . ."

I stood beside Kemie's hospital bed and stared down into her face. She hardly resembled the beautiful woman that I knew. Every time I looked at her for too long, I got misty-eyed, so I turned away and faced her mother.

"So—" Brenda Bryant said as she forked food into her mouth from a Styrofoam plate. "—that was the dude you told me about?" She nodded at the TV screen.

"Yeah. His name was Chris, and it was his brother, Phil that Kemie killed."

"I know all of that, but the news said there were three people killed inside the house."

I shrugged my shoulders. "It's Christmastime. There was a family gathering, and I decided to crush everybody. A family that prayed together lived their last days together. One sin was attributed to them all. If my baby dies—their whole bloodline dies."

"The police are probably looking all over for you."

"And I'm right here at the bedside of my injured girlfriend. I've been here all day and I got a witness to prove it."

"A witness? Who?"

"You. You were with me all day, right?" I asked as my eyes bore straight into Brenda Bryant's eyes.

"Of course—yeah, you were here with me."

"Besides, you heard the people on the news—the police are lookin' for Santa Claus. Did the doctor make his rounds today?"

Brenda Bryant nodded.

"What did he say? Anything new?"

Shaking her head, Brenda Bryant said, "He said that Kemie is still hovering between life and death."

"Well, I sure hope she lives, because if not, many will die."

********

The food that Marnie cooked was pretty good.

We sat at the table in her living room eating smoked turkey wings, stuffing with gravy, macaroni and cheese, broccoli with cheese sauce and cranberries. The hot buttered rolls melted in my mouth, and I never realized how hungry I was until I sat in front of the food. I half-listened to Marnie as she talked about her day.

"—and that girl is terrible. She all of a sudden done decided that she wanna be gay. I don't know what the hell is goin' on, but nowadays bitches act like that shit cute. Bitches with other bitches, niggas with niggas. This shit is crazy. My mother act like she don't even care about my little sister being a dyke. That's my girl and all. I love my mother to death, but as girlfriend gets older, she's getting dizzy and more dingbatish. Then my punk ass uncle Todd got drunk and started fighting his wife. I hate it when he comes to any family gathering. He always gotta show his ass. And he got the nerve to have like seven kids and all them little muthafuckas bad as shit. My uncle Lump came—"

At the mention of the name Lump, I knew that Marnie was referring to Champ's father. "Have you heard from—Reggie?"

"Damn, I'm glad you mentioned him. He called my phone and said that he couldn't get in touch with you, but told me to tell you to call him. He left you a number." Marnie got up from the table and grabbed her phone off the couch.

She scrolled through her phone and then said, "I programmed the number in my phone. Here it is. 202-527—"

I programmed the number into my cell phone under Champ's name. Since it was almost 11:30 at night, I decided to call Champ first thing in the morning. Hopefully, he had some info for me about where I could catch Lil Cee. I wanted to bring the New Year in the right way, with all my enemies in the ground. Standing up, I grabbed Marnie and pulled her in close and kissed her. We kissed for an eternity it seemed before Marnie broke the kiss.

"Get off me, nigga. You don't love me," Marnie complained as she tried to wiggle out of my embrace.

I held her tighter, ignored her, and kissed her on her neck.

"You think I'm stupid, huh? Well, nigga, I'm far from it. I'm hip to you. You're using me to fill a void in your life

**86**

because your girl ain't available right now. If Kemie was to wake up tomorrow, I'd be yesterday's news. You'd throw my ass to the curb with the rest of the garbage in your life. You don't want me.

"You don't need me. Say it, Khadafi. Go ahead. Say it! Tell me the truth. Admit it to me and yourself. Tough ass nigga, go ahead and keep it real with a bitch." When I didn't speak, Marnie fought her way out of my embrace. In her eyes were large tears forming.

"Why are you doing this to me? Why play with my emotions like this? Huh? What have I done to you—so bad to make you not love me and want to use me? Do you feel sorry for me because of the baby? Is that why you're here? I heard all about your girl being pregnant and losing the baby. I can't stand here and tell you that I'm sorry to hear it.

"Well, I don't need you, Khadafi. I don't. I don't need your pity, your time, your fake ass affection or your dick. I feel so stupid, so anything. I let you fuck your way back into my life, my bed, my comfort zone and you don't even love me."

I stood there looking at Marnie, and my heart broke for her. But only some of what she said was true. I did love her. I did want her. But my heart was and would always be with Kemie. So without saying a word, I grabbed my coat off the couch and left.

********

I woke up in my own bed with a vicious hangover. Once I got home last night, I downed a whole bottle of Krug champagne, and I never drink champagne. After getting off my knees, hurling in the toilet, I felt better. A little. I showered and dressed after cooking a vegetable and cheese omelet. The next order of business was to call Champ.

"What's up, cuz?"

"Dirty Redds? What's up, slim?"

"Champ, what did I tell you about that Dirty Redds shit?" I asked and smiled, already knowing his answer.

"I can't remember all that shit. Muhammad, Ismael, all that shit the same to me. Anyway, I got some good news for you and some bad news. "Which one you want first?"

"Gimme the good news first."

"Cool, I came up on a CO bitch at the halfway house. She used to work down Lorton before going up the jail and then the halfway house. Her name is Naomi Smith. She made a few moves down Lorton and she knows I know it. So I slid up on her and put a bankroll in her face. She bit. Gave a nigga some pussy and that information that you were looking for. Lil Cee's address."

"Okay. And?"

"That was the good news. The bad news is where the address is," Champ said.

"How bad could it be? That nigga don't live with the chief of police, do he?"

"Naw. But he might as well, because the address that he gave the people and they verified it is in another state."

"Another state?" I repeated incredulously.

"Your man Lil Cee left here and moved to Georgia. Norcross, Georgia to be exact. So either you get on the next thing smoking to Georgia, or you forget about Lil Cee. Holla back if you ever need me again. I'm gone."

The cell phone dropped from my hand. I couldn't believe it. If Lil Cee was in Georgia, who the hell was in DC shooting at me?

# CHAPTER FOURTEEN
## Lil Cee

*Norcross, Georgia*

T en . . . 9 . . . 8 . . . 7 . . . 6 . . . 5 . . . 4 . . ." I counted.
". . . 3 . . . 2 . . . 1. . . Happy New Year!" Kia shouted
and popped the cork out of the bottle of sparkling apple
cider that she shook. Apple cider spilled from the bottle onto
the floor. She lifted the bottle and poured the cider out on top
of my head.

I laughed and grabbed the bottle from her. After wrestling
it away, I poured the remaining cider over her head.

"Boy, stop! My hair! You gon' mess up my hair!" Kia
shrieked and ran around the living room.

Chasing her all around the room, I finally tackled her onto
the couch. We both laughed and kissed. Then I remembered
something else. I reached down and felt Kia's stomach."I
didn't hurt you when I tackled you, did I? Was I too rough?"

"No, boy, you good. The baby is good. We good. I am the
happiest woman alive. You could never hurt me."

We kissed some more and then lay quietly on the couch
snuggled up. Minutes later, I listened to Kia's light snore and
felt both happy and sad. I was happy to be alive. Happy to
have Kia by my side and happy to be almost a father. Ever
since Kia told me about the baby, I'd been floating on a cloud
that defied all time and space.

# THE ULTIMATE SACRIFICE III: NO REGRETS

But for all my happiness, pain still lived inside me. Love is pain. The pain inside me was so great that it threatened to overwhelm me at times. Times like now. I allowed myself a moment of weakness and got emotional. Tears slowly fell down my eyes. What the hell? They say that men cry in the dark anyway, don't they? I cried for all the people that I'd lost. I cried for my mother, a great lady who loved life and died much too soon for no reason at all. I cried for a little girl named Charity Renee Gooding, my little sister who was three years old when she died. Thirty-six months old when she was killed. Killed by a monster. A monster named Luther Fuller. That monster also killed my brother.

I thought about 'Church' and remembered his every eccentric move. His calm demeanor and religious personality. I remembered him in every situation that we'd face together until that one fateful night. It was the night I planned and practically had to drag him, kicking and screaming to the book release party. All because I wanted to celebrate a little and see Wale and Rare Essence perform. I never imagined that I'd run into Khadafi there.

I never imagined that he'd tell me to my face how he killed my family and why. I never imagined literally beating him to death until I was actually doing it by the bar inside the hotel. I never imagined that he'd beat us to the parking lot and gain the advantage over us at the game that we also tried to play. I never imagined that as I cowardly ran away, that the man that I loved like a brother, Church, would be gunned down in the parking lot of the hotel. Body left cold and lifeless as his blood spilled on the asphalt. I never imagined any of that on my way home from prison. On that long bus ride from FDC Houston. Things didn't quite turn out how I had hoped. I hoped to just kill Khadafi and Ameen's brothers and that would be it. But fate had a way of changing the course of your life when you stopped at a fork in the road. Sometimes it decided for you. And with things being as hectic as they were, it was time to abandon ship.

Trying not to wake Kia, I got up and walked over to the balcony and opened the glass door. I stepped out onto the balcony and surveyed the surroundings of a foreign place. Then I wondered how I had ended up here. With tears still in my eyes, I remembered.

Having never been outside of DC as a free man, it was taking me a minute to adjust to living in a slower environment like Norcross, Georgia. Before we left DC, Kia and I had both decided on living in Atlanta. Mostly because of the black Mecca implications and all the so-called opportunities that a new start would present. But somewhere along the way, on Interstate 85, Kia saw a sign that read Decatur, Macon, Lithonia and Norcross and the number of miles we had left to reach each place. Out of nowhere, she said, "Let's not got to Atlanta, baby. Everybody who leaves DC goes there. My girlfriend said that Atlanta is a baby New York, DC, and Maryland all mixed up into one. Let's go somewhere that nobody has ever heard of." Kia closed her eyes, opened them a few seconds later and said, "I like the sound of Norcross. Let's go to Norcross."

"What if they are still lynching black folks in Norcross?" I asked.

"We are from the Nation's Capital. If anybody knows how to lynch a muthafucka right back, it's us," Kia replied and closed her eyes again.

That's how we ended up here in Norcross. And it turned out to be a pretty good spot to lay back and raise some kids.

I stood on the balcony of our two-bedroom apartment in Albany Gardens, right across from the Piggly Wiggly supermarket and wiped my eyes. Tears wouldn't bring my family back, and I was getting tired of crying. I wanted to be happy, but grief and anger always got in the way. Having settled in Georgia, getting acclimated to a new place with a baby on the way should be reason to smile. To dream. To fly. To conquer.

But I couldn't let go. Two things stood in the way of me breaking away from my past and focusing on my future. Both of those things were 800 miles away, back in Washington, DC. One was named Khadafi, and the other was called revenge. And no matter what, I was determined to have both.

All in good time, I'd have them. I could wait. Kia was able to get a job at the local high school cooking for the students, something she said she always wanted to try. I had plenty of money left to me by my mother, and we had a child on the way. So pretty much, I had a lot to live for. But is life really worth living if you ain't willing to die for a cause? That's the question that haunted me every day.

# Chapter Fifteen
## Shawnay

"Did you get the money I wired you?"

"Yeah, I did. Khadafi, you didn't have to do that. I don't need your money. That's not the reason why I told you about Kashon," I said into the phone.

"I never said that you did. And I know you don't need my money, but I just wanted to do something for my son. You know I don't believe in all that holiday shit, so I waited until the New Year to spread some love. I wanna see you and Kashon bad, but —"

"You don't have to explain anything to me. I know all about the life you live."

"True dat, but there is a lot you don't know, and I can't explain it to you. So I stay away to stop any of my beefs from coming to your front door. If my enemies ever found out I have a son—"

"What? What would they do?" I asked.

"Listen, that would never happen, and it's good you are all the way in Virginia anyway. When things slow down, I'ma—"

"You don't have to make me any promises that you can't keep, Khadafi. I'm good. Kashon is good. We gon' be okay. Just do what you gotta do to survive—whatever it is that you are involved in. Once you do that, you can be a father to your son. I would never deny you that."

"Have you heard anything from Ameen?"

"I haven't talked to him, naw. But he's in contact with my daughter, and he thinks that I don't know about it. The lieutenant at the jail be giving him the straight out phone calls all the time. Kenya—my daughter tells me everything they talk about."

"So he knows about Kashon? And who his father is?" Khadafi asked.

"Kenya calls herself tryna hide all that, but I'm sure she's told Antonio about my son. Kenya—well, neither of my daughters know who Kashon's father is, so the answer to that question is no. But knowing Antonio like I do, if he knows that you and I were messing around—"

"If he knows? If he knows? You say that like it's a mystery. He knows. Trust me on that. He knows."

"I kinda figured that, but I couldn't be 100% sure. I know that he sent the dude to kill me—"

"He what?" Khadafi interjected.

I told Khadafi about the night the dude with the beard came to my front door with the gun and the message from Antonio. "He said that betrayal is—"

"worse than slaughter."

"Yep. That's what the dude said. How did you know?" I asked, curiously.

"Because that's something that everybody in our circle said and believed. We lived the Omerta and that mantra betrayal is worse than slaughter. It means that we would rather die before we betray a friend. I know it well. And I also know the man you described."

"You know him?" I repeated.

"Yeah. His name is Harold, but we called him Umar. Ameen sent Umar to kill you because of me. I betrayed him, but he must've attributed that betrayal to the both of us."

"How? Did he send somebody to kill you?"

"Naw. He couldn't. Well, he didn't, but he tried to do it himself."

Now I was really confused. How had Antonio tried to kill Khadafi. I asked him.

"I never told you this because I didn't think it was important for you to know. But now that you've told me about Umar coming to your house, you should know. When I got locked back up, the judge from my first case gave me a twelve months hit at my revocation hearing. I thought that I'd be sent to a medium level prison or somewhere sweet to serve the year. But what I didn't know is that the Feds send you back to the prison that you came home from if you violate. I ended up back in Beaumont. I went outside to the rec yard. I knew that Ameen was still in the hole there. After all, I was still in contact with him. But I had absolutely no clue that he knew about me and you. Speaking of which, I still don't have a clue as to how he could've found out about us. But anyway he knew. He came outside and the COs put him in the cage right next to me. He can't rec with nobody because of the status he was on for the murder—"

"Murder? What murder?" My head was spinning.

"That's a story for another day and conversation. Let me finish this one. Ameen came to the fence and we talked. Out of the blue he said, 'It's something you're not telling me, slim.' I asked him what he was talkin' about. 'Shawnay,' he replied. 'You promised me you'd take care of her, slim.'

"'I did take care of her,' I told him. 'You didn't hear about it?' I asked.

"He said, 'I heard about it, all right. You took real good care of her. You took such good care of her, that you fucked her.'"

"But—how—did—? Who told him?" I asked.

"I just told you that I was wondering the same thing, but I still don't know. But what I do know is that Ameen told me that I violated the trust and bond between us and that's when he stabbed me."

For some strange reason a migraine headache formed in the back of my head and worked its way up. I looked around for a second and then remembered that I was still at work. "Stabbed you? Ameen—Antonio stabbed you?"

"Seven times and almost killed me. Remind me to show you my scars the next time I see you."

"But how? You just said that y'all were in two different cages."

"A dude that was in the cage with me put me in a headlock and pent me to the fence. That's when Ameen stabbed me through the fence. A lieutenant saved my life. I was fucked up bad. I had a shit bag on for over a year. And my insides still fucked up. After he stabbed me, they separated us and put me in the hospital and put him in the SHU."

"You said something about a murder. Antonio was in Texas charged with another murder?"

"Yeah, but the key word is was. He's no longer charged with it. He went to trial about three or four months ago, and he beat it."

All of a sudden, a light went on in my head. And something else made sense. "The lawyer. Ruby Sabino. That's why Antonio told me to give the lawyer fifty grand of the money you gave me, because of the murder. I remembered thinking to myself that that was a lot of money to give a lawyer for an appeal. But Antonio never mentioned a word about him killing nobody."

"That's because he didn't kill anybody. I did."

"Wait. If he didn't kill anybody and you did—how is it that you're out here and he just fought a murder charge in trial?" I was perplexed.

"I said that whole subject is a conversation for another day, but since you won't let it go . . . I killed a dude, details not important. The prison saw us on camera going to where the murder was committed.

"The prison officials snatched not only me, but Ameen, Boo, and Umar, too. Well, there was a fifth dude with us, but he—well, we thought he snitched because they separated him, but it turns out that he didn't snitch. He's the one who helped Ameen beat the case. I'm getting ahead of myself—I know. In the SHU, Ameen made the decision to take the murder charge and free the rest of us—"

"But why? Why would he do that? I mean—knowing that he had an appeal coming up and everything? Why?"

"The three of us—me, Umar, and Boo—all of us were within a year of going home. Ameen had the most time left, and he decided that all four of us didn't need to stay in prison for one murder—"

"But he didn't do it!" I exclaimed.

"I know that. We know that. He knew that. But the people at the prison didn't know that. They were charging all four of us with the murder. So Ameen made the Ultimate Sacrifice and confessed to the murder. When he did that, the peoples let the rest of us go. That's how we got home. Before I left him, Ameen's last words to me were, 'Take care of my family.' That's why he feels betrayed by me. Because he gave himself to free me—free us, and all he asked was that I take care of you and his daughters. Me, falling for you—doing what we did, crossed the line. I knew better—but you were irresistible."

"Khadafi, listen—it wasn't your fault. I'm as guilty as you. I—"

"Naw, you listen. I'm a real nigga, a street nigga. I knew the code and where the lines were drawn. And as bad as I wanna kill Ameen for what he did to me—I accept the fact that I betrayed him. He was supposed to bring me that move in Texas. Shit, I would've done the same thing. But what's done is done, and neither one of us can change any of it. Kashon is here, and we all have to live with that."

I thought about everything Khadafi had just said and figured that he was right. There was no way to change anything that had happened.

"You couldn't have known this, but if it makes you feel any better—or any worse—the dude who tried to kill you—"

"The one with the beard?" I asked.

"Yeah. He's dead. Somebody killed Umar about a block away from where you used to live. As a matter of fact, he got killed that same night."

"Killed by who?"

"I don't know. But I have a few ideas. Ameen blamed me for that, too," Khadafi responded and then got quiet. Then finally he said, "Shawnay, I'm sorry for everything."

"Don't be. We're two consenting adults, and as human beings we all make mistakes, but just like you said earlier, we can't change anything we did."

"I wish I could've been the fly on the wall and seen Ameen's face when he found out about Kashon, if he knows about him." Khadafi giggled.

"Like I said before, I know my oldest child, and knowing her like I do, she told him. I bet money on that. And now he probably wants me dead even more."

"You and me both. I know he down Beaumont fucked up—"

"Beaumont? You mean to tell me you don't know?"

"Know what?"

# Anthony Fields

"Antonio ain't in Beaumont no more. He's at DC jail. On appeal." Suddenly Khadafi wasn't giggling anymore.

# CHAPTER SIXTEEN

## Ameen

The old saying goes—don't nothing come to a sleeper but a dream."

At first I thought that I was dreaming when I heard the voice, but then I opened my eyes to see Lieutenant Worthy standing at my bars. I wiped the sleep out of my eyes and swung my legs off the side of the bunk. I went to the sink and brushed my teeth. "That's what I was doing, chasing a dream. Anything is better than my reality right now."

"This shit ain't shit," Worthy replied and smiled.

Spitting toothpaste in the sink, I looked up and replied, "That's easy for you to say. You go home every day after work."

"All I'm doing is getting some pussy every day and you're not. If I could bring you a bitch in here, I would. You know that."

"Pussy would be good, but I'd rather take the freedom."

"Well, I can't help you with that, but I can ease the pain a little with a degree of freedom. Your paperwork cleared this morning. You're going to open pop' today."

"That's definitely a good thing. I appreciate this shit, Worthy."

"Like I said earlier, that shit ain't shit. The move sheet comes out about one o'clock, but you won't move until about 2

100

p.m. Until then, you just lay back and think about what I told you about how DC jail works now. This ain't the jail that you're used to. Don't let one of them young niggas trick you into killin' 'em. They gon' tell on a nigga from the grave. And whatever they don't tell the cameras will catch."

"I got you, big boy," I said before making wudu and preparing to offer my prayer that I missed. "I gotta pray, Worthy."

"I can dig it. Just let me say this and then I'm outta here. I got a meeting to go to. I might not get back down here before you leave, so again, remember what your lawyer said about shit lookin' good for you. I'm stressin' this shit to you because I know how you get down, and this jail ain't on that type of shit no more. Stay focused and keep your eyes on the door that you wanna go out of. When you finish praying, just hit the wall up top and Cooper is gonna let you out. Go 'head and work the phone until you ready to clean up the tier. I'ma holla back."

"I got you and thanks again."

"I'ma come and check on you in a few days."

"A'ight. That's a bet."

Five minutes later, after offering my prayer, I was ready to hit the road running to accomplish my mission. I thought about everything that Worthy had just said and knew that he was right, but I had an obligation to my men and the Muslims that I needed to fulfill. But what about your obligation to your family? Don't they count, too? I shook off the thoughts in my mind and thought about being released into a general population setting after being locked down for so long. An untamed beast being let out into the wild after being in a cage for over three years. Things were bound to be real interesting real soon. I reached my arm out through the bars and tapped the wall over top of my cell. The cell door opened and I ran up to the office to get on the phone.

I called Rudy's office and spoke to him for about ten minutes. There was no change in my appeal status. I was still waiting for the nine judges to decide my fate. I made a few other calls before I decided to call Shawnay. I dialed her at work.

"Virginia Hospital Center, Shawnay Dickerson speaking. Hello?"

Just like all the other times I called, I couldn't bring myself to speak.

"Virginia Hospital Center, may I help you?"

I hung up the phone. As bad as I wanted to speak to Shawnay, for some strange reason I couldn't. I couldn't quite find the words that I needed to say. I was afraid of what her response would be when she learned the caller was me. I wondered if she still had any love for me. I wondered if there could be reconciliation between us after all we had been through. I wondered if I could control my emotions after seeing her son and knowing that the father of that son was my enemy. I wondered if I'd kill her. I dialed Shawnay's number again and after hearing her voice again, I hung up.

******** 

"Southside!" the tall female CO hollered at the bubble in the middle of the hallway intersection that split the north and south sides of the second floor. The south side grill opened, and two other dudes and I followed the CO down the hall.

"Southwest two, you got two coming in." She looked down at the cards in her hand and said, "Thomas and Felder, go 'head in."

I stepped into the sally port and dropped my bag. The dude with me did the same. A cop came out the unit bubble and searched our bags. Then after a brief 'do your own time speech,' we were assigned cells.

"Thomas, you're in thirty-seven cell on the bottom left, and Felder, you're in fourteen cell on the top left."

Faces were smashed against the fiberglass windows on the doors that led to the inside of the unit. I smiled to myself as I saw all the young dudes ice grilling me with false bravado that would instantly change if I whipped out both of the big ass knives that I had in my shoes. The sally port door slid open. I picked up my bag and entered the unit. The crowd that had gathered at the door to see who came in parted as we made our way in. I hit the steps to the top tier and made my way to the fourteenth cell. At the back of the tier, three dudes congregated there as if they were up to something. Quickly scanning their faces, I couldn't spot a potential enemy, but one dude did look familiar. I needed to get the knives out of my shoe. "One of y'all sleep in this cell?"

"Tonio Felder, what's up, nigga?" one of the dudes said. It was the one that I recognized. He had a smile on his face. "Don't tell me you don't remember me, nigga. What's up?"

Just as I was about to go for my shoe, I looked up and placed the face. I returned the smile. "Mike Boone, what's up, slim?" We embraced.

"Nigga, I ain't seen your ass since Cedar Knoll or Oak Hill."

"I'm hip. I heard you was out Lee County, though. I almost didn't recognize you, slim. Your face got big as shit. You got the mumps or something, slim? Your shit swollen?"

"Nigga, fuck you. That's all your ass wanna do is jone. I'm hip to you," Mike replied while laughing. Then he introduced the other two dudes with him. "This is Tim-Tim right here and this scared ass nigga right here is my man Rah-Rah. His codefendant, Donnell Porter was down Oak Hill with us."

"Donnell is my man." I turned to the dude Rah-Rah. "Ain't Nell in the SMU in Lewisburg?"

"Yeah, him and our other codefendant, Velle."

I turned to face the brown-skinned, stocky dude. "You're Timothy Doyle, right?"

"Yeah."

"My man sent me some pictures to Beaumont with you in 'em. He spoke real highly of you. Good to meet you."

"Likewise," Tim-Tim replied.

"They put you in fourteen cell, huh?" Boone asked. "That's a good look. They put you in the cell with a good man. He's on a visit right now, but y'all should get along good. Trey been in a long time. He know how to bid. All of us are back up here on a writ. Tony Hammond called us back. The last thing I heard about you, they say you caught a body down Beaumont."

"I beat that shit in court. They said I killed that rat nigga Keith Barnett, but it wasn't me. I just took the beef so that some good men could go home. Now, I'm back in court tryna see if these people are gonna let a nigga get back."

Boone was in the middle of saying something when I heard the Muslim call to prayer. "I'ma have to get back with y'all good men in a minute. I gotta go and pray."

\*\*\*\*\*\*\*\*

Later that day, my celly, Trey Manning and I stood on the top tier side by side and stared out into the open common area of the block. I had heard a lot about Trey, and all the good men that I knew respected the baby-faced gangsta, who had been in prison for twenty-two years on a murder beef.

"—this shit is crazy, Ameen. These niggas is on some bullshit. They love and respect the rats. I can't get over that shit. All they wanna do is look at hot nigga DVDs and movies. Read hot nigga books and shit. Just like they do in the Feds.

We been up this jail for about two months, and other than the fact that a nigga get to see his peoples twice a week, this joint weak as shit."

"I heard."

"I'm ready to blow this joint and go back to weak ass Canaan. At least—"

I leaned on the rail of the top tier and keyed in on all the faces that I saw. Where are you, Cochise?

"—these young niggas are fucked up, slim. They running around talkin' 'bout they Bloods and Crips and shit. You see all them youngins' over there by the gym?"

My eyes looked over to where Trey referred to. "I see 'em, slim."

"They Bloods. Pirus and Nine-Trey Gangstas or some shit like that. I asked the dude that's supposed to be the leader where they got Bloods at in DC, and his lil punk ass gon' tell me they all over the city.

"I hate them niggas, slim. In the Feds, we be running them niggas asses up. Rats and gang members. That's what the future holds for us, rats and gang members. I need to get the fuck outta jail. Them niggas over there by the phones is Crips. Hoovers, Rollin' Sixties, Shotgun—you name it, they it. I can't believe—"

Suddenly, I smelled something that smelled like a decomposing body was nearby.

"What the fuck?"

Trey burst out laughing. "That shit ain't nothing. I farted. That dirty rice shit I ate for lunch fucked my stomach up. But anyway—"

Out of nowhere, a commotion in the day room caught my attention. The dude that came in the block with me earlier was running around one of the tables, but he was quickly cut off by two young dudes with street knives out. About four dudes total converged on the dude and attacked him with knives. He tried desperately to fight off his attackers, but they were too determined to maim, to kill. With every punch he threw, one of the dudes plunged a knife into his unprotected body. I watched as the condemned man finally screamed out a bestial, guttural cry and collapsed.

As soon as I saw the thick purple blood hit the floor, I knew the dude had made his last stand. The four dudes didn't know that the man was dead. Either that, or they didn't care because they all stood over him and took turns slamming their knives into his prone body. In seconds, the unit was flooded with correctional staff. "Everybody get to their cells. Now!" a white shirted lieutenant shouted.

Trey and I made our way down the tier to our cell. I knew that a shakedown was coming next, so I reached down and untied my shoes. "Do you got a spot in the cell to put these joints up in?"

"In the cell? Naw. But Boone is on detail—" I pulled the knives out of my shoe. "Gotdamn, slim! What the fuck? You had both of them bad muthafuckas on you the whole time we been standing on the tier?"

I nodded.

"Put them joints up somewhere—anywhere. All they gon' do first is the body search. They ain't gon' shakedown until tomorrow. By then you can give them joints to Boone and let him put 'em in the spot."

"That's a bet," I responded as I took my two knives and stashed them in my mail.

Trey took off his jumpsuit and lay in the bed. "Between me and you, slim, I knew that shit was about to happen."

"Oh yeah?"

"Yeah. The dude that came in the block with you was named Cornell Thomas. He used to be thorough back in the day. I guess the bid got to him later on, because he ended up telling on a good man named Fat Koola. On a body. Cornell was a nigga that came up in the trenches when Lorton was Lorton, and the real hyenas and wolves roamed that muthafucka. Him and Koola knew each other from the bricks as kids.

"In 1990, Koola left New Mexico and ran into Cornell, who was just leaving Leavenworth. They ended up being cellies in El Reno. For whatever reason, Koola started telling Cornell about some cold case murders that he had never been charged with. Cornell decided to get a time cut off Koola. When he got back to DC, he contacted the US Attorney and became a world class rat. Now he running around tryna act like he ain't done nothin'."

My mind was on the story that Trey had just told and that made me think of Lil Cee. Thoughts of Lil Cee sparked thoughts of Umar and Boo. Then thoughts of Umar and Boo brought me back to my main objective, killing Cochise Shakur. I hadn't seen him yet, but I was positive that he was in the unit. He probably was in his cell and hadn't come out yet. Or he was in court. Either way, it was all good because he wasn't going nowhere and neither was I. At the moment, time was the only thing that I had a lot of, so patience is and always would be a virtue. The sounds of snores broke my train of thought.

A few minutes later, cops were at the door.

"I need both of y'all to strip. Sarge, pop fourteen cell."

# CHAPTER SEVENTEEN
## Detective Tolliver

The Anacostia branch of the Park Police always had several helicopters on deck, ready to fly at the beck and call of the DC police department. They also employed the best ex-navy divers in the area. I stood at the railing by the rough waters of the Potomac River and waited for the divers to resurface. Keeping my fingers crossed, I prayed that the divers would find what I knew to be on the river bottom. The guns used in the Canal Street murders. Although I failed science, I was wise enough to know that the gun—if recovered—would not reveal any fingerprints. The salty river water would have aided in the decaying and erosion of not just the print, but also the metal used to fashion the guns. The best thing that could come from the finding of the guns would be to try and trace the serial numbers and try to map out a time line and lifeline for the guns, in hopes that someone could be tied to one of them. Or all of them. That would be a big break. And a big break is exactly what I needed.

Leaning on the rail, the triple homicide on Christmas day ragged my mind. It had to be connected to my case. My suspects. Christopher Lamont Bowman was one of the biggest drug dealers in the city and well known to the local FBI and Metro Police. According to the FBI liaison, a secret conspiracy was being built on Bowman and his Colombian connects. The FBI believed that something went awry in the underworld business, and someone targeted and executed Chris Bowman and his entire family.

"Maybe his connect learned of the conspiracy case and eliminated its weak link," one agent said.

"Maybe Chris Bowman stole drugs or money from the connect." Another agent smirked. Theories were tossed around during the investigation, but only the facts remained that Chris Bowman, his mother Alberta Ida Mae Bowman, and his sister Cheryl Bowman were all dead.

I never said a word to my fellow officers, but nobody and I mean nobody saw the connection that I saw. Then there was the thirty-three-year-old woman found the same day, lying beside the dumpster, shot in the face. Witnesses reported seeing a lone man dressed as Santa Claus entering the house on 'V' Street and leaving. The fake Santa was seen driving a dark colored Mazda MPV van. A MPV van matching that description was found days later in a parking garage at Howard University hospital.

The van had been wiped clean. That wasn't the work of out-of-town Colombian hit men to me. That was the work of Luther Fuller or Tyrone Carter. Which one, I didn't know, but the connection to Luther Fuller couldn't be dismissed. An earlier investigation into the death of Phillip Bowman, the man found dead in an abandoned tenement in Capers projects, revealed that Phillip was romantically linked to Rakemie Bryant. Him being killed in Capers validated the fact that he was killed because of Rakemie. For some reason that escaped me. I couldn't shake my intuition that Chris Bowman and family was killed by the same gunman. Maybe Chris Bowman found out about the link between his brother, Rakemie Bryant, and Luther Fuller. Maybe he retaliated and we didn't know it. Maybe Khadafi found out that Chris Bowman was on to him. Maybe TJ killed the family for Khadafi? There were too many likely scenarios to count. And I had no hard facts to present to anybody, so I just kept everything to myself. If the Feds wanna believe that Christopher Bowman and his family were killed by Colombians because of something Chris Bowman did, who was I to tell them not to? I just filed my assumptions and my theories in the back of my head. The file in my brain on TJ Carter and Khadafi Fuller was expanding daily. And there was one thing that I had to give the two men credit for, and that was the fact that they never left a lot of clues behind at a crime scene. In a sense, they were just lucky that way. It happened all the time with criminals past and present. History dictated that. But just like all the other legendary psychopaths, serial killers, and murderers, TJ and Khadafi's luck would run out. And when it did, I planned to be there to bust their asses. A splash of water broke my musing. I looked out at the water and saw a head appear.

Removing the tube in his mouth that was connected to the scuba gear, the diver said, "We got something at the bottom. My partner should be up any minute with the finding."

A minute later, the second diver surfaced. In his hand was a mesh waterproof bag. "You were right, detective. Pop open the champagne. Here's your weapons that you said were down there."

The second diver handed the bag to his partner, who was now sitting on a small dock a few feet from me. The first diver to surface, who now had the bag tossed it my way. The bag landed beside me with a thud. Like a little kid, I tore into the bag and opened it. Stopping briefly to put on latex gloves, I pulled five weapons from the bag and laid them out on a sheet of plastic, side by side.

Having read the ballistics report on the shell casings found at the scene and the bullets pulled from the victims, I already knew what I'd find. But actually having those weapons in front of me was a different feeling altogether. There were four handguns and an assault rifle. I fingered the first gun, a Hi Point 9-millimeter, and then the second one, a Glock 40. The third and fourth guns were a Ruger 9-millimeter and a Sig Sauer .45. The assault rifle, which had done the most damage to the victims was an AR 15.

"I knew it! You bastards came here, dumped the guns, and killed Mark Johnson. But why?" I asked aloud.

I spoke briefly with both divers, shook hands, and then left the Harbor Marina. It was time to see what story the guns could tell me.

# Chapter Eighteen

## Khadafi

The temperature outside had dipped below 20 degrees and would be like that all week according to the weatherman. DC was in for a blizzard-like storm, he said.

I watched the rest of the news and then clicked the TV off. Lying in my king size bed, I thought about the lyrics to Luther Vandross's song, "A House is not a Home."

"—a chair is still a chair/even when there's no one sitting there/but a house is not a home when there's no one there—"

I was seriously missing Kemie, but I tried to think about other things like Lil Cee and whether or not he'd really run away to Georgia. I thought about Ameen and the conversation I'd had with Shawnay. What if Ameen won his appeal and came home? How would he deal with Shawnay? My son? And would he come after me? And vice versa? I thought about Phillip's brother, Chris Bowman, his sister, and mother. A whole family I'd killed, all because of the sins of one son. I thought about Bean and Omar, my two friends that I killed for their sins. At last count, that was a total of six people who died because of my love for Kemie. Rakemie Bryant. My heart, my soul mate, my love. No matter what thoughts I conjured to try and get my mind off Kemie, they always came back to her 360 degrees. So finally, I gave in to my thoughts of Kemie and went all in. I put both hands behind my head and watched TV.

In my mind, it rewound parts of my life and showed me Kemie as a little girl, when I would always mess with her in elementary school. I saw us as a couple in our teenage years, the dates at Crystal's Skate Rink, the carnival on Benning Road, and others. I remembered the day I took Kemie's virginity and stole her innocence forever. I saw all the visits in various visiting rooms at prisons all over the country. I smiled to myself as I remembered the day that I first came home, and at the airport arrivals gate, Kemie pulled up in the candy apple red Nissan. I remembered that first kiss like it was yesterday.

I saw Kemie and me in New York shopping, us at the car lot, the day I copped us both Rovers. Then suddenly I remembered something else. Getting off the bed, I walked over to Kemie's walk-in closet and rummaged around on her top shelf. Where is it? Finally, I found the small box where she kept all her personal trinkets. Opening the box, I peered inside. Moving stuff around, I found exactly what I was looking for. The plastic DVD case was stained a little from wear and tear over the years. But overall it was intact. I put the box back in the place where I found it. Turning the DVD over in my hand, I walked out the closet, went to the DVD player, and popped in the DVD. I sat down on the bed and waited. The plasma TV screen came alive with images of Kemie dropping to her knees and pulling my zipper down. "Is the camera on?" she asked.

"Yeah, it's on," I replied.

"I'ma give you something to dream about for the next ten years."

It was the tape that we made when I first came home in '08. Kemie had been reluctant to fuck me on camera, but I had talked her into it. After her initial reservation, Kemie performed like a porn star. I watched her suck my dick and got aroused. Before I even realized what I was doing, my dick was out and in my hand. Slowly, I stroked myself until a crescendo built up, and I busted a nut all over my hand. I watched the DVD and beat my dick again while watching it. After the DVD faded to black, I undressed and went to the shower to clean myself up.

While getting dressed, I heard my cell phone vibrating. I picked it up and saw that the caller was TJ. "Cuz, what's up?"

"What's up, slim?"

"You. I ain't heard nothing from you since the funeral."

"I been on some other shit, but I'm back. I gotta lick for us."

"Is that right?"

"Yeah. It's a sweet joint, too." Plus, I think I got a line on whoever it was that got at our women—"

"Who?" I bellowed into the phone.

"These phones, slim. C'mon, you know I ain't saying nothing on this jack. You out and about?"

"I'm about to be. Where you tryna meet up at?"

"Down Capers. Meet me over Esha's house at about seven o clock," TJ said.

"That's a bet." I looked at my watch. It was sixteen minutes to three. I ended the call and thought about what TJ said. Did he really know who had shot Kemie and killed Reesie? My blood started to boil, and I had to will myself to calm down. I walked over to my safe and opened it. Peering inside, the stacks of cash that sat bundled together reassured me that life was good. I still had keys of dope, coke, and over two hundred pounds of weed. I was nowhere near broke and didn't really need to go on another caper, but outlaws lived the life of the most hunted. So I had to give in to the nature of the beast. Plus, I had to keep TJ on his toes. If he ever realized that I was stacked so heavy with drugs and money, then I'd have to watch over my shoulder for the day he'd come after me. And I couldn't let that happen. Not now, not ever.

********

I was about ten minutes early for my meeting with TJ. By the time I parked my truck outside of Esha's house, it was 6:50 p.m.

Jumping out the truck, I nodded and dapped up all the good men congregated on Esha's porch. Turning the doorknob, I walked into Esha's house. There were all of ten women huddled in the living room. All of them hood rats.

"—and that shit is crazy because—" Lil Keisha was saying.

"How the fuck that's gon' be crazy, but what he did to her ain't crazy? She was suppose to do that shit. Fuck that nigga, girl. I would've done the same thing if he would've done that to me," Esha responded.

"Yeah—I know, but—"

"Ain't no butts. Girlfriend did what she had to do. I say give the bitch an award for biting that nigga's dick off."

"I'm sorry, Esha, but I'm with Keisha on this. You don't bite off the dick that feeds you," Shampoo added.

Esha stopped braiding Cookie's hair and turned to face Shampoo, as if her head was connected to a swivel. "Bitch, is you lunchin'? Smoking boat again or what? Don't bite the dick that feeds you? What the fuck is that?"

"I always thought it was the hand that feeds you," another girl said.

"It is the hand," TT said as she sat her forty ounce Red Bull down. "But with that nigga and that big ass dick—Esha is right. When a nigga toting like that and know how to work the muthafucka, he feeding a bitch dick, all day every day. Not food."

There was no way in the world I was gonna stand there and listen to a rack of opinionated hood bitches debate about a nigga's dick.

"Esha?" I called out, silencing the room.

"Hey, boy. What's up?" Esha asked.

Then all the women in the room spoke to me and I spoke back.

"Ain't shit. I'm waiting on TJ to come through. When he do, tell him that I'm upstairs playing the Madden joint, a'ight?"

"A'ight. And make sure you leave a few dollars on the dresser up there. Electricity ain't free around here, you dig?"

"I can dig it. I got you," I answered and disappeared up the stairs.

I heard one of the women say, "Girl, that nigga Khadafi be fly as shit. Always."

Somebody else said, "No bullshit. I need to see what that dick do. "I heard he got it good."

I laughed to myself when I heard Esha say, "Y'all horny, dusty ass hookers need to chill out. Kemie ain't dead yet and when she gets well, ain't none of y'all tryna see that girl about that nigga."

I set up the PlayStation 3 and played Madden against the computer. Before long, I was so caught up in the game that I lost track of time.

My watch read 9:27 p.m. by the time I glanced at it, and I realized that TJ hadn't showed. What happened to him? I checked my cell phone to see if TJ had called. He hadn't. I tried calling him, but received no answer. Downstairs, I asked if anybody had seen TJ. Everybody in the room said no.

"Esh, I left the money on the TV upstairs. If TJ comes through, tell cuz to call my cell phone."

"A'ight, boy, you be safe," Esha responded.

Outside, I walked over to my truck and pulled off. I decided as I pulled off to go down Southwest and holler at my man Strong about him copping some weed I still had from the Canal Street caper. Driving down 'M' Street, I turned off onto Third Street and pulled over. I pulled out my cell and called Strong. I saw his burgundy Dodge Charger sitting on the corner.

"I'm getting out my truck now. Come outside—" I was saying as I stepped from the Escalade. I was about to say something else to Strong, but suddenly I heard shots a split second before slugs slammed into my back and leg. Letting go of my phone, I reached under me and gripped my gun. Lifting myself up, I pulled it as I waited for the gunman to finish me off. I expected to be hit in the head at any moment, but for some reason, the coup de grâce never came. But what did come was kicks that rained down all over me.

"Bitch ass nigga! Talk that gangsta shit now!"

I recognized the voice instantly. Absorbing the kicks, I played dead.

"Why did you kill my brother over that freak ass bitch of yours? Huh? Answer me, nigga!" I felt a foot nudging me in the side.

"Turn over, nigga. I wanna look you in your face and make sure you dead." This was my one and only shot at living. I had to make it count. I braced myself and turned over, simultaneously pointing my gun at the man above me and firing.

*Bok! Bok! Bok!*

I watched Devon stumble back, surprised. Quickly, I jumped to my feet and covered the distance. He fell to the ground, holding his stomach. I could see crimson stains spread across his shirt. All my bullets had found a home. Instinct told me to get out of there, but I had to know why Devon moved on me and who told him about me killing his brother.

"Cuz, listen to me," I said, standing over him. "I'ma call an ambulance for you. I don't want to kill you. Just tell me who told you I killed your brother. Who started all of this bullshit?"

"Don't let me die, Redds. Don't let me die," Devon stammered, visibly afraid.

"I'm not, cuz. I'ma help you get help. I didn't mean to shoot you. Who put you on me?"

"TJ told me. TJ said you killed Bean and my brother. I believed him. That's why I came at you. I was angry I—"

I couldn't believe my ears. It couldn't be. "You lyin', cuz. You lyin'. TJ ain't told you no—"

"He did. And when I didn't believe him, he proved it."

"How?" I asked incredulously.

"He took me with him to PG hospital. The night he tried to kill you. In the rain. I was there. I shot too as you ran back into the hospital. TJ said—"

"It doesn't even matter now, cuz. Because he was right, I did kill Omar. And I killed Bean. I'ma kill TJ, and I just killed you." I pulled the trigger and hit Devon in the head twice. I heard sirens in the distance. A movement on the side of me caught my attention. Strong walked around the truck and saw me walking away from Devon. For a quick second, I looked at Strong and tried to decide whether to leave him or—I made the decision in seconds. I lifted my gun again and fired. Strong dropped to the ground, lifeless.

Marnie's apartment was only a few blocks away, so I drove there. Besides, I needed answers that only she could give me. The bulletproof vest strapped to my body had saved my life. Without it, I'd be dead and that was scary to me. I felt blood running down my leg and above my waist somewhere, but where I didn't know. I dragged myself out of the truck and up

the stairs of Marnie's building. I hoped that she was home. I
hadn't had time to check for her car. I banged on her door.

# CHAPTER NINETEEN

## Marnie

I was on the couch watching Sons of Anarchy when the banging on my door started.

"Who the fuck is it?" I leapt off the couch and went to the door. Looking through the peephole, I saw that it was Khadafi. I opened the door prepared to curse his ass out, but then I saw the puddle of blood on the floor at his foot.

"You're bleedin'," I blurted, alarmed at the sight of blood.

Khadafi walked gingerly into my house leaving a trail of blood behind him on my carpet, but I was more concerned with his well-being.

"Who did you tell?"

I saw the scowl on Khadafi's face and knew that whatever was on his mind was way serious. "What—?"

"Who the fuck did you tell?"

The look on Khadafi's face, his disheveled appearance, and the blood on my rug was starting to scare the shit out of me. "Tell what? Who did I tell what?"

"The night that I was here—the night that you told me about Kemie creeping with the dude Phil. That night I told you that I killed Omar and Bean because I felt that they crossed me by fuckin' Kemie. You were the only person—"

"Don't come up in here with this bullshit, Khadafi. I didn't tell nobody shit," I lied.

Khadafi reached out forcefully and grabbed me by my shirt. "Stop fuckin' lying to me, cuz! You were the only person that I told the shit to. Who did you tell?"

"Khadafi, baby, please. You're scaring me, and you're bleeding. You need help. Get the—"

"Marnie, I need to know!" he shouted and then lowered his voice. "I need to know who you told. Somebody just tried to kill me, and I don't know why."

"Khadafi let me go."

"Who did you tell what I told you?"

I hesitated for a minute but then came clean. "The only person that I said something to was Reesie. I told Reesie."

"Fuck!" Khadafi muttered as he shed his wool coat and sweater. "You told Reesie and she must've told TJ. Damn, cuz. I wish you hadn't done that. Help me take this vest off. My back hurting like shit. As a matter of fact, go and get an old sheet or something."

I left to get the sheet and then came back and helped Khadafi take off his bulletproof vest. Khadafi sat down and moaned as he pulled off his boots, and then slid his pants down. He was also bleeding from the shoulder.

"You got blood on your shoulder, too," I said as I inspected his leg wound first.

Blood was coming out of the hole there. "Let me see if the bullet went all the way through."

"It didn't. I can still feel it in my leg. By the bone." Khadafi tore a piece of the sheet into strips and then handed me one. "Here, to stop the bleeding."

"A tourniquet. I know all about it. I am a nurse. Duh?"

"I'm starting to feel a little dizzy, too."

"You need to go to the hospital then," I pleaded.

"I can't. I just killed two muthafuckas. They gon' know it was me. Why did you tell Reesie what I said?"

# THE ULTIMATE SACRIFICE III: NO REGRETS

I ignored Khadafi until I had completely wrapped the sheet around his gunshot wound. "She was my best friend, Khadafi. It just came out the night that I cried on her shoulder. The day that you said you were leaving me and going back to Kemie."

Khadafi shook his head. "And she told TJ. He told Devon—and he just tried to kill me."

"Who? TJ? Devon? Who just tried to kill you?"

Khadafi explained to me how he confronted Devon after Esha told him what Devon had been telling people around Capers. He told me about the attempt on his life and how he had just killed Devon.

"You just said that you killed two muthafuckas. Who else did you kill besides Devon?"

"A friend of mine named Strong. He showed up right after I killed Devon."

"I'm confused. The dude Strong was your friend, right? So why did you kill him?" I asked, looking confused.

"Because he saw me kill Devon, and although he was a friend, I couldn't leave him alive to tell the story. That's how cases get built on niggas. You know our motto is 'Leave no witnesses!'"

"Well, I'm just glad that you're okay."

"The vest saved my life—again. Check the vest. There should be at least two rounds stuck in the material."

I checked the vest and just like Khadafi said there were two slugs embedded in it.

"Before Devon died, he told me that TJ was the one who told him that I killed Omar and Bean. Him and TJ were the ones that tried to kill me as I left PG hospital one night. All this time and I didn't even know it. I can't believe it. He smiled in my face at Reesie's funeral. He hugged me and smiled in my face, and all the time he wanted me dead. Tried to kill me. But what I don't understand is why he sent Devon or why he hooked up with Devon to get me. TJ could've tricked me and killed me at any time. He set me up, that much I do know. He called me and ran some shit to me about a lick we could go on. He told me to meet him down Capers at seven o'clock. He never showed, but he had to know I'd come. So why didn't he kill me himself? He could've ambushed me easily. He put Devon on me. Devon must've followed me to Third Street. As I got out the truck, he tried to kill me. TJ is fucked up at me about Bean. He wants to kill me about me killin' Bean."

I stood over Khadafi and checked his leg wound. The bleeding had stopped. Everything that Khadafi had said crowded my brain. My thoughts raced a mile a minute as I struggled to connect the dots, but eventually I did. I had always wondered why TJ tried to kill Kemie. Now I knew why. He wanted to hurt Khadafi and take away the one person that he knew Khadafi loved the way he loved Bean. Then kill Khadafi. It was a feeling that I could definitely identify with. I couldn't lie. But I wanted Kemie dead for different reasons. As I cleaned and bandaged the old shoulder wound that Khadafi had aggravated, I struggled with the decision that I knew I had to make. And that was whether or not to tell Khadafi what I saw the night Kemie was shot. I tended to the man that I loved with the most tender love and care that I could muster, and along the way, I decided to tell him what I knew.

"I got something to tell you and you can't be mad at me. Promise me that you won't be mad." I stood up, turned my back, and paced my living room floor.

"Whatever it is, I promise you that I ain't gon' be mad at you. You already put my life in jeopardy when you told Reesie that I killed Bean and Omar and didn't know it, so how bad could it be?"

# THE ULTIMATE SACRIFICE III: NO REGRETS

"I put your life—Khadafi, that's not fair! Okay, then again, I'ma grown woman. I fucked up and I can admit that. If it's worth anything, I'm sorry—"

"Fuck that shit. You made a mistake. Go ahead with whatever it is that you need to tell me."

"The night that you left me to go home to Kemie—I was devastated. I mean really, really devastated. I was hurt bad. My pain was so deep and severe that it became real to me, like a real person. I cried and cried and finally, I decided to kill myself. I never told you any of this because I didn't want you to pity me and stay with me out of sympathy. That would have hurt me even more.

"Marnie, I—"

"Boo, just let me finish." I stepped over to Khadafi and kissed him. Then I put two fingers to his lips and held them there. "Let me say this while I still have the nerve to say it. After the thought of killing myself passed, the thought of killing Kemie emerged in its place. I told myself that she was the reason you didn't want me. I thought about all the pain she caused me before and decided that she was the cause of all my pain. So that night I decided to kill her. If Kemie was gone, things with you would be different, I told myself. I planned her murder in my mind a thousand times. I had the murder weapon and everything. Do you remember the gun that you gave me the day that you told me that somebody shot your Range Rover up on MLK Avenue?"

The look in Khadafi's eyes was evil. Pure evil. It frightened me and chilled me to the bone. Khadafi nodded.

"That was the day that you had just copped the Infiniti truck. Well, anyway, I kept the gun. You never asked for it back, so I kept it. That was the gun that I planned to kill Kemie with. One day I drove to y'alls house—don't look at me like that. Of course I know where y'all live. The house is in Tacoma Park.

I was at your house—well, outside your house the day Kemie rushed out and jumped into her truck. That was the day that they discovered Reesie dead—"

"Man, hold on, cuz. What the hell was you doin' outside my house?"

"Boy, get over it. I was there, okay? I followed Kemie that day to Reesie's apartment building and again when she pulled off about fifteen minutes later. She went up Alabama Avenue and took that straight out to where she eventually pulled over and parked. At the liquor store across from the Hobo Shop. I drove past her truck and noticed that Kemie had dropped her head down onto the steering wheel. I kept going over to Marlboro Pike. There, I got out the car and ran back over to Kemie's truck. I tapped on the window to get her attention—"

Khadafi leapt up from the couch and shook his head. "Marnie, please don't tell me that you shot Kemie. You shot Kemie?"

"I wanted to shoot Kemie," I said and walked across the room. I had to get away from Khadafi for a while. "I needed to shoot her, but I couldn't. I wanted her dead. I willed myself to shoot her, but again, I couldn't do it. I'ma whole lotta things, but I guess a killer ain't one of 'em. Dejected, I lowered the gun and walked back to my car. Halfway there I heard gunshots. I turned and saw a person with a gun shooting into the Land Rover. I could see the sparks as they erupted from the gun's barrel. I was close enough to feel the vibrations. The person then ran to a car. The person and the car were well known to me.

"The street was well lit, and my eyes weren't deceiving me. The car was a black Buick Roadmaster."

"TJ shot Kemie? That's what you're tellin' me?"

I nodded and watched the cloud of hurt descend upon Khadafi's face.

"He shot her and then ran back to his car and pulled off. I saw him. And at that moment, I was happy. I was afraid. I don't know what I was feeling, all I know is that I knew that you and I would finally be together. You, me, and our child. I vowed to myself to never tell a soul what I saw."

Khadafi sat back down and put his face in his hands. I wondered if he was crying. "On my dead mother, I'ma kill him. I'ma crush that nigga. His ass is mine."

I sat down on the couch beside Khadafi and tried to console him, but he was having none of it. Khadafi turned to face me and looked me in the eyes. "Did TJ see you that night? If he ran up after you walked away then that meant that he saw you, right? He had to. He had to have sat and watched the whole episode unfold. He had to have known that you were following Kemie. He knows you. He knows your car. While you were following Kemie, TJ was following y'all. But the question is, does TJ think that you saw him?"

"I don't know. We never locked eyes or anything, but I can't say for sure whether or not he saw me."

"Cuz, you gotta bounce," Khadafi said suddenly. "You can't stay here no more."

"Go? Bounce? Can't stay here no more? Why?" I asked him, vexed.

"Because TJ will eventually come for you. I'm surprised that he hasn't already. Trust me I know this nigga. He knows that you're pregnant by me. He knows how I feel about you."

"But how?"

"How? Because I told him. He was my man and I told him a rack of shit. If Kemie were to die then that would make you a witness to murder, and our motto is . . ."

"Leave no witnesses. I heard that before already."

"Well, now, TJ has more reasons than one to kill you. Once he finds out that I survived the hit by Devon and in turn killed him, he'll probably make the quantum leap and know that Devon told me everything. TJ knows that I will question a victim before they die. He watched me do it several times. Then he'll come looking for me. TJ knows that he can get to me through you. You are in danger. You and the baby. That's why I say that you gotta bounce."

"But where will—"

"You can go down North Carolina to your people's house. Yeah, go to Wilmington. You can stay there until I tell you it's safe to come back."

"My job—my apartment—" I stammered in disbelief.

"Fuck all that shit, Marnie! What's gonna happen to that shit if TJ kills you?" Khadafi exploded. "You can always get another job, another apartment, but you can't get another life if TJ takes this one. Don't worry about none of this shit. I got money for you and the baby, y'all gon' be a'ight. Go and pack whatever you wanna take because you're leaving tonight."

I jumped up. "Tonight?"

"Yeah, tonight. That's if TJ ain't outside waiting to smash both of our asses."

I thought about arguing with Khadafi further, but unfortunately I decided against it. He was right. Everything that he said was true and I knew it. That's when I realized that I wasn't ready to die just yet. I rushed into my bedroom and started to pack.

# CHAPTER TWENTY
## Khadafi

C hange of plans," I told Marnie as I loaded the last bags into the trunk of her car. I needed to secure myself just in case things went bad.

"You say you know where my house in Tacoma Park is, right?"

Marnie nodded. "1736 Woodlawn Drive."

"When all of this is over, I'ma ask you how in the hell you know where I live, but right now, I want you to go there."

"To your house? Why?"

"Listen, we'll talk when I get there. We are going to go there separately. I wanna make sure that you're not being followed."

"Well, who's gonna make sure you are not being followed?" Marnie asked.

"Let me worry about all that. Here." I pulled the spare key off my key ring and gave it to Marnie. "Park in the carport beside the house and let yourself in through the door right there. Go in and make a left. That hallway will lead you to the living room. Wait for me there."

Pulling Marnie close, I kissed her. "Go. I'll be coming through the door no more than five to ten minutes after you."

I watched Marnie pull off and then limped to my truck. My leg was stiff, throbbing and hurt like hell. And so did my back. The muscles there screamed out for relief. Despite my pain, I was happy to be alive. Again, I had cheated death. A bulletproof vest and a dumb ass nigga had spared my life. Devon wasn't a killer. He only pretended to be one. Pretenders always made vital mistakes that led to their demise. If only he'd known to finish the job with head shots and no questions, he'd be alive and I'd be dead. Goofy muthafucka, fuck him. I pulled into traffic and stayed three to four cars behind Marnie, all the while checking all my mirrors for any possible threats.

Fifteen minutes later, we finally reached Takoma Park. I watched Marnie enter my house and then I circled the neighborhood about ten times before being satisfied that all was well.

I parked my truck beside Marnie's Chrysler and entered the house. When I reached the living room, Marnie was standing in front of our wooden armoire looking at photos of Kemie and me. She heard me walk into the room. Without looking at me, she said, "You and Kemie look really happy in these pictures."

I knew exactly what road Marnie wanted to go down, and I wasn't going to go there with her.

"I don't know how this shit'll turn out, but it's do or die for me. I have to go after TJ. That's not even in the talk. He violated and tried to bring about my death. It's either him or me. So listen to me, if I die or go to prison, you have to be the one who holds me down. If I die, fuck it, I'm gone, so I don't give a fuck after that. Promise me that you'll get my body to the Muslim brothers—the Masjid on Benning Road. Tell the brothers that you want an Islamic burial for your baby's father. Whatever the cost, pay for it and donate a few dollars to the Masjid.

"How much is on you. If I die, you take everything and make sure that my unborn child has everything he or she wants and needs. And there's another thing—" I grabbed a pen and wrote down Shawnay's phone number. "Nobody knows this but you, not even Kemie. I have a son named Kashon. He's almost a year old."

"You have a son?" Marnie asked.

"I don't feel like getting into the specifics, but yeah, I have a son. And you have to promise me that you will give his mother, Shawnay, some of this money. I want to make sure that my son and your unborn child know each other as siblings. That's not too much to ask, is it?

"I guess not, no."

"Good. Listen, this house is in Kemie's name. Let her family fight over it." I led Marnie into the basement. "In these boxes are drugs, Marnie. All different kinds of drugs. If something happens to me—death or prison—I want you to come here and get all of this shit out of here. Put the boxes in storage until you decide what to do with it. But never tell a soul about its whereabouts, you feel me? You'll have the spare key. Nobody else has a key to this house but Kemie, and she is at the hospital. C'mon, let's go upstairs."

Upstairs, I led the way to the bedroom. I went to the closet and opened my safe. Emptying out its contents, I put everything in a bag and laid it on the bed. "That's over three hundred thousand dollars. I just told you what to do if I don't survive—"

"But why do you have to go after TJ? Why can't we both leave?"

I cut Marnie off. "I ain't never ran from a nigga and I ain't gon' start now. Besides, TJ won't stop until I'm dead. Plus, I owe him for Kemie."

"Kemie? Kemie! Is this shit about Kemie? Fuck that bit—"

My hand reacted before my brain did. I smacked Marnie hard in the face.

"Nigga—" Marnie screamed seconds before she rushed me, both arms swinging wildly. "Don 't—you—ever in your life hit me."

I gave in and let Marnie get her frustration out. Then I grabbed her and held her. "I'm sorry—I didn't mean to—"

"Get off me! Let me go! You brought me here to beat me up?" Marnie screamed hysterically. "You hit me because I said what I feel. Let me go, Khadafi!"

I held on tight as Marnie tried to force herself from my embrace. Kissing all over her head and face, I eventually got her exactly where I wanted her. "Marnie, I love you. I need you. Please forgive me . . ."

********

The sunlight coming through the window was the first thing I saw when I opened my eyes. I glanced at the clock on the dresser 10:21 a.m. Beside me, Marnie slept peacefully. After sex for hours and a shower, Marnie massaged my whole body until I fell asleep. "Marnie, wake up."

Her body stirred and then her eyes popped open. "Where—" She looked around the room. "I thought I had dreamt—"

"Time to get up. Call your job and say whatever you need to, but make it quick. I want you on the road soon. And I want you to take my Escalade. I'ma call Alex and have the title transferred over to you. It's paid for."

"But what about my car?" Marnie asked groggily.

"I'ma trade it in, along with my hoopty and get something that nobody has ever seen. I never got the chance to finish what I was saying last night. I told you what to do if I die, but on the flip side of that coin, if I make it, but end up in prison, you'll have to hold me down. That means pay my lawyer, send me a few dollars here and there. Can you handle that?"

"You know I can."

131

"Good. So call your people in Carolina and let them know you're coming today. I'ma load all of your stuff into the Escalade, plus the money. Don't tell anybody about the money. Your family, nobody."

"I'm not stupid, Khadafi."

"Good. Then you'll just chill in Carolina until you hear something. Keep in touch with somebody up here, Esha, Dawn, Keisha, somebody. Their nosey asses will know something about me or TJ. If things go my way, I'll call you. If you don't hear from me in a week, well—it is what it is. Either I'm dead or in jail. Call up to DC jail and check and see if I'm there. If not, and you don't hear from me, call the Muslim brothers. You get up and get yourself together and I'ma make us some breakfast. Then you hit the road."

********

With Kemie in the hospital surrounded by family and tight security, and Marnie about an hour away from her destination, it was time for me to go into beast mode. I paid my neighbor two hundred dollars to drive my DTS to Legend Imports on Silver Hill Road, while I drove Marnie's Chrysler 300. I traded both cars in for a 2012 Buick Lucerne, black on black with 35% tints. I needed to make one more stop, and it was the most important one.

********

"What type of heat do you need?" Dice asked.

"I need something proper. Here take these." I handed Dice one of my 9-millimeters and the .40 cal' that I'd taken off Devon. "They hot, but I cleaned both of them up. I got another handgun. I need something light, but deadly. With a clip that hold at least fifty. You got something like that?"

Dice went into his backyard and came back with a bag. He opened it to reveal all kinds of handguns, machine guns, and rifles. "I got a baby SKS that hold sixty in a banana clip. Bad muthafucka. That joint will spit on call, and you don't have to burp it.

"I got a mini 14 Ruger sub joint that only hold thirty-five in the clip, but it hold .762's. They like AK bullets. It's a chopper disguised as a machine gun. I got Macs, Techs, Heckler & Kochs. You name it, I got it."

Twenty minutes later, I left Barry Farms projects with a brand new SKS and enough shells to start another Vietnam. Pulling my hat down low, I pronounced myself ready for war.

"I'm coming, TJ. Ready or not, I'm coming."

# CHAPTER TWENTY-ONE

## Ameen

B all!" one of the dudes on the basketball court yelled
out. "I called ball. Respect my call."
"You be crying like shit, blood. No bullshit. You make
a nigga not even wanna play this shit," a dreadlocked young
kid with a rack of tattoos on his face responded.

"Stop hacking me then, you bum ass nigga, and I won't
have to call ball."

I leaned on the wall of the gym and watched the basketball
game in process. The area was small and with only one
basketball court, dudes played only a three on three.

The dude who had earlier called 'ball' was a human
highlight reel with an NBA-like game, so everybody in the
unit gathered to see him ball. All eyes were on him except
mine. Mine were on his teammate. The big dude with the long
hair. I had watched him for days, and now I was starting to
feel like too many days were passing. Something an old head
convict told me the day I hesitated to put the knife in a dude
who disrespected me in the chow hall came immediately to
mind. "Patience is a virtue, Ameen. But when you wait too
long it becomes cowardice." I surreptitiously eyed the man
who'd been recently found guilty of killing my partner, Boo
and his family. Cochise Shakur's conviction had been
publicized in all the local newspapers. The way he cavalierly
talked about those killings on the tier down South One

propelled me forward. I left the gym and went directly to the bottom left tier where Boone, Tim-Tim, Trey, and Omar Van Hagen were all working out.

"Boone, I need to holla at you, slim."

"What's up, Antonio?" Boone replied as he got up from a set of burpees.

"Not here, slim. In the cell." The look on my face probably told Mike Boone that I was deathly serious, because without another word he led me to his cell.

Once the cell door closed, he said, "What's up, slim?"

I needed a good solid man to assist me in my quest to kill Cochise Shakur, and I knew that Boone could be trusted. Not that my celly couldn't, I just felt that I'd known Boone longer and had seen him respond while in the trenches.

"Listen, scrap, I need your help. I got a move I need to make, and I need another set of eyes and ears. I wouldn't even ask you if I didn't have to, but basically you are the only dude besides my celly that I trust in here. My celly is about to go back to the Feds and see the parole board. They took back his five-year hit and gave him a rehearing. He should be able to get an assumption date at least. Slim been in prison twenty-two years, and I respect the game too much to involve him. Not saying that your situation is any less fruitful, I'm just asking for your assistance. Eyes and ears."

Boone dropped his gloves on the metal desk by the wall. "What you tryna do, slim? I'm with you."

"There's a dude in the block that I came out here specifically to get. He killed a couple of my men and some other people. I been chasing slim since we was down South One together. I just couldn't get to him. But now I can, and I'ma dog him with or without your help. I just need you to keep watch for me. That's it."

"First, you gotta tell me who you talkin' 'bout, slim. I gotta few men in the block myself, and you know I ain't wit' you smashing no Muslims."

"He ain't Muslim, and I've never seen you say a word to this dude. His name is Cochise," I said and waited to read Boone's facial expression.

"The big nigga with the long braids? The one that just lost on all them bodies?"

"Yeah, one of them bodies was my man. He was like a brother to me. He killed my man's seven year old daughter and his grandmother. There's no reprieve or clemency for that. Allah forgives sins, not me. So what's it gonna be? Are you wit' me or not?"

"Fuck it. I'm trained to go. I'm with you, slim. Run the game plan down to me."

For the next thirty minutes that's exactly what I did.

\*\*\*\*\*\*\*\*

"Outside rec! Outside rec!" I heard the CO calling for rec and I jumped up.

"You going outside, Trey?" I asked my celly as I put my extra jumper on, and then brushed my teeth.

"Naw, slim. It's too early for me. I don't be fuckin' with that eight in the morning rec shit. I'ma lay in. Just get the door closed when you leave."

"That's a bet, slim," I replied, spitting toothpaste in the toilet. Within ten seconds, I reached under my mattress and pulled my twin bangers. I put a blade in each of my shoes and put them on. Sticking my arm out the door, I hit the metal over the top of the cell to get the CO's attention. "Pop fourteen cell for rec," I said.

A few seconds later, the cell door popped and I stepped out.

"Sarge, close fourteen cell back." I waited until my cell door was secure before proceeding to the sally port with all the other convicts. Then I went out in the hall and got searched by the rec officer.

I met up with Boone outside. We said very little to one another as we circled the square rec yard and did pull-ups. The rec yard sat on the ground floor of the jail. Cement blocks served as benches. Other amenities included tables for tabletop games, a volleyball net, a basketball court, and a radio."

A crowd formed around the jukebox as everybody listened to the latest hip-hop on WPGC 95.5. I pretended to rock and sway every time I passed the jukebox, but truth be told, I was hyped and focused on Cochise Shakur, who was engaged in a whole court game of basketball.

Outside recreation was only for an hour. So when my mental clock chimed in my head and let me know that the hour was almost up, I went to the cement block, turned my back to the yard and kicked off my shoes. I pulled out the ripped bed sheet and unrolled it. Then slowly and methodically, I wrapped one knife handle and then the other.

After both knives were wrapped and ready to go, I put them up my sleeve. Walking up to Boone, I passed him a knife. I nodded to him and looked in Cochise's direction on the court. Boone nodded in understanding. Ten minutes later, the rec officer called an end to rec. I walked over by the door that led up the stairs to the second floor. The dimly lit stairwell was a known death trap at the DC jail, and it was about to become one again today. Flipping the knife over, I palmed the blade end, but I kept the handle hidden up my sleeve. I stood alone and watched all the prisoners head in my direction to the door. Cochise Shakur was at the rear, engaged in a conversation with Boone. I watched Boone stop walking as he spoke to Cochise and wondered what he was saying.

Whatever he was saying was working against Cochise, because him and Boone ended up being the last two people to approach the entrance to the stairwell. I walked into the stairwell and climbed the stairs to the first landing. There I stood waiting for the door to open and Cochise to walk in. The lone rec officer had opened the door to the stairwell and climbed the stairs to open the door on the second floor that led to the unit. I could hear voices as I walked down the stairs. The door opened. Cochise stepped into the stairway, distracted because he focused on Boone, who walked behind him. I reached the bottom ground in seconds and plunged my knife deeply into Cochise. Caught by surprise, his eyes showed alarm and fear as I repeatedly stabbed him. Boone hit him in the back and I worked the front. Cochise tried to fight back, but he was in a losing battle and he knew it. Suddenly, he collapsed to the floor. I stepped over him and aimed my knife straight at his throat. Then I plunged it in, twisted it, and left it there. Sure that he was dead, I stepped out of my extra jumpsuit and wiped blood off my hands.

"Help me get him up!" I shouted to Boone. "Put him in the coat basket."

At the bottom of the stairs was the basket that held the coats for people who went out to rec. We lifted Cochise and put him in the basket. I took a coat and cleaned the blood off the ground, and then threw it in the basket over Cochise. Then quickly, Boone and I raced up the stairs to catch up with the others. Cochise Shakur's murder had taken months to plot, a few days to plan, but only three minutes to execute.

As I walked back into the block, step for step with Boone, all I thought about was the fact that all the punishment Cochise took before he died, never once did he scream or holler out. I respected that in him. Cochise's body was found an hour before the four o'clock count. The entire DC jail was placed on lockdown. And suddenly, I felt a sense of déjávu. It felt like 2007 in Beaumont Pen, when Keith Barnett got killed. All over again.

# CHAPTER TWENTY-TWO
## Khadafi

Timing is everything and mine is off a little. As soon as I pulled back into my spot across from the court where Esha lived, I spotted TJ going into Esha's house. Silently, I cursed because I'd have liked to have caught him before going inside, but what the hell. His death certificate was still signed and sealed. His cockiness and arrogance made my blood boil. This nigga knew how I got down, and his lack of regard for my gangsta was insulting.

He had to know that eventually Marnie would tell me about him shooting Kemie. TJ was slipping bad, or either he just had a death wish. Maybe he had a casket already picked out and a plot out in Harmony beside his family that was already paid for, but he just needed a muthafucka to put him in it. Or did TJ believe that I was too afraid to cook his ass?

Well, even wild animals will sacrifice their blood and gnaw off a limb when trapped. Survival is the first law of nature in the land of the beasts next to self-preservation. Then comes the preservation of those we love—Kemie, Marnie, Shawnay, my son Kashon, my unborn.

I chewed bites of my mozzarella chicken sandwich and stared at the door that TJ had just entered. The tinted windows on the Buick Lucerne allowed me to watch, but not be seen. Thoughts of TJ sending a boy to do a grown man's job made me smile. He had to know that sending Devon at me would bring about Devon's demise. He had to know that Devon couldn't kill me. So that made me conclude that TJ wanted Devon to die. Probably because he was running his mouth too much, and eventually word would get back that they were the ones who shot at me at the hospital. Maybe Devon had become too much of a liability to keep around.

As I finished my sandwich, I decided that that had to be it. TJ had to know that I'd smash Devon.

The desire to trap my prey came upon me as the thought of going inside Esha's house and killing TJ crossed my mind. But I suppressed that urge. Namely because I'd have to crush Esha, too, and I didn't want to do that. Unconsciously, I pulled a rolled blunt out of my pocket and lit it after downing the last of my Dr. Pepper soda. I puffed on the blunt and let the hydro take me to another state. An introspective state. Then the questions came. Had TJ really killed Reesie, and why? Had she become a liability too? Or was TJ just slowly becoming unglued? Was his mental capacity diminishing? It had to be, because why would he shoot Kemie and leave me alive to find out about it? Why not just confront me about whether or not I killed Bean and Omar?

The suicide angle came back to mind and that open casket waiting for TJ. Then something inside me said, "Fuck all that. Knowing the answers to all them questions is not going to change what we need to do today."

The weed choked me as I muttered in agreement with my conscience. Nothing could change the path that I was about to take. I picked up the SKS off the floorboard of the Buick and fingered it. Over sixty bullets were in the clip, and only one needed to find its mark, TJ's head. I put the blunt out and focused on Esha's front door. As soon as TJ walked out the door, his time was up.

# CHAPTER TWENTY-THREE

## TJ

I know all about what happened to Devon, Esh. I heard the story just like everybody else did," I said, exasperated and trying to figure out exactly what Esha was getting at.

"Well, somebody told Pee-Wee and nem' that you sent Devon at Khadafi and that's why Khadafi killed him. "Is that true? Did you tell Khadafi to come down to my house so that you could set him up to be shot by Devon?"

"Esha, you horse playing right now—"

"Ain't nobody horse playing. I'm dead muthafuckin' serious. I remember the day that Khadafi came in here and said, "I'm waiting for TJ to get here. Holla at me when he do." And he went upstairs to play the Play Station. You never showed up, and after a couple of hours, he left. That was the same day I heard that Devon got killed down Third Street. When I first heard it, I'm thinking, Okay, them Southwest niggas on some bullshit again and they probably blamed Devon in some way for Black Woozie getting killed up here. I'm thinking they wanna kill anybody from Capers. Then today, I hear from Pee-Wee that niggas—"

"Niggas like who, Esha?"

"How the fuck do I know? All I know is that niggas is saying that you told Devon that Khadafi killed his brother and Bean. Devon ran his mouth and Khadafi got word of it. That part I know for sure because me and Khadafi talked about it.

142

They say that Khadafi went down Third Street and confronted Devon about the rumors. You were supposed to have gassed Devon up. They saying that you gave Devon a gun and everything. Then he went after Khadafi the day Khadafi was here, and we both know the rest of the story. So I'm asking you, is any of that true?"

"I know one thing. Muthafuckas in the hood be running their mouths too much." I instantly regretted involving Devon in my beef with Khadafi. "Naw, that shit ain't true. Not the part about me gassing Devon up to go at Khadafi, but I did tell him that Khadafi killed his brother and Bean. He decided to see that man about that. That ain't on me. He jumped out there and Khadafi killed him. Why should I care?"

"Why should you care? I can't believe you just said some shit like that," Esha said and threw both hands in the air. "Ughh! Y'all niggas kill me. All of us grew up together and be around each other every day. How can you be so uncaring about one another? This shit is crazy. They must be putting something in the water to make all of us in the ghetto turn on one another. I need to move away from all this shit. I'm not feeling all this snake shit. And the killings . . . Look at all the deaths we been experiencing in the hood lately. In the last few days, months, and years. Bean, Omar, 'Quette, Reesie, Kemie is on her death bed, they say. This is some geekin' ass shit, and I'm tired of it all. I swear to God I am. Are you sure that Khadafi killed Bean and Omar?"

"Yeah, I'm sure. He admitted it to Marnie. Marnie told Reesie and Reesie told me. And I believe he did it, so he's gonna pay for it."

Esha looked at me incredulously. "He gon' pay for it, huh? So I guess now you wanna kill Khadafi. Based on something that was said but you don't know for sure. What if he didn't do it?"

"Fuck all that. He did it, and I know he did it. If he told Marnie he killed Bean, then he killed Bean. Khadafi ain't gon' lie about no shit like that. Man, fuck that snake ass nigga, Esh. Why the fuck are we standing here even talkin' about this nigga?"

"Because TJ, I'm sick of all the killing. I've had it up to here, and somebody gotta try and talk some sense into y'all thick ass skulls. All of us are a family. Remember that? Now you standing here sounding like you wanna beef with Khadafi. All because of some he said, she said shit about him killin' Omar."

"I ain't beefing about Omar. Me and Omar wasn't never really that close. That's the real reason why I gave Devon the opportunity to get at Khadafi. For his brother. My beef with Khadafi is about Bean. Bean was a big brother to me. He raised me, and Khadafi betrayed the world by taking him away from us."

Esha looked at me and then dropped her head. She turned and walked across the room. Shaking her head in disbelief, she said, "Betrayal is worse than slaughter. That's something that Khadafi always says, ain't it? Betrayal is worse than slaughter. He said that he would rather be slayed than betray one of his men. That's what he said." Esha walked over to the bookshelf on the wall and pulled down a book. She opened it and turned a few pages. "The dictionary defines betrayal as: to help the enemy of, to expose treachery, to deceive, specifically to seduce and then desert; to reveal unknowingly as in to betray a trust. You say that Khadafi betrayed the world by killing Bean, right? Well, guess what, TJ? You're wrong." Esha looked up from the book with tears rolling down both sides of her cheeks.

"Khadafi did all of us a favor by killing Bean. You think that Bean was your big brother, huh? He was your man, right?

144

He loved you, right? Wrong! He wasn't your man, TJ. He wasn't your big brother, and he definitely didn't love you. He didn't love Khadafi, Damien Lucas, Quette, Omar—none of y'all. The only person that Bean loved was Bean. You call Khadafi a snake, but boo, Bean was the biggest snake of all. You just didn't know it. Back in the day when you went to Atlantic City to celebrate your birthday, that was the week—"

"—end that my family got killed." I finished Esha's statement reflectively.

"Three dudes broke into your father's house and killed everybody because you wouldn't tell them where your money was."

All of a sudden, Esha had my undivided attention. I had never told a soul that my family was killed because I wouldn't give up the money.

"They killed your stepmother first—then your little brother and lastly your father."

Something inside me snapped and I rushed Esha. I grabbed her by the neck and choked her. "How do you know that? I never told—"

"Let my neck go—and I'll—tell you."

I let Esha go. "Tell me!"

"I know because Bean told me."

"You're lying!" I hissed through clenched teeth. "To protect Khadafi."

"TJ, think about what you're saying. How could I be lying and know what I just said? Khadafi was in prison when your family got killed. What you don't know is that me and Bean was fuckin'. We hid it from everybody and mainly creeped around, but it's true. The night everything happened, he came to my house drunk and high. Bean had started fuckin' with that dope, and it was getting the best of him. But I didn't care because when that nigga had that dope in him he would fuck

145

the shit outta me. That's what it was. I was gone off the dick. Bean told me everything that happened in your house that night—what he'd done. Bean was jealous of you. He raised you to be a thug, but you turned out to be a pretty good hustler. When you got that heroin plug with the dude Manny Stone and didn't put him on, he was fucked up. He ranted and raved about how much he had given you, how much he had done for you, what he'd lost fuckin' with you, and how you didn't appreciate him. I knew that he was fucked up with you, but I never imagined that he would do the shit he did. I never thought in my wildest dreams that he'd let greed and jealousy eat at him that much to where he'd go that far. Bean went around Barry Farms and got three dudes, C-Dubb, Black Scrubb, and a dude named Nayroo, to go in your father's house. Bean waited outside while they did what they did. He gave them the order to kill your people. He was still outside the house even when you called him on his cell.

"He told me that you were crying like a bitch. Bean told me that he called you back and acted like he'd just discovered your family dead. He laughed about the whole thing, TJ. He laughed at you. And that laugh is nothing I will forget as long as I live. The next day, after you got back from Atlantic City, you and him went on a mission to find the people responsible, or at least the people that you suspected. You got at a few dudes that you thought may have been involved, and the rest of the dudes y'all killed were dudes that Bean didn't like. He made up stories and fed them to you, knowing that he could play on your emotions. The part that fucked Bean up the most was that he never got his hands on your money. Every day after that, you rode around looking for people to kill and the person that needed your greatest kill was seated right next to you. This is a secret that I've lived with for the last seven years.

"The only other person who knows this story is my mother. I don't keep nothing from her."

As the realization of what had been done to me and my family by the person that I trusted most, hit me like a ton of bricks, my knees buckled. My eyes watered.

"But—but Bean—"

"What TJ? Bean wouldn't have told me all of this? Well, he did. He didn't care about me knowing because he knew I'd never say a word. I just told you I was under his spell. I was dicknotized. And besides, the most important thing was that Bean knew that I knew that if I said a word to you or anybody, he'd kill me." Esha snapped her fingers. "Just like that. I was afraid of Bean, TJ. Especially after he did what he did to you, to your family. I watched Bean kill people. I knew how much he loved killing. So I kept quiet. Bean was a dirty muthafucka. He knew that me and Kemie was friends and he started fuckin' her while he was fuckin' me and do you think he cared? No. Guess where he brought her to fuck her sometimes? Here. In my house. Just to fuck with me. He'd do extra shit to make her moan loud just because he knew that I'd hear her. He also knew how Khadafi felt about Kemie. He didn't give a fuck. He'd fuck Kemie and then write Khadafi a letter and put pictures of them in it and then give it to me to mail off. The weekend that you went to Atlantic City for your birthday, Bean called Reesie and told her that you took two bitches with you. Reesie didn't tell you that?"

I shook my head, numb and devastated by everything I'd just learned. The pain in the middle of my chest turned to anger. "You stood here a few minutes ago talkin' about snake shit this and snake shit that and how sick of it you are. And you mean to tell me that all this time you been breaking bread, eating and chillin' with a nigga, smiling in my face, and you knew the whole time who killed my family and you never said a word. Bean been dead three years, and you never told me none of this shit. Why? You let me walk around here with all these 'I miss you, Bean' T-shirts on and watched me pour out liquor on his behalf, and all this time you knew what that nigga did to me? To my family? You knew how much that shit fucked me up. Changed my life. You fuckin' knew. You—"

"TJ, when you got locked up, Bean was still alive. When you came home after doing almost five years last year, I thought about tellin' you. But then I thought to myself, What good would it do? So I made the decision to leave the past in the past and worry about the future. Our future. But now that all this wild shit is happening, and everybody has turned into Bean reincarnated, I felt now was the time for you to know that Khadafi is not your enemy, and that he did the world a favor by killing Bean. Khadafi didn't betray you, TJ. Bean did. Bean was your enemy. Not Khadafi. You didn't know it then, but now you do."

I listened to every word that Esha said and analyzed it in my head. Here I was trying to kill Khadafi for betraying me by killing Bean and all the while I should've been thanking him. I had to get in touch with Khadafi and tell him what I'd just been told. Everything except the part about me wanting to kill him. That part I'd keep to myself, but there would be no such pardon for my home girl. What gave her the right to keep me in the blind for so long about a situation that affected me? What gave her the right to cover up my old skeletons with new dirt? I remembered the day that I promised myself that I would never shed another tear. It was the day that I left the cemetery. But as the tears in my eyes fell, I couldn't deny their existence. I let them fall and didn't bother to wipe them away. The beast inside me raged and roared and was ready to rear its head. My body shook slightly as I reached under my sweater and gripped the 9-millimeters that I had there. I pulled one out.

Esha's eyes widened as big as teacups as she shook her head.

"TJ—nono!'"

"You ain't no better than Bean, Esha. You became just as guilty as him the day you decided to keep quiet. And for that, I can't let you go on livin'." I raised the gun and fired a round into Esha's face. The bullet hit her in the eye and knocked her body backward.

Life is a fickled thing, and it's funny how shit happens. Esha tried to save Khadafi's life by revealing what she knew about Bean and my murdered family. She had to know that by telling me her secret after all this time that she was gambling with her life. In the end, she decided that that was a gamble she was willing to take. Her life for Khadafi's. In a way, I guess that was her very own sacrifice because she had to know that I'd kill her. I needed to find the three dudes that went in my house and killed my family. They were now my targets.

Backtracking, I wiped down whatever I thought I touched and left through the back door.

# CHAPTER TWENTY-FOUR
## Khadafi

Something moved on the side of Esha's house that caught my attention. Instantly, I perked up as I saw TJ leaping the small fence adjacent to the tenements. Why is he coming out the back of Esha's house and not the front like he went in? I watched as TJ furtively scanned the sidewalk as he jogged down the little dirt hill that led to it. Baffled but focused, I lifted the SKS and stepped out of the car from the passenger side. The sun was starting to set, and the streetlights hadn't come on, but it was still pretty well lit outside. My eyes wouldn't fail me. I skulked alongside the Buick until I reached the street, and then I made my way quickly across and up Seventh Street. Once I was in a position that I liked, I lifted the SKS and let it go at TJ.

*KOK. KOK. KOK. KOK. KOK. KOK kok kok kok kok kok kok kok kok kok.*

I watched as TJ glanced over his shoulder a split second before diving in the dirt beside the curb. He rolled over and then darted behind a parked car. I moved swiftly to cover the ground between us because I didn't wanna give TJ time to pull his pistols. I underestimated the speed of a fearful man, because in seconds TJ sprinted across the street and ducked down behind another car, and his twin guns were now visible. All I could do was let the SKS go at the car to try and force TJ

150

to abandon his position. I needed him out in the open where I could crush him.

"What the fuck you doing, slim?" TJ shouted from his hiding spot. "This is how you treat your friends, huh?"

"God protect me from my friends 'cause I can handle my enemies. Remember that, cuz? Stop tryna play dumb. You know what it's hitting for!" I let off a quick burst of bullets.

"You trippin' slim!" TJ responded.

"Naw, cuz, you trippin'. You done tried to kill me at the hospital, but you missed. You won't get that chance again."

"According to who? Devon? You let Devon poison you against me. He wanted you dead, not me. He shot at you, not me."

"It don't even matter, cuz. Devon's dead and soon you will be too."

Suddenly, TJ stood with a handgun in each hand. "You die first, slim." He spit both guns in my direction, and I had to run for cover. Then suddenly, I stopped in my tracks. What the fuck am I running for? I got a muthafuckin' choppa. Real niggas do real things. I turned and let the SKS go.

KOK. KOK. KOK. KOK. KOK. KOK. KOK. KOK.

TJ screamed out something I couldn't make out as he took off running through the cut toward Sixth Street. I was just about to chase him when I heard the first siren closing in on me. Quickly, I turned and ran back to the Buick. Just as I tossed the SKS into the passenger seat, the cops pulled onto the block. I calmly strapped myself in with the seat belt and pulled away from the curb. The police car behind me flashed its blue and red lights signaling me to pull over, but I wasn't tryna hear that shit. I drove up the street as if I was color blind, with thoughts of getting rid of the submachine gun. At the top of the block, I spied two police cars parking in a way that would literally block my exit. If I was a regular nigga, I would've stopped my car, but I'm an outlaw. I made a split decision and stepped down hard on the Buick's gas pedal.

The powerful V8 engine responded immediately, and barreled me forward until I rammed right through the slight space that separated both front ends of the police cars. The Buick was banged up a little, but took a licking and kept on ticking. I shot up Seventh Street and turned onto Eighth Street. Checking my rearview mirror, I saw that now about ten squad cars had joined the chase.

"You gotta get rid of the SKS," my conscious repeated over and over as I hit 'M' Street at over 100 miles per hour, with a line of DC police cars on my ass. Out of nowhere, thoughts of LaLa came to mind and the day he led the cops on that high speed chase. The day he lept off the bridge. At the Washington Navy Yard, I bucked a sharp right and hit the Eleventh Street bridge, almost colliding with another car as I did so. I was grateful that rush hour traffic was over and done with. My destination was unknown, but my conscious was still talking to me. Then, like I had an epiphany, I slowed the car. The water. Like LaLa, I had to get to the water. But not to jump over the bridge into the water. I needed to get the SKS to the water. In the water. To be caught with it was an automatic mandatory minimum sentence of ten to fifteen years in prison. When I hit the brakes, all the police cars behind me slowed and eventually stopped. They blocked all oncoming traffic, leaving me as the only car on the five-lane bridge overpass. My mind raced at a hundred miles a second as I thought out my next move and then implemented it. I turned my car to face the curb and railing. The cops were now out of their cars with their weapons drawn and aimed in my direction. I reached over and grabbed the SKS. Using the under panel of the dash and gas pedal, I wedged the SKS slowly into place. The car inched forward. Opening the car door, I kicked at the

SKS and forced it all the way onto the gas pedal. Then I leapt out the car. I didn't even stay to watch what happened as I got up and ran, but I heard the car crash into the railing and seconds later into the water. Mission accomplished.

My lungs filled with cold air as they expanded, and my leg that I got shot in started to throb with pain. Then suddenly, I was tackled from behind. As I was being led to the police transport vehicle, all I could think about was TJ.

********

Inside the police precinct, I was processed in. I refused the Miranda questioning session and a phone call. All I could think about was how lucky TJ and I both were. It was as if Allah had purposely spared us time after time for a reason. I had TJ dead to right with a choppa in my hands and didn't hit the muthafucka one time. What the fuck? The holding cell that I was in was full of niggas and getting more crowded by the hour.

I slid down the wall at the back of the cell and sat with my face in my knees and thought. The arresting officers told me that I was being charged with reckless endangerment, eluding the police, and destruction of government property. Which were all misdemeanors, but they said that more charges were forthcoming. Fuck 'em. Bring it on. I pulled off my North Face coat, balled it up, and used it as a pillow to put behind my head. Then I lay down. Staring at the ceiling, I wondered how long it would take for the cops to retrieve the Buick from the bottom of the Potomac River, or even if they would or could. Since the window was down, would the SKS wash out of the car and get lost? As far as I knew, nobody had gotten hit down Capers, so I was good on that.

A few minutes later, a female cop came to the bars of the holding cell with a clear plastic bag containing my belt, shoestrings, cell phone, watch, and a wad of money. She counted out a hundred dollars and handed it back thru the bars.

"I forgot, but here take this. You're allowed $100 on your person. The total amount of this money is fifty-three hundred dollars. Now minus the $100, it's $5,200. Here . . ." She handed me a piece of paper. "Sign this right here."

I looked over the inventory receipt and signed it. I turned to leave, but heard my name being called. Looking over my shoulder, I saw a plain clothes cop dressed in what appeared to be winter linen standing in the spot where the lady cop had just stood.

"Let me holler at you for a minute," he said.

With a mean mug on my face I walked back to the bars. "What's up?"

The cop reached through the bars and tried to hand me a business card. After a minute or two of holding the card suspended in midair, he pulled his arm back.

"My name is Detective Maurice Tolliver. I'm working a case where your name came up, and I was just wondering if you'd like to talk about it. You know—clear a few things up. We can go up to my office and discuss a few things. You thirsty? I can get you a beverage of your choice. Hungry? I can get you some food—or a cigarette if you smoke. I believe that we can help each other if you're willing. So—"

"Help each other?" I repeated.

"Yeah. Help each other. I think that we can definitely help each other out. Like I said, if you're willing."

"How can you help me?"

"I can make the paperwork on the charges you just caught disappear, and in the next hour or so you can be walking out that door a free man. I can work magic. By the time I'm finished you'll think I'm a magician."

# ANTHONY FIELDS

All I could do was stand there at the bars and look at this creep ass cop disrespecting me. I envisioned myself blowing his head clean off. "A magician, huh? Yeah, I bet you got all kinda tricks up your sleeve. You want me to help you and by helping you, help myself?"

"That's usually how it goes around here. Yes. "

"I already know that. That's why so many niggas in the world need their muthafuckin' heads blown off. For helpin' themselves by helping y'all. You'll never count me amongst the broken men. So therefore I don't need your help."

The curly haired detective that looked like Laz Alonzo to me, came closer to the bars and hissed, "I forgot that you're one of them tough Southwest niggas, right? I can respect that. But make no mistake about it, you gon' need some help. Either from me and the government, or a good defense lawyer. The only difference is that I'ma offer you some help right now that may save your ass later. Look at gangsta dudes like Pappy, he copped to over eight murders and told on Kevin Grey, and now he's back on the streets. Why? Because he wanted to help himself after he caught that gun and coke beef on Hadley Terrace. He needed help then, and you need help now. If you want that help, I'm here to provide it. But the catch is that you have to want to help yourself now and not later, because by then I'ma be mad at your tough ass and I'm not gon' wanna help you. I'm the only muthafucka around with a shovel strong enough to dig you out of the deep shit you're about to be in. Do the right thing, Khadafi, and help yourself out. Because when I catch TJ, I'ma offer him the same deal, and maybe he's not as tough as you. What's it gonna be? It's first come, first serve."

The first thing that struck me was the fact that the detective called me Khadafi, and he mentioned the name TJ. Not Tyrone Carter, but TJ. This nigga knew us intimately. All of a sudden, name recognition kicked in, and I remembered where I heard the cop's name from. A couple of days before the all-white party at the Omni Shoreham, TJ and I went out Tyson's corner in the Escalade the same day I copped it. While I was shopping, Kemie called me.

"What's up?" I said into the phone.

"The police, that's what's up," Kemie replied. "A detective by the name of Maurice Tolliver been calling me all day."

"For what?"

"For what? For what? About the truck, nigga. The Infiniti truck with all the bullet holes in it. The one—"

Maurice Tolliver.

The same detective who had called Kemie's phone. He knows me, Kemie, and TJ. I wonder what else he knows. I looked into the detective's face and smiled. After all, he was the person that probably had the gun that was recovered from the truck, the one that had my prints on it. That's why he's so cocky. He had the gun and the words of some rats probably. That's why he said I was in deep shit.

"Ay, cuz, you can take that shovel and whatever else you got and stick it in your ass. Whatever it is that you think you got against me, come on with it. See, I'm not Pappy. I'm not Steve Graham. I'm not Moe Brown, or none of them rat ass niggas. I'm me. I still live by the code of them old-timer mafia niggas.

"I live the Omerta. So you can take your help, your food and beverages and your cigarettes and save 'em for the next nigga. When it's time to rumble, I'll lace my boots up tight and fight. That's all I know, cuz. So get the fuck outta here with that bullshit, and you and everybody with you can eat my dick. How 'bout that?"

Then calmly, I walked away from the bars and left the detective standing there looking dumb as shit.

# CHAPTER TWENTY-FIVE

## Detective Tolliver

While my Canal Street murder weapons languished on somebody's shelf down at the forensics lab in Quantico, I still had to link murder suspects with a crime scene and possible murder weapons. And that wasn't turning out well at all. "—you and everybody with you can eat my dick."

Khadafi's words replayed in my head as I climbed the precinct stairs en route to the conference room on the fourth floor. I couldn't lie to myself and say that I was surprised that Khadafi turned down my offer to help himself by ratting on TJ. For a brief second, I thought I had him, but then he went off on me. Smiling to myself, I had to respect his gangsta. And his arrogance. I couldn't blame him for being arrogant. He and TJ had eluded the whole DC police department for months. I vowed to myself to take them both down, and I planned to keep that vow, no matter how much arrogance and dignity Khadafi showed.

You and everybody with you can eat my dick.

As I walked into the conference room, my presence ceased all conversation and harmless banter. "Thank you all for staying. De La Cruz, you're the arresting officer. Please tell me everything that happened."

Officer Enrique De La Cruz leaned back in his seat and flipped through a notepad in his hand. "At 6:17 p.m., a call went out over the radio about shots being fired in the vicinity of Seventh Street Southeast. I radioed that I was in the area and would respond. At the time, I was coming down Pennsylvania Avenue, about six blocks away. As I pulled down 'I' Street, I could hear rapid gunfire—"

"Rapid gunfire?" I repeated.

"Yeah, as in automatic machine gun rapid fire. Then suddenly it stopped. I observed a man dressed in all black clothing getting into vehicle on the corner of Seventh and 'K'. I decided to stop that individual, but the man pulled away from the curb driving a new model Buick that was black in color. I radioed in that—"

"Was there a weapon visible? When he entered the vehicle, was there a gun visible?" I asked.

"—Uh, I didn't see one, but he was moving pretty fast as if he was evading the cops. I radioed in and that's when the roadblock—"

"Roadblock?"

"Yeah." Officer Terry Vance said as he stood. "I was responding to the scene, too. I radioed my position inland and decided to set up a roadblock at the end of the block. Another car was in the vicinity. We talked on the walkie-talkie and set up the roadblock. We parked our cars front end to front end."

"And the driver never stopped?"

"No." Terry Vance snorted and sat down. "He drove right through it."

"I continued to give chase," De La Cruz added. "I followed him while several other cars followed me. The Buick turned right onto Eighth Street and proceeded to 'M' Street. He was going approximately ninety-eight miles an hour. He turned right onto the Eleventh Street bridge. About a mile or so across the bridge, the car stopped. Everybody froze as if suspended in time as the Buick backed up and then turned and headed for the sidewalk and railing. He jumped out and the car jumped the curb, crashed through the railing, and went over into the water. We tackled the driver and arrested him. He gave me a false name when I asked him for ID. He said his license was at home and that his name was Alvin Vaughn. Other officers at the scene recognized him. They identified him as Luther Fuller. That's when I called you."

I paced the conference room floor. My mind was in overdrive. "Okay. Did anybody see Luther Fuller firing a gun?" I asked.

"So far, nobody has come forward, detective, but you know how folks are in that area. Nobody wants to talk to the cops," a male patrolman I'd never seen before said.

"There has to be a reason why he drove the car off the bridge," I said almost to myself as I paced. "He had something in the car that he didn't want found. He didn't want us to catch him with something. A gun or guns possibly? A body in the trunk? Drugs?"

"Can't we just get the car out of the river?" De La Cruz asked. "I mean, like you say—he purposely sent the car over the bridge for a reason, right? Let's get the car and see why or what he was hiding."

"It' not that simple, De La Cruz," I answered without breaking stride in my pace. "The department has to pay for divers and equipment to retrieve the car. If we go after that car and we don't find jack shit, then we wasted the taxpayer's money and the chief will have our asses for lunch and dinner. Even if we do go after the car, that won't happen for a week at least, and we have to charge Fuller, who's called Khadafi in the street, with something that will hold him. Three misdemeanors won't do it. And I need him off the street. I—"

A head popped into the conference room. "Moe, pick up your cell. Emily Perez is trying to reach you," Ed Delany said and closed the back door.

"Thank you all for talking with me. I will contact you if I need anything else. I need y'all to talk to people in the neighborhood and see what you can find out about the gunfight that occurred there." I thought about the handgun that I got out of the blue Infiniti truck with Khadafi's prints on it. It would give me a little time to try and break the case open without murders happening. But eventually, the charge wouldn't stick because the Infiniti was not in his name. He wasn't in the truck when it was found, and the gun also had other prints on it. I walked into my cubicle and picked up my phone just as it vibrated. "Hello?"

"Tolliver, it's me, Emily Perez. I think you better get over here. We're all on Seventh Street in Capers projects."

My gut fluttered, and I knew that something was wrong. "The gunfight earlier. You've found a victim?" I surmised.

"I don't know about that, but what I do know is that we just discovered a body inside a house down here . . . And the identity of the deceased is known to us all."

"Who is it?"

"Ronesha Lake, also known as Esha. Shit is about to get crazy."

"I'm on my way."

# CHAPTER TWENTY-SIX
## TJ

By the time Dawn pulled up to pick me up from the McDonald's on South Capitol Street, I noticed that I'd been sitting inside the fast food joint for almost three hours. Time not only flies when you're having fun, it flies when your head is full of questions that you can't answer and harsh realities that you don't wanna face. In my head, I could hear the sounds of the choppa that Khadafi had just spit at me earlier reverberating over and over again. I heard the words that I said and the words he said. I could feel my heart rate continue to climb while in the midst of the heated gun battle. I could feel the courage inside me strengthen and congratulate itself for standing fast in the face of adversity. But above all else, I could hear every word Esha said to me before I killed her. The questions in my head were too numerous to ponder or answer. So I sat at the table in McDonald's eating cold fries and sipping a Sprite for hours. My cell phone vibrated and I knew the caller was Dawn. I'd already seen her pull up. "Yeah?"

"I'm outside," Dawn replied.

"You want something outta here?" I asked as I stood and dropped my food and drink into the trashcan.

"Naw, I'm good. I was at home cooking when you called."

"I'm on my way out."

I slid into the passenger seat of Dawn's Hyundai Sonata.

161

"Damn, nigga, I don't get no hug, kiss, or none of that shit, huh?"

"My bad, Dee. I'm a little under the weather right now. I got you later though."

Dawn pulled out of the McDonald's parking lot. "What the fuck happened to you? Your shit look like you been playing football in the dirt of something. And where's your car?"

"I was on my way in Esha's house when Khadafi ambushed me. He pulled out a hammer and tried to kill me. I ran through the cut and didn't stop until I got here. I been here for a few hours before I called you."

"What the fuck did you do to Khadafi to make him pull that shit? Y'all niggas be together every day."

"Khadafi is on some other shit, Dee. He killed Bean, Omar, Devon, and now he's trying to kill me."

"I heard that shit before, but—" Dawn said and turned the corner as if she was going to Capers.

"Where are you going?" I asked.

"Around the way to get your car and talk to Esha—"

"No! Don't go around there. Khadafi might be still out there, and both of my guns are empty."

"TJ, Khadafi got locked up. About two hours or so ago. Lil Keisha was driving past on the bridge and saw the police putting Khadafi in the backseat of a police car. So you don't—"

I cut her off. "Still, don't go around there. Go to your house."

"What about your car?"

"Ain't nobody gonna fuck with my shit. They know better. I'll get it tomorrow. I'm hungry and I'm tired. Plus I'm horny. Go to your house." I was lying through my teeth, but I had to say whatever it took to get Dawn's nosey ass away from Arthur Capers. I didn't want her to be the one who found Esha

162

dead. I didn't know whether to be happy or sad that Khadafi had gotten locked up. I knew that I had to kill him, but deep down inside I wasn't sure if I really wanted to. Then a new reality dawned on me. Khadafi knew all my secrets. He was an accomplice to almost all my murders. He was a witness. He was now an enemy. I had to kill him for that reason alone. It was the reason why I'd killed Reesie. I was too far gone down the path that I'd laid. It was too late to turn back. I had to kill him and everybody else that threatened my survival and freedom. But first, I had bigger fish to fry.

"Damn, do me a favor, boo, and drive through Barry Farms. I need to holla at one of my men . . ."

Never imagined that he'd let greed and jealousy eat him up that much to where he'd do what he did . . . Bean knew niggas from all over the city. He went around Barry Farms and got three dudes. I still remember their names . . . C-Dubb, Black Scrubb, and a dude named Nayroo. Bean put them on you and then waited outside while they did what they did. Killing your family . . .

On Eaton Road, I spotted a friend of mine named Dice. He was my gunman that kept all the latest guns and hard to get accessories. "Pull over right here. I need to holla at slim right there." Dawn pulled over and I hopped out the car.

"T Jizzle, what's up dawg?" Dice said as I walked up.

"What's up, slim?" I responded and gave him a pound.

"Shit ain't shit. They got a slow song playing and I can't even two-step to it."

"I can dig it. Pretty much the same here. I need to holla at a coupla your men, though. I got something lined up, and I need a few good men. Other good men sent me this way," I explained.

"Who you lookin' for?" Dice asked.

"Black Scrubb, Nayroo, and C-Dubb. Those are the names I was given."

Dice's facial expression changed into something that resembled annoyance. "Are you sure about them names, dawg?"

"Positive."

"And you said that some good men gave you them names?"

I was starting to sense something was wrong. "Yeah, that's what I said. Why? What's up, Dice?"

"I'm just saying, dawg. Whatever good men that gave you two of them names need their background checked out. C-Dubb got killed a couple years ago after a nigga in the hood found out that he was a rat. He told on the homie Lil Kenny on a body. Kenny sent the paperwork home and let everybody read it. Dubb got crushed about a week after that. Nayroo ain't no rat as far as I know, but he ain't built for no gangsta shit no more. Slim hit a helluva lick years ago and was doin' the muthafucka. His connect dried up, and he decided to take a trip up top to New York. He got caught on the turnpike coming back. Nobody understood how he got outta that mess, so niggas ain't fuckin' with him. Since he lost everything he had on that move up top, he went broke. That started fuckin' with his head, so he started smokin' boat. Slim been on some lunchin' shit ever since."

"Is that right? Interesting story, but whatever happened to him?"

"Who Nayroo? Slim be up the hill. On Birney Place. He probably outside right now."

"I can dig it. I appreciate you, slim, but you didn't say what's up with Black Scrubb."

Dice picked up a beer that had been sitting on the ground and took a swig. He threw the twenty-two ounce Miller

Genuine Draft back again and finished it. Then he flipped the can over to the dirt and grass part of the sidewalk.

"That's my man, Anthony. We call him Black Scrubb—and whoever gave you slim's name must've been outta town for a while, because slim been on his laid back shit for years now. Something happened years ago that fucked slim up, so he put the guns up and got on his good husband, good father shit."

"I can respect that, but I still need to holla at him because what I got lined up might change his mind."

"Maybe, maybe not. Especially now because he got caught up on some domestic shit, and he's still in the halfway house behind it. He probably on paper and some shit. You might wanna holla at someone else."

"You know what, I think you right. My bad, slim. I didn't mean to waste your time. I'll holla at you again soon," I said. "I need a few of them thangs." I gave Dice some dap and turned to leave.

"Whenever. You know how to find me. And tell Khadafi that I got some new shit, better than the joint he bought the other day."

I stopped dead in my tracks. "Khadafi bought some joints from you the other day?"

"Yeah, about three days ago I sold him a brand new SKS. A joint I call the baby SK. That joint come with a banana clip that hold sixty shots. Bad muthafucka."

You're telling me. "I'll be sure to let him know what you said. I'm out, slim. You be cool."

********

As soon as we walked through Dawn's apartment door, her house phone lit up. Dawn dropped her purse, kicked off her tennis shoes, and walked over to the phone.

"Hello? What? You're talkin' too fast and I can't—wait? No! How? Who—" The phone dropped from Dawn's hand as she burst into tears. She dropped to her knees and placed her hands over her face.

I already knew what someone had just told Dawn on the phone, but I acted as if I didn't. "Dee, what the fuck is up?" I shouted as I walked over to her.

Dawn looked up at me with a tear-stained face and said, "Esha's dead! Somebody killed Esha!"

# CHAPTER TWENTY-SEVEN
## Detective Tolliver

NNOOOOOO. My baby! Eessha! DDEARR GOD NOOO!"
This was the hardest part of my job, and no matter how many times I witnessed it, it never got any easier for me to deal with.

"EEESSSHHHAAA!"

The distraught, painful look of a parent as they identified the remains of a dead child, it's purely indescribable. The lifeless shell that remained, that was once so full of life. It was probably the worst thing a parent could witness. Children were not supposed to precede their parents in death. Most parents felt that their children should bury them and not the other way around. I agreed with that. Maybe that was one of the reasons why I never tried to produce a child. Like any man desiring to live the so-called American Dream, I'd often thought about having a normal family, with two or three kids, a wife, and a dog. But over the years, the harsh realities of the inner city and the things I witnessed as a cop day in and day out derailed that train of thought. The world that we live in is a cruel, cruel place, and I could not bring myself to create another human life to grow up and suffer in it. Call me a pessimist or call me a realist, but whatever you call me, you'll never call me a 'grieving parent.'

# The Ultimate Sacrifice III: No Regrets

I glanced down again at the face of Ronesha Lake and tried to remember what she looked like before she took one bullet to her left eye that ripped through her brain and exited her head at the back. Then I pulled the white sheet back over her head and turned to face her grieving mother. Bayona 'Bay One' Lake was inconsolable.

"Ms. Lake, again, my name is Detective Maurice Tolliver. I need to ask you a few questions. I know it's kinda hard for you to do right now, but in my line of work, solving the crime in the first twenty-four to forty-eight hours is something we strive for. After the first forty-eight hours, the trail goes cold and it becomes harder to bring a suspect to justice. I knew your daughter from the neighborhood, and she didn't deserve this. Every—" Bayona Lake collapsed in my arms and was sieged by a fit of dry heaves and soundless screams. My heart broke for her. "Ms. Lake, do you know anybody that we should look at for this? Does anybody in particular come to mind that may have wanted to hurt Esha? Any enemies that you know of?"

"EEESSSHAA! Oh my God! Esha! I—swear—to—God I'ma, I'ma, I'ma. Muthafuckas gon'—kill—my—daughter."

"Who killed your daughter? Do you know? Help me get the person who did this to Esha. Help me bring her killer to justice."

Suddenly, Bayona Lake wiped her eyes and straightened herself up. She freed herself from my embrace. But just as I thought that she was ready to talk to me, I was wrong. Ronesha Lake's mother gathered her wits and simply turned and left the room.

********

I lay in the bed that night and tried to figure out what Ronesha Lake had to do with all the recent events that were going on between Capers and Southwest? Why would somebody wanna kill her? Was it because TJ and Khadafi were known to hang out in her house? Was she targeted because of them? Or was she targeted by one of them? What did Esha know that could possibly get her killed? Did she have something to do with the gunfight that had taken place earlier? There were no bullet holes in her windows or doors, so Esha wasn't hit with stray bullets. Two different kinds of shell casings were found at the scene of Seventh Street. My guy that works in ballistics eyed the casings and told me that they were 9-millimeter shells and .45 caliber casings fired from a sub machine gun. The shell casing found inside of Ronesha Lake's house was from a 9-millimeter. In a few weeks, we'd know if the 9-millimeter shells found outside matched the one found inside Ronesha's house. And we'd be able to see if there were any prints left on the shells after they were loaded into the gun. It would be asking for too much for Khadafi's prints to be on the shell casing that killed Ronesha, so I didn't even ask.

But I needed answers to my questions and prayed that I'd find them soon. I needed to know where TJ was and who Khadafi was shooting at on Seventh Street? If it was Khadafi doing the shooting. We still didn't know that for sure, yet. Then I thought about somebody shooting at Khadafi at PG hospital and Devon Harris's murder on Third Street in Southwest. He was a known Capers knucklehead, and his death had to be tied in with everything in some kinda way.

Thoughts of the slain Ronesha Lake brought back images of her grieving mother. After she broke down over her daughter's death, she picked herself up and put a look on her face that chilled me to the bone. Right before she left the morgue. I sat up in bed and grabbed my cell phone off the night table beside my bed. I dialed the office.

"First District Police Department, how may I direct your call?" a male voice said.

"This is Detective Maurice Tolliver. Who am I speaking with?"

"Dan Poindexter, Moe. What do you need?"

"Hey, Dan. You drew the midnight shift this week, huh?" I asked.

"Yeah, but fuck it. It beats driving around Fifth and 'K' Streets chasing johns and male prostitutes all night. You calling to chit chat, Moe, or do you need something?"

I laughed to myself.

"Dan, I need you to run a name through the system for me and see what you get, okay?"

"Wait a sec, Moe. Okay, give me the name."

"Bayona Lake. That's Bayona spelled b-a-y-o-n-a . . . Lake. Put her alias in, too. It's Bay One . . . spelled b-a-y . . . o-n-e. Run that."

I heard Dan punching what I gave him into his keyboard. After a brief pause, he said, "Bayona Louise Lake, also known as Bay One, female, birthdate, August 17, 1963. No current address, no job on the record, several arrests over the last ten years. Let's see here. Possession of heroin, possession with intent to distribute cocaine base, marijuana and PCP, possession, possession, possession, disorderly conduct, assault, assault with a deadly weapon, gun possession, distribution, possession of marked money, assault, CPWL, manslaughter and second degree murder."

"What happened in the manslaughter case and the second degree murder?"

"Says here that she beat the second degree in trial and copped to the manslaughter. Bay One did seven years out Maryland in the early nineties. Last offense was a possession about two years ago. What she do now, Moe? Kill somebody else?"

"I'll let you know when I find out, Dan. Hey Dan, thanks again, buddy. Good night." I hit the end button and put the cell phone back on the table. I was right back at square one. There was a lot going on behind the scenes, and for the life of me, I couldn't figure out any of it.

Maybe with Khadafi off the streets, even for a little while, things would loosen up and a break in the case would come from somewhere. Maybe not. But it wouldn't hurt to think positively. Seconds later, I was asleep.

# CHAPTER TWENTY-EIGHT
## Marnie

I stood in the living room of my cousin's house in the Garden Lake Estates section of Wilmington, North Carolina, and stared out the window at the Cadillac Escalade SUV. All the money was still in the back cargo area behind the third-row seat. Even after being in Carolina for the past six days, my nerves were still shot. I couldn't sleep right or eat right, and that gave me more stress because I knew I could be hurting the baby. I rubbed my stomach and felt my unborn child moving around. My and Khadafi's unborn child. Everything that I saw made me think of Khadafi. So far, I hadn't heard a word from him since the day after I arrived in Wilmington. I called him and we talked. He told me that he was looking for TJ still. That was five days ago and my heart yearned to hear his voice to know that he was okay. I walked to the couch and grabbed my cell phone. I dialed Esha's house and got no answer. That's strange, because somebody was always in Esha's house. Next, I dialed Keisha's cell phone and it went straight to voicemail. Then I tried Dawn and Shawn. Nobody was answering phones and that made my nerves get worse. Khadafi's last words to me came to mind. "Just lay in Carolina until you hear something. Keep in touch with somebody up here, Esha, Dawn, Keisha or somebody. Their nosey asses will know something about me or TJ. If things go

172

my way, I'll call you. If you don't hear from me in a week, well, it is what it is. Either I'm dead or in jail."

Silently, I prayed for the best, but expected the worst. Please, Khadafi, don't be dead. Please, baby, I need you. The baby needs you.

"Marnie, you ready to go," a voice behind me asked.

I turned and faced my cousin Danielle. Our fathers were brothers. She was about an inch shorter than me and a little lighter. But other than that, my favorite cousin, that had me by about three years was my spitting image. "Yeah, I'm ready, Dani. Let me go to the bathroom before we leave though. This baby has to be chillin' somewhere right on top of my bladder."

"That's how it goes sometimes, girlfriend. Go handle your business so that we can bounce. Tenth and Castle is gonna be filled with niggas and bitches even though it's wintertime. I'ma have to figure out some back routes just to get us to Independence Mall, all because it's nice outside."

I tossed my phone onto the couch and went upstairs to the bathroom. Still, silently praying for Khadafi.

********

"Oh my God, cousin! Check these bad muthafuckas out right here."

I grabbed the shoe out of Danielle's hand and looked at the label inside. Proenza Schouler.

"Do you think the snake skin on there is real?"

I checked the price tag and whistled. "Shit, for $1,175, that better be real python on 'em. You like these shoes, huh?"

Danielle's face lit up like a little kid on Christmas. "Do I? I gotta dress that would go perfectly with them. But girl, on my budget, I can't afford no shoes like that."

"Well, guess what, Dani? Today is your birthday. These shoes go with that handbag, right? Go and get it."

# The Ultimate Sacrifice III: No Regrets

"Get the fuck outta here, cousin! You on joke time. That bag cost like two grand, I know."

"Didn't I just say Happy Birthday?" I asked, smile beaming.

"But it ain't my birthday, Marnie, and you know it."

I grabbed Danielle's hand and walked her over to the counter. "Good afternoon," I said to the lady at the counter. "I need that handbag right there. The python Proenza Schouler. Yes, that one. Thank you. And I need these heels in a size—" I looked at Danielle.

"A size seven. But—" Danielle said.

"A size seven. Yes, ma'am, thank you. No buts, Dani. Let me do this. I haven't been down here in years. And you and I haven't shopped together in more years than that. You are my favorite cousin. I love you, and you always welcome me in your home when I come."

"You are my cousin. We're family. You don't have to thank me for that. I love you, too, crazy ass girl, but you don't have to spend your money on me. You gotta baby coming—"

The lady returned with Danielle's shoes.

"Dani, go try the shoes on so that we can go to the next store. The day has just begun."

As I watched my cousin try on the shoes, it made me feel good to be able to do something for her. At twenty years old, Danielle left college and put her dreams on hold to raise my eight-year-old cousin, Demarion. Our other cousin, Emanuel Barnhardt, whom the streets of Wilmington called Lil Black got knocked by the Feds and sent to prison for a long time. Demarion's mother was a young girl that Black had in his stable of bitches. But once Black went to prison, the girl decided that she had too much life to live, and an eight-year-old son didn't figure too well in that equation. She wanted to put Demarion up for adoption, but Danielle wasn't trying to hear that. Demarion was family, and family always looked out for their own. Danielle sacrificed her life so that our little cousin could have a good life. And ten years later, she was still doing just that.

"Do they fit?"

"Is the president married to the baddest black bitch in the world?" Danielle asked as she stood and walked around the store in the heels.

"Good. Let's get them and go. We got other stores to hit."

******\*

By the time we turned onto Greenfield Street, I was so deep in thought that I hadn't heard a word of what Danielle had said.

"So are you down or what?" Danielle asked again as we got out of her Toyota Prius that was filled with shopping bags.

"Down for what?"

"Damn, Marnie, I swear sometimes, girl. I think you do that shit on purpose. Didn't you hear a word I just said? I'm tryna hit the New World Nightclub and I want you to go with me. What do you say?"

"I'm not doing no loud ass nightclubs—"

"I'm tryna show you how we get down in the Port City, girl. New World is gonna be off the hook. Niggas—"

I opened the back door and grabbed a handful of bags. "I'm cool on all that shit."

"Girl, put them bags down. It's bad enough that I let you lug all that shit through the mall. Demarion is gonna get the bags."

We walked into the house.

"De? De? Demarion Barnhardt! Boy, get your ass down here!" Three minutes later, Demarion came lumbering down the stairs. "What's good?"

"Boy, don't what's good me. What took you so long to come downstairs?" Danielle asked.

"I was on the phone and the music was on. I couldn't hear you," Demarion said and leaned in to kiss Danielle.

Danielle pushed him away playfully. "Boy, don't be putting your lips on me. I don't know what you doing nowadays with your lips. And especially since I saw that new girl you had over here last week. She wasn't exactly pretty."

"Aw, stop hating on me, cousin D. I'm a smooth operator, and I get all the girls. The one you saw last week was replaced by another one this week."

"I just hope your ass remember to strap it up, 'cause I ain't tryna raise nobody's kids. You're grown, so I'm finished raising kids. You are definitely your father's child. Now take your smooth operator ass outside and get them bags out the car."

"Did y'all get me something? Oh, my bad, what's good, cousin Marnie?" Demarion said moments before he hugged me.

I hugged him back. He was a good kid and I liked him a lot. "Yeah, we hooked you up. Wait until these little country bitches see your new Yves Saint Laurent high top tennis shoes and them new Gucci low tops."

"For real?" Demarion beamed.

"No, for play," Danielle said and nudged him toward the door. "Go get them bags."

Demarion opened the door and stepped outside and then stepped back in. "Ain't that your cell phone on the couch, cousin Marnie?"

I looked at the phone lying on the couch. I had forgotten all about it. "Yeah, that's mine."

"That bad boy been ringing off the hook for a while. Somebody's really trying to reach you."

With that said, he ran outside. I picked up my cell phone and saw that I had eight missed calls. Three calls from Keisha, one from my mother, and four calls from a number that came up as 'private'. I dialed Keisha's phone and prayed that she answered. She did.

"Hello?"

"Marnie?"

"It' me, girl. What's up?"

Keisha told me everything that had happened since I'd been gone. About TJ and Khadafi shooting at each other down Capers, about Khadafi getting locked up on the Eleventh Street bridge and sending his car over the bridge. And about finding Esha dead in her house. I was happy to hear that Khadafi was still alive, even if he was locked up. That was the news I needed desperately. But I was also devastated to learn that our girl Esha had been killed. I was overwhelmed with emotion. "Keisha, what happened to Esha?"

"Somebody shot her, Marnie. They say she got shot in the face. And girl, Bay One has been on a nut out here. That's why ain't nobody been answering their phones. Bay One been calling everybody's phone all day ever since she found out. She's hurting bad, Marnie. Esha was her only child."

I swiped at the tears that formed at the corners of my eyes. My pain was deep. In the last sixty days or so, I'd lost several of my closest friends. "Who could have killed her?"

"Marnie. Bitch, we been up for days, drinking, smoking, crying and thinking. Can't nobody figure out who could've killed Esha. Everybody loved Esha. We thought that a stray bullet might've hit her since TJ and Khadafi were outside her house shooting, but the police told Bay One that her house has no bullet entry or exit holes, so whoever shot Esha, meant to do it, and they did it while inside her house."

"Keisha, are you thinking what I'm thinking?" I asked.

"Girl, we all grew up together in the same streets. We done lived the same lives and danced to the same music. We've experienced the same heartaches and pains. So of course, we're thinking the same thing. Did Khadafi or TJ kill Esha? And if so, what for? Am I right?"

"Do you really believe that one of them did it? And do you know what Khadafi is locked up for? Was it for shooting at TJ? And if TJ ran and got away like you said, where is he now? What the hell did Khadafi run his car over the bridge and get locked up for? Has he been down Capers?"

"Bitch, if I knew the answers to all that shit, I would be Madame Crystal Ball. Where the hell are you at?" Keisha asked.

Out of town, but I'm on my way home. I'll call you back when I get there." Immediately, I disconnected the call and told Demarion to take my bags to the Escalade.

"Where are you rushing off to?" Danielle queried.

"It was good spending time with y'all. I had a ball, but it's time for me to leave. My lover needs me, and when love calls, you gotta answer."

********

It took me almost nine hours to get back to DC from North Carolina because every hour I had to stop and use the bathroom. All the while I paid no mind to the fact that I had over three hundred thousand dollars in a bag in the back of the truck. I hopped out the truck in front of my apartment building and glanced around in all directions hoping that death wasn't lurking around the corner. My heart rate sped up as I thought about what Khadafi said about TJ.

"Go? Bounce? Can't stay here no more? Why?" I asked him, vexed.

"Because TJ will eventually come for you. I'm surprised that he hasn't already. Trust me, I know this nigga. He knows that you're pregnant by me. He knows how I feel about you."

"But how?"

"How? Because I told him. He was my man, and I told him a rack of shit. If Kemie were to die then that would make you a witness and our motto is—"

"Leave no witnesses. I heard that before already."

"Well, now, TJ has more reasons than one to kill you. Once he finds out that I survived the hit by Devon and in turn killed him, he'll probably make the quantum leap and know that Devon told me everything. TJ knows that I will question a victim before they die. He watched me do it several times. Then he'll come looking for me. TJ knows that he can get to me through you. You are in danger. You and the baby. That's why I say that you gotta bounce."

To me, TJ had become the boogey man. I looked all around the area again before walking to the back of the truck and opening the back hatch. The street was well lit by the streetlights that heavily lined my street. My watch read 3:21 a.m. and I was tired as hell. I decided to leave all the shopping bags in the truck, but I wasn't leaving the money in there. Lifting the duffle bag, I put an arm through each of the nylon handles and carried it like a backpack to my front door. It was heavy, but I managed. I quickly put the key in the front door before glancing around again. The street was deserted. Closing the door behind me, I made sure that it locked. Then I walked up the stairs to my house. Inside my apartment, I finally dropped the bag, sat down, kicked off my shoes and exhaled.

# CHAPTER TWENTY-NINE

## Marnie

The next morning I found out that Khadafi was in the DC jail's intake block on the third floor. His visiting days were Tuesday and Thursday. My heart smiled at the fact that today was Tuesday. The visiting hours were from 12:30 to 3:30 p.m. and from 4:30 to 7:30 p.m. I decided to go as soon as possible. That gave me enough time to wash, condition, and blow dry my hair. I curled it into layers and then gave myself a pedicure and manicure. As I painted my toenails a deep shade of red, I thought about how much Khadafi liked pretty feet and wished I could rock my open toed heels, but it was still too cold outside for that. Despite the slight bulge in my stomach, I wanted to look good for my baby Khadafi, so I rocked a gray wool, Prada ensemble that accented my ass and hips. On my feet were black wool and silk Prada heels with patent leather bows on them. At 12:10 p.m. I was ready to leave.

********

Khadafi walked through the door of the visiting hall with a bright orange jumpsuit on, but the sight of him still made my pussy wet. His cornrows had seen better days, and his skin looked a little ashy brown, but my heart still skipped a beat. I loved him for better or for worse. Khadafi sat down on one of the stools, picked up a receiver, and waved me over.

Smiling, I sashayed over to the stool in front of him. Only a thick fiberglass partition separated me from the man I yearned for. I picked up the connecting receiver.

"Don't ask me how I knew, but I knew you would come up here today."

"Oh, so you clairvoyant now, huh?" I asked.

"Naw, when I called you yesterday and couldn't reach you—"

"That was you calling from the private number?"

"I called about four times before I gave up."

"Yeah, that was you. I was at the mall with my cousin Dani and I left my cell phone at her house. I saw the missed calls when I got home."

"You were at the mall, huh? So how much of my money did you spend?"

"How much of our money did I spend, you mean? I spent this much." I raised my left hand and separated my index finger and thumb about an inch.

Khadafi smiled. "That translates to about ten grand or so, right?"

"About that. What happened to your hair? Are you gonna tell me what happened to you? And have you heard about Esha?"

The look on Khadafi's face said it all. He dropped his head momentarily, and then looked me straight in the eyes. "These phones might be bugged, so I can't say too much. I heard about Esha on the news. I can see the TV from my cell. Ever since I got here about four days ago, I been locked down. They say I gotta do seven days on total lock down before I can go to open population. I go back to court in forty-five days for a status hearing. The judge ordered me held without bond on these misdemeanors because the government claimed that more charges were forthcoming, and I am a flight risk. They got me on three charges, eluding the police, reckless endangerment, and destruction of government property. They got a gun charge that they're trying to put on me. They say they found a gun in my Infiniti truck last year when it got shot up down Capers. The gun has my prints on it, and they can tie the truck to me. All I'ma say is that I might be here for a while and even places like this ain't safe. I believe I know who killed Esha. You and I know him well."

I pulled the receiver away from my mouth and silently mouthed one name. "TJ?"

Khadafi nodded. "I watched him go in her house. He stayed in there for about fifteen to twenty minutes, and then I heard a single gunshot. The dude left Esha's house through the back door, and I found that strange because he entered through the front door. I caught him coming out—well, let's just say that he got away. I had a feeling that something bad happened, I just didn't know what. When I saw the news the other day and they said Esha's name, I knew it was him. And that's fucked up that he did that to Esha. I can't imagine what she must've said or done to make him do that. Listen to me. This is what I want you to do. I don't know where TJ is, so I don't want you nowhere near Capers. But I want you to get in touch with Bay One and tell her what I just told you. About Esha. Word for word. Then I need you to get in touch with two lawyers for me. Can you remember their names, or do you want me to wait until we talk on the phone?"

"I'll remember them. Go ahead."

"Call Bernard Grimes first and try to retain him. If he can't take my case, call a dude named Jonathan Zuckerman. They both should be in the yellow pages—"

"Don't nobody use the yellow pages no more, but I'll find them online. Bernard Grimes and Jonathan Zuckerman?"

"You got it. Tell them what I just told you about the three charges and tell whichever one that agrees to take the case to come and see me. Ask him how much he charges to retain his services and then meet him and pay him. That's most important. When you leave here, I need you to Western Union me some money for my books. Send a grand. That should hold me for a minute, and then Western Union $300 to my man Tony Hammond. His government name is Navarro Hammond, and he's here at the jail with me. Write me some letters and send me some pictures."

"What kind of pictures do you want, brotha?" I asked salaciously and licked my lips.

"Whatever kind you wanna send, except nude joints. They won't let them in. Send some lingerie joints."

"Boy, my stomach is getting big. You ain't tryna see that shit."

"Why ain't I? Send them. You are my baby, and you're having my baby. Ain't nothing to be ashamed of on my end. You are a bad muthafucka, pregnant or not. My dick getting hard just thinking about your body. Is that pussy wet?"

"When? Now?" I asked.

"Right now," Khadafi said and smiled.

"I don't know. Let me see." I lifted my skirt and then went under it to my panties. Moving the center to one side, I pushed a single finger into my pussy and pulled it out. It was coated with juices. I showed the finger to Khadafi.

All he could do was shake his head. I got courageous and decided to give him a peek at my pussy. Moving the chair back a little, I lifted my skirt, lifted up and slid my panties down my legs. Then I pulled them over my heels and put them in my lap. Khadafi's eyes were big as boiled eggs. I licked my lips again and then put the finger that was just in my pussy, in my mouth. I pulled it out and lifted my skirt enough to where he could see my shaved pussy. He had to stand up a little to see it good and he did. I put my skirt down and picked up my panties. I dropped them into my wool coat pocket.

"Does that answer your question?"

"I can't believe this bitch-shit. I'm locked up in here and all that good pussy is out there with you. I guess you did answer my question. What color are your toe nails?"

"You wanna see them, too?" Then without waiting for an answer, I crossed my legs and undid the strap on my heels. I pulled the heel off and wiggled my toes.

"My favorite color. Cuz, you fuckin' my head up right now. You gone have me in the cell slick-jacking and shit."

"Slick-jacking? What's that?"

"That's me on the top bunk playing with my dick while my celly is on the bottom bunk sleep. I could wait until he can go out the cell, but fuck that. I can't wait another two days before I beat this dick."

"Boy, you are a mess."

"Naw, I'ma be a mess tonight once I beat my dick and cum all over myself."

I laughed at the image Khadafi just gave me as I put my shoe back on and strapped it up. Then another thought crossed my mind. My smile vanished. "From the look of you and the good mood you're in, I take it that your girl is gonna be okay, huh?"

"I called the hospital and talked to her mother. Her condition hasn't changed much, but everybody believes that Kemie will come out of her coma."

Except me. "That's good for her. So I'm supposed to hold you down while you're in here, just so you can go back to her when she comes home?"

"Can we have a good conversation without you bringing that shit up?" Khadafi hissed.

"Nah, nigga, we can't. It's the truth, ain't it?"

"That ain't the truth, cuz—"

"I told you about that cuz shit. Nigga, I'm your woman. Well, one of 'em. Not your buddy in the street. Respect me as such."

"Like I was saying, that ain't the truth, Marnie. I'd never leave you. We are bound by blood, a child, and sacrifice. Kemie will have to respect that."

"That bitch ain't gonna respect shit but an ass whipping and you know it." I was starting to get heated. And from the look on Khadafi's face, he was too. I decided to ease up and go on to steadier ground.

"In any event I got you. I'ma play my position and be the ride or die chick on the side. I know my place. I gotta call the lawyer and get him to take your case. Pay him, send you some money, write you, visit you, and send you semi-naked photos. And I gotta contact Bay One and give her a message from you. I got you, boo. Just like a good side bitch is supposed to be."

"Go ahead with that bullshit. I love you, Marnie, and you mean more to me than you know. That's why I sent you out of town. Hold on. Something just dawned on me. TJ is still out there. Your life is still in danger."

# CHAPTER THIRTY

## Khadafi

"My life is still in danger? Why?" Marnie asked incredulously.

"For the same reasons that your life was in danger before. Nothing's changed. Other than the fact that I'm in here and TJ knows that. I can't protect you from in here."

"Don't worry about me. I can protect myself. I still got the gun you gave me, and it's fully loaded."

"Didn't I just tell your GI Jane ass that these phones be tapped! And you talkin' 'bout 'don't worry about you.' Your ass gonna be over GTE locked up and having a baby."

"If I can be in a cell with you, I'd gladly accept prison. Does that tell you how much I love you?"

Marnie's words reached down inside me and threatened to make a gangsta get mushy, but I held it together. "Yeah, it does, but right now we gotta keep you alive. I want you to go somewhere and lay low."

"I'm not gonna be a prisoner in my own home, Khadafi."

"I didn't say go home. And didn't you just say that you'd gladly accept prison for me?"

"Naw, nigga. I said I'd gladly accept prison if they let me be in the cell with you. It's a big difference."

"Listen, cuz. Marnie, you don't know TJ like I do. I told you that before. He just killed—my bad—these phones. Just do what I told you to do. Keep that joint with you at all times, and if you ever see him, start bustin'. But in the meantime, you gotta limit your dealings with all the bitches from around the way, because one of 'em might betray you unknowingly. I should be able—"

"FULLER! LUTHER FULLER, your time is up!" a male CO bellowed.

"—to call you again soon. Don't forget to tell whichever lawyer you retain to come and see me soon. Remember everything that I told you and come back up here Thursday. And don't give nobody none of that pussy." I stood up and placed my right palm on the glass.

Marnie stood and I did the same. "I love you, cuz. Hold me down."

"I love you, too, baby. And you ain't gotta tell me to hold you down. I'm trained to go and know exactly what to do. I got you."

"FULLER! Don't make me call you again!"

"Damn, he geekin' like shit, ain't he?" Marnie said and screwed her face up.

"Don't even sweat that nigga. They a little power struck around here, but it's cool."

I stood in front of the glass and watched Marnie walk away. From head to toe, my bitch was a bad muthafucka and I really dug her. I never meant to catch feelings for her, but somewhere along the way I did. When I told Marnie that I loved her a few moments ago, deep in my heart I knew that I meant every word.

"You gon' lose your visits bullshittin', Fuller. Let's go!"

Marnie waved one last time before disappearing onto the elevator. That was my cue to leave. I walked out of the visiting hall thinking about how shit would be disastrous once Kemie got out the hospital and came home. Shit between her and Marnie was going to heat up and probably turn deadly, and I had to do all I could to prevent that. The solid steel door closing behind me brought me back to where I was and the danger lurking behind every door. Every corner. I knew that I had done a rack of shit to niggas in the streets, and they knew it, too. So my enemies were plentiful. Including the most dangerous one—Ameen. I knew that he was in the jail somewhere. DC jail held over 2,500 muthafuckas in eighteen units on three floors and somewhere in that equation was Ameen. At some point we were bound to meet, and knowing Ameen like I did, he'd definitely be ready to move. Ever since I first walked through the door to the jail, I vowed that I wasn't gonna lose my life here. The cemetery outside across from the jail couldn't have my bones. Not yet. I had to find a way to get Ameen before he got me.

"Northwest!" I yelled into the sally port to get the CO's attention. A second later, the grill opened and I walked into the unit. My head pounded and my heart was heavy. For the life of me, I could not figure out why TJ would have wanted to kill Esha. What the fuck had she done to him? I thought about the day that I saw TJ creeping out of Esha's back door. He looked suspicious. What made me know that he was Esha's killer was the fact that none of us ever used Esha's back door, because you gotta climb over too much shit at the back of her house to get to the back door. TJ didn't want to be seen leaving her house. But he was seen. By me. I instantly cursed under my breath, mad at myself because I let him get away that day. I had a muthafuckin' choppa and still let him get away. That wasn't like me. Maybe something inside me didn't really wanna kill him. I handed the CO in the bubble my visiting pass and ran down to the bottom tier. The CO hit the glass bubble and said, "Fuller, you live on the top tier."

I turned around and threw up one finger as if to say, "Gimme a minute." I jogged the short distance to thirty-one cell. Inside the cell, Tony Hammond sat on the bottom bunk playing cards with his celly. "Tony, what's up, cuz? You got that for me?"

The well-known convict with the salt and pepper wavy hair and a ready smile, rose and lifted the mattress on the top bunk. He pulled out a Scrabble game and passed it through the cell door to me. "Everything is in there, youngin'. You gon' get that money to me, right?"

"No doubt about it. Ain't nothing changed with me since we was in Atlanta."

"A'ight, young Khadafi. That's what's up. I know you about your business. If you need anything else just holla at me."

"I will, and Tony, keep this just between us, a'ight, cuz?"

"No doubt, youngin'. No doubt."

My celly was at court, so I could pretty much move around the cell freely. Dropping the Scrabble game on my bunk, I removed the lid. Inside the black cloth bag where normally the wooden letter pieces would be, there was a small bundle. I unwrapped the bundle and did a mental check to make sure that everything was there. It was. I picked up the street knife and palmed the handle. The flip out blade was about six or seven-inches long and shiny as shit. A big smile crossed my face. Whenever I did run into Ameen again, whether it was in the hall or in a unit, there would be no more Beaumont rec cage moments. He'd never catch me off guard again. This time, we'd both get hit. And if I died, then so would he.

# CHAPTER THIRTY-ONE

## Ameen

"These dudes in this joint talkin' bout you, slim."

"Is that right? What they saying?"

"They say you killed that dude Cochise and put his body in the coat cart downstairs."

I leaned in the doorway of twenty-five cell and watched as David 'CooWop' Wilson dumped packs of tuna fish into a Styrofoam tray. "You know how these 'talk-got-it-dot-gov' ass niggas is. They just bored, and gossiping is their favorite pastime. How many people you cooking for?"

Wop added mayo, honey, pickles, jalapeno peppers and cheese to the hook up and stirred it all up to mix it. "I'm hip to these niggas. I'm just putting you on point that these niggas got your name in their mouths, and in a few, the wrong ears gon' hear that shit. Ain't nobody getting none of this hook up but me, you, and Trey. Oh, and Boone."

"Ay, slim. Is what they say about Keith McGill true?" I asked.

"Yeah, he told on a dude named Smith-Bey from down Minnesota Avenue. Him, John Green, Monyay, Baby Kairy and all them niggas hot as shit. That nigga—"

One of the young Muslim brothers appeared out of nowhere. "Ameen, somebody want you out in the sally port."

"Good looking out, ock. CooWop, I'll be right back." I walked up the steps and looked out the door to see who was in the sally port. To my surprise it was an old friend.

"I heard you was up here. What's up, good looking?" I said to Tony Hammond.

"Ain't shit. These people tryna give me some play since Convict died."

"Michael Paige died?"

"Yeah. Slim died of cancer about two months ago. But look, that ain't why I came through. I got a kite for you. It's some news you can use. I'ma put it in this trash right here, and all you gotta do is get the detail nigga to give it to you. I'ma holla back at you soon."

"A'ight, big boy. You be cool."

Later that evening, Mike Boone brought the kite to my cell.

"What's that?" Trey asked me as I opened the sealed envelope.

"This is that kite that I was tellin' you that Tony Hammond left me." I pulled the paper out of the envelope and read it:

Young Ameen,

That young boy Khadafi is in the block with me. They got me on detail in the intake block, so I see everybody that comes in, ya dig? He's been here for about four or five days. I'm not sure exactly what he's back in on and how long he'll be here, but he says it may be a while. Although you and I never discussed what happened between y'all down Beaumont, I heard all about how he went home the first time and betrayed you by going at your woman. Since we all live by the 'betrayal is worse than slaughter,' the universal laws apply to all the good men. They are ingrained in us for a reason. The sacrifice that you made for your men, Khadafi included, was admirable and what was expected of a true soldier like you. So when you did it and we heard about it, none of the good men were surprised. Only the suckas misunderstood it. I also heard about what you did to him in the rec cage when he came back to Beaumont. Again, nobody was surprised at what happened. You did what was expected of you. Your enemy survived, and now he has grown strong. He's here, he's armed, and he probably knows you're here. So be careful. You are a good young dude, Ameen, and that's rare in this day and age. So I gotta lot of love for you. Never be the fool and never be afraid to be afraid. A fool is the only one who denies his fears. A real man embraces it and is unafraid to admit his fear. A fool scoffs at danger and ignores it. That's why Tony Fortune is not alive today. That's why Broadus is not alive today. That's why Cadillac is not alive today. In the face of a legitimate threat, a real man ignores nothing. Always remember these words, and you can thank the wise old owl later.

Why do I call myself the wise old owl? I'll tell you. The wise old owl lived in the oak. The more he saw, the less he spoke. The less he spoke, the more he heard. That's why the wise old owl outlived all the other birds.

Make this kite self destruct in two minutes.

Take care soldier. We are in NW 3. Your man is in 12 cell.

With respect,

The wise old owl

I laughed to myself and balled up the letter, and then I flushed it down the toilet.

"What he talkin' 'bout, slim?" Trey asked.

"You remember the dude I was tellin' you about? The one that was my man until he went home and started fuckin' my baby mother?"

"Yeah. The nigga you caught in the cage and busted his ass?"

"Yeah, him. Khadafi. He's in the intake block with Tony. Tony told me that he got his hands on a hammer, so he must know that I'm here. Either way, it's time to cook this beef between us."

"Ay, slim, you know I'm tryna make it out this muthafucka, but if you need me, I'm with you. No questions asked."

"I respect that, big homie, but I'ma handle this one solo. I already got an idea of how I wanna get him. And this time, ain't no fences gonna be in between us. This time, I'ma make sure that he dies."

# CHAPTER THIRTY-TWO

## TJ

How dare these niggas. They gon' kill my family and leave me alive to one day find out about it. Like I'ma bitch or something. It's all good though, because I get to fuck these niggas around one by one. Their families can respect my gangsta later. Black Scrubb and Nayroo, two dead men that had no idea that they were about to become dead men. One of my biggest regrets had to be that I wasn't able to kill C-Dubb. I filed his name in the back of my mind and pondered the thought of finding and killing some of his family members, kids, or whoever was linked to his blood.

The way Hope Village halfway house was run, I knew meals were served in the middle of the building's cafeteria. So all the dudes in the halfway house had to come out and walk to the cafeteria to eat. Yesterday, I waited outside and watched them during all three meals. But I didn't know who Black Scrubb was. The second day I staked out the halfway house, I spotted someone I knew. Ronald Herndon aka U-Conn Ron. I got out my car and walked over to U-Conn as he walked to chow. We embraced and kicked it for a minute.

Then I told him that I was looking for a dude who is supposed to be my half-brother and they called him Black Scrubb. U-Conn pointed a dude out to me that was as black as coal, wearing blue jeans, butter Timbs, and a thick leather jacket. From the angle where we stood, all I could really see was the side of his face. But he had a distinctive walk, one that I had on memory already. By the time U-Conn went inside the building to go and get Scrubb, I was gone. I didn't want the dude to see me. I wasn't concerned with U-Conn telling the dude who I was, because all he knew me by was Tyrone and not TJ. Now here I sat in the woods directly across from the halfway house, ready to split this nigga's shit. It was a new day. A day that Black Scrubb would not get out of. Silently, I asked myself, What if the dude Scrubb figured out who I was and never came out, or worse, he bolted and left the halfway house sensing danger? Well, we will see, won't we? As I sat, stood, and crouched, all I could see in my head was Bean's wicked smile. Every night since I killed Esha, it was all I saw. And all I could hear was his laughter. Laughing at my gullibility, my loss, my pain.

". . . he said that you was on the phone crying like a bitch. He laughed at you, TJ. And that laugh is something that I will never forget."

I'll never forget it, either, Esh. I eyed the red-brick building that I had seen Scrubb go back into after he left the cafeteria with U-Conn Ron. I remembered the puzzled look on his face and how he had looked all around looking for Tyrone. But Tyrone was nowhere to be found. I was back in my car down the street and hiding. Well, today he would see me, or at least parts of me. I tied my dreads into a ponytail and tucked them inside the back of my ski vest. Glancing at my watch, I knew it was almost time for the halfway house dudes to eat dinner. I crossed my fingers and hoped that Black Scrubb was hungry. Having been in the woods all day, I was pissed that he hadn't come out to either breakfast or lunch, and I was starting to lose faith in catching him today. But not enough to abandon my position. Come outside, Scrubb. Go to chow.

# The Ultimate Sacrifice III: No Regrets

In anticipation of seeing Scrubb, I pulled a black nylon cap down over my head and fitted clear ski goggles onto my eyes. I looked like I was in Aspen skiing. No witnesses would be able to describe me physically, other than a man dressed in black wearing goggles and a hat. The wind had started to pick up a little, but I wasn't worried. The temperature could drop all it wanted to. I was dressed for the elements. My insulated gortex boots and cargo pants sealed in body heat.

About thirteen minutes later, a CO unlocked the front door of the building from the inside. Then the first wave of dudes started to trickle out slowly. And then another wave and another, but still no Scrubb. I cursed under my breath. Where the fuck is this nigga?

Then, as if he heard my pleas for him to come out, he did. That's right, slim. Go get your last meal. I pulled both of my guns and stretched. I needed to get the kinks out from sitting and crouching for so long. It was almost 5 p.m., and in the projects next to the halfway house, people were everywhere, but I didn't give a damn. I thought about the fact that I only needed one gun to kill this nigga, Scrubb, and maybe I should put one back in my pocket, but then I figured that having two guns visible would make all the other halfway house niggas get the fuck out the way as I crushed Scrubb.

Whatever they were serving in the cafeteria must have been pretty bad, because it didn't take long for dudes to start coming back outside. And Scrubb was with them. It was time to pounce. I let Scrubb get about six-feet away from his building before I made my move. I was a black blur coming out of the woods and crossing the street. Dudes leaped over gates and scattered, but I was focused on Scrubb, who surprisingly saw me and didn't run. I stopped directly in front of him. Seeing him up close fueled my anger even more. I shot him in the forehead and when his body dropped, I stood over him and emptied the clip in his ass. Seconds later, I was running through the woods that lead to Suitland Parkway.

********

"I just killed one of the dudes that brought y'all that move, Pop. I gave you my word that I'ma make it right. Well, then again, I can never make it right because nothing I do is gonna bring y'all back—but I can make it better. Out of the three dudes, Pop, two are dead. The dude named C-Dubb was already dead by the time I found out who the dudes were. Black Scrubb died today, and the dude named Nayroo is next on my list. The crazy part about it all is that Bean put it together. That's crazy, huh? The same nigga that came in your house and ate your food, slept, chilled and called you Unc. He was the one that set it up. All because he got mad at me because I wouldn't put him down with the dude Manny Stone and that Ghostface Killaz dope they had. Ain't that a bitch? I thought he was my man, Pop.

I thought he was my brother. He tricked the shit outta me. I was so blinded by loyalty, love, and respect that I never saw the betrayal coming. I wish I could exchange places with y'all, Pop. No bullshit. I wish that I could make a deal with the devil and give him my soul just to bring y'all back. I wish I could do that, Pop. I wish I could." I wiped tears from my eyes and rearranged the flowers that I had just laid on the graves of my family. As I walked away and started down the hill, headed back to my car, I thought about Khadafi, and the fact that he tried to kill me. Initially, I thought that we could talk and try to get past our misunderstanding, but now I see that that couldn't happen. Too much blood had been shed and since he came at me as I left Esha's, that meant that he knew everything I did. And it also meant that he wanted me dead, so there was no room for discussion. Well, you ain't said nothing slick to a can of oil, Khadafi. I was gonna let you go, but now I'ma finish what I started by killing you and everybody you love.

# CHAPTER THIRTY-THREE

## TJ

D C police were called to the scene of a brazen broad daylight murder. Right here in front of a building operated by the DC Department of Corrections as a halfway house, thirty-nine year old Anthony Payton was shot and killed as he returned from the evening meal being served in a cafeteria nearby. Witnesses tell CUS News that a man dressed in all black clothing ran out of the woods across from the building and ambushed the victim here. Authorities are continuing to investigate this horrific crime . . ."

"You ready to go yet?" I asked Dawn as she walked into the living room of her apartment and clicked the TV off.

Dawn nodded.

"You remember what I need you to do, right?"

"I'm not deaf, dumb, or mute. I heard everything you said. Identify the dude, Nayroo, and then let you know who he is."

"Good," I said and stood. My guns were in my waist, and I was ready to commit my second murder of the day.

********

How could I get into the hospital and kill Kemie? What if she woke up and told the police that I shot her? Where the hell do I find Marnie? And why didn't I kill her the night I shot Kemie? I had no answers to the questions in my head. I wondered how long I'd have to wait to get my chance to kill Khadafi. The Remy Martin XO was keeping my body warm and buzzing. I drank straight from the bottle as I sat in Dawn's car and waited for her to return. I looked at the digital clock on the dashboard and wondered what was taking her so long. Ten minutes later, the door opened and Dawn ducked into the driver's seat. She smelled of PCP, and her eyes were a little glassy. "Did you find out who he is for me?"

"Of course I did," Dawn retorted and started the car.

"So what does he look like? Is he out there now?"

"Yeah, he's out there. Just chill out for a minute. I'm about to show you who he is." Dawn pulled the car out onto Martin Luther King Avenue and then turned onto Birney Place.

"What the fuck is that smell?" I asked, already knowing what it was. "And what took your ass so long to come back."

"Got damn, nigga. Who are you? The IRS? Am I being interrogated?"

I decided not to respond and skip it before I got mad and crushed Dawn's ass, too. She had no idea she was playing with a lit fuse that was ready to explode. What she said in the next few minutes would decide if she lived or died. The car became silent, and I figured that Dawn did in fact know me well enough to understand when she needed to play her part and let me do me.

"I'ma jump out up here and get a couple sacks from the light-skinned dude up here with the dreads. Directly behind him on the front porch of the building is another dude leaning on the green door. He's wearing a burgundy Redskin hat and a green old ass starter coat. That's the dude Nayroo."

Suddenly, the car stopped and Dawn hopped out. She walked over to the sidewalk and said something to a light-skinned dude with blond colored dreads. Behind him, just like Dawn had said, stood a dude dressed as she described. Nayroo. Nice to meet you, homie. Enjoy your last few minutes of life. When Dawn got back to the car and pulled off, I said,

"Drive over to the entrance of the Ellos apartment building and park right there."

"TJ, what the hell are you about to do?"

"The less you know the better. That way you have deniability. Park right out front and wait for me. Be ready to pull off when I get back." I exited the car and walked over to the front door of Ellos. The doorjamb was broken, so the door mechanism wouldn't lock. I walked right in the building. Knowing the building like the back of my hand, I quickly jogged down the hallway on the first floor and found the staircase that led down two flights of stairs and the basement door. Outside, I found a rock big enough to wedge into the backdoor to keep it open. Once that was done, I jogged around the backside of the building to the front and darted across the avenue. Park Chester projects had a cut that ran straight through from MLK Avenue to Birney Place. I crept through the cut until Birney Place was visible. It was a little after midnight and nobody was outside but niggas hustling. I didn't want to draw fire from some niggas standing around, so I couldn't mask up. All I could do was act like I was on foot coming to buy drugs. My hair was tied up and pressed down with a nylon cap. Earlier, I had changed clothes, but my attire was still all black. I came out of the cut and casually walked down the street where my target was. Nobody in the crowd knew who I was, so I was good. Nayroo stood alone on the porch.

"What's up, dawg?" the light-skinned dude that Dawn had spoken to said. "What you need?" The atmosphere tensed momentarily.

"Who got that 'love boat' out here?" I asked.

The tension eased. Dudes went back to what they were doing.

"I do. What you tryna get?"

"Gimme something for fifty."

As soon as the light-skinned dude reached in his dip to get the drugs, I pulled both guns. I hit light-skinned first and watched his men scatter. Then I ran over to the porch and cornered Nayroo. The look on his face was priceless. I raised both guns and hit his ass up. His body did the Harlem shake and then dropped. I leapt up the five steps and stood over his fallen body. Head shots came next. Then I ran back up Birney Place and hit the cut. Minutes later, I walked out the front door of the Ellos building. I casually walked up to Dawn's car and got in.

"TJ, please tell me that you had nothing to do with the shooting that I just heard. Please fuckin' tell me that you didn't just kill that dude you had me point out to you?"

"Get away from here, Dawn. Take me to your house."

"My house? TJ, them dudes . . . Well, one of 'em—he knows me. He knows I just came around there and asked who was Nayroo."

"They can't link you with nothing. Just chill out, Dee. Everything is gonna be a'ight."

"You . . ." Dawn inhaled deeply, exhaled, and pulled out of the Ellos driveway. She drove down the avenue way too fast.

"Slow down, Dawn. You gon' get us pulled over. Calm down and be normal," I pleaded. That's when I looked in the rearview mirror and spotted a car that I'd seen earlier. A money green Nissan Altima coupe was about three cars behind us, and I was 100% sure that it was the same car that I had seen when I pulled into Dawn's apartment complex earlier. Who could it be?

"Everything is not gonna be okay, TJ. Them niggas know me. They are going to put me with whatever you just did. You never said . . ."

"Listen, there's a car following us, and we need to shake it. If it was the cops, they'd be pulling you over by now, so they're not cops. I got enemies everywhere . . ."

"See, I told your ass them niggas know me! It's probably one of them."

"It ain't nobody from Park Chester because I saw the car at your house earlier."

Dawn whipped her head around and almost lost control of the car. "At my house? Aw . . . hell naw! What the fuck you done got me mixed up in, boy?"

"Just turn your ass around and drive. You know the area. Lose the green car about three cars back."

Glancing in her rearview mirror, Dawn spotted the car and made evasive maneuvers that made me proud. She hit a few corners and sped up then slowed down. Once we were uptown somewhere by Malcolm X Park on Sixteenth Street, the green car was nowhere to be found.

"A couple of clocks up is the Carter Barron Amphi Theater. It's deserted at this time of night. Pull in the parking lot and go around the back so we can make sure nobody is still behind us," I told Dawn.

"Them Park Chester niggas are gonna kill me. They . . ."

I burst out laughing and couldn't stop.

Dawn stared at me like I was going insane as she parked the car. "What the fuck is so funny? The fact that those Park Chester niggas is gonna kill me?"

"Naw, I'm not laughing at that," I said as I continued to laugh.

"Well, what the hell is so hilarious? Tell me so that I can laugh, too."

"I'm laughing at how shook you look. Keep talkin' 'bout 'them niggas gon' kill me'."

"What's funny about that? They are gonna kill me—"

"They are not. Trust me, them niggas are not gonna kill you."

"How can you be so sure?" Dawn asked me.

"Because they won't get the chance." I raised the gun in my right hand and blew Dawn's brains all over the driver's side window."

********

Killing Dawn wasn't part of the plan. She caused her own death the minute she revealed that the light-skinned dude knew who she was. Her rants and raves were true. The Park Chester niggas would put her with the murder of the dude, Nayroo and the light-skinned nigga's shooting. At some point, they'd find her and then under duress from either them or the cops, Dawn would break and give me up, and there was no way that I could let that happen. I didn't want to kill Dawn, but killing her meant nothing to me. I was devoid of all emotion, feeling, or remorse. The day I was forced to kill Reesie, the only person that I loved as much as myself, I completely lost my soul. So everybody else that I killed after her was as easy as swatting a fly off my face. Reesie, Esha, Dawn, three women that I loved and grew up with had died by my hand. If I had any tears left inside me, I'd cry, but I didn't have anything inside me but emptiness. My heart was a hollow shell. The hand I was dealt in this life drained me of my joy, my love, my soul.

I lay on Dawn's couch and thought about the green Nissan Altima that I'd seen following us. Was it my paranoia or was I simply imagining things? Who could the person or people inside the car be? Khadafi was in jail, and all of my known enemies were dead. I thought of all the possibilities and couldn't settle on anything definite. I thought about Dawn's body slumped over, head bloody, and the fact that I took her house keys and came back to her house after killing her.

Maybe it was because my car was parked outside. Maybe not. Maybe I have a perverse desire to conquer the dead in every way. The realization dawned on me then that I'd also killed the last two remaining dudes that were involved in my family's deaths. Suddenly, a tremendous calm washed over me. "Now, y'all can really rest in peace, Pop." My only regret was that I didn't get the chance to kill Bean myself. Death had a way of going around in circles. It always came back around, and one day it would find me. But until that day came, I still had work to do.

********

"Excuse me, ma'am. I'm here to visit my cousin. Can you tell me what floor and room she's in?"

The lady dressed in hospital scrubs who sat behind the counter looked up from her computer screen. "What's your cousin's name?"

"Rakemie Bryant. R-A-K-E-M-I-E Bryant."

"Ms. Bryant is in room 512. That's on the fifth floor. Just get on the elevator behind you and press five."

"Thank you." I turned to leave, but the lady called me.

"Sir, I need you to fill out this form right here, so that I can give you a visitor's pass. You cannot move throughout PG hospital without one."

I filled in all bogus info on the form. "Uh . . . what day is it?"

"January 27," the lady replied.

After passing the form back to the lady, I was given a visitor's pass. I caught the elevator to the fifth floor and followed the signs that lead to room 512. Outside the room were several people that I recognized as Kemie's family members. Before I could decide whether to leave or stay, Reesie's little sister Tera came out of nowhere and called my name. That brought stares from the rest of the family.

Kemie's mother walked up to me. "What are you doing here, TJ?"

I couldn't read the expression on her face, but I knew that Kemie couldn't have said my name because the cops would be somewhere nearby. "I just wanted to check on Kemie."

"She's still in the same shape, comatose. When she comes to I'll be sure to let her know that you stopped by, but do me a favor and don't come by again. You were the last person to see Reesie alive, and seeing you brings on a lot of bad energy for me and for my family. So again, please don't come back."

Without another word, I turned and walked away. But I would definitely come back, and the next time it would be to kill Kemie.

# CHAPTER THIRTY-FOUR
## Lil Cee

T his won't hurt a bit." The OB/GYN said to Kia as I watched Kia lay on the examination table and relaxed as much as she could. Her shirt was pulled up to where her breasts were almost visible. Her bare stomach was revealed for all to see.

"I'm gonna squirt a little of this gel onto your stomach . . . and then . . . It's kind of cold, huh? Okay. I'll take this little gadget here and pass it onto your stomach. Do you hear that?"

The unmistakable sounds of a heartbeat came out of speakers attached to a computer and monitor.

"Is that the baby's heartbeat or mine?" Kia asked.

"That's the baby's heartbeat, sweetheart," the female doctor beamed. "And it sounds very healthy and strong to me. All of the baby's vital signs appear to be normal. Now look at the screen here. This area is the baby's head."

"Oh my God, Charles! Look!" Kia said excitedly.

I stared at the monitor and tried to make out the images that the doctor pointed at.

"This would be one of the arms. And here's a leg. The baby is lying on its side, sort of. For you to be in your first trimester, the fetus is developing well. Would you like to know the sex of the baby? I usually recommend that young parents know the sex of the baby. To me, it helps in the parental bonding stage, but it's entirely up to you two."

Kia looked up at me as if to let me make the decision. I nodded. I was curious to know anyway.

"We'd like to know what the sex is," Kia answered and stared at the screen.

"Okay. Good choice. Let's see here . . ." The doctor moved the computer mouse-looking thing all over Kia's stomach to get the right angles. "Here we go . . . right here. See the area here?"

Kia and I both stared at the monitor. But I couldn't make out a thing.

The doctor pointed at the screen. "It appears that you two are the proud parents of a little girl. See here . . . This is the tiny form of the vagina. Congratulations on the baby girl."

When one life ends . . . another begins . . .

I thought about those words and how my mother adamantly believed in that. So I couldn't help but wonder if God blessing me with a daughter was to replace my little sister? Looking over at Kia, she was all smiles, and that in itself made me feel good.

********

"I'll have the shrimp and lobster alfredo, a side order of jumbo spice shrimp and the garlic bread sticks with the mozzarella cheese inside of 'em. Gimme some melted butter and cocktail sauce with my jumbo shrimp, and a large raspberry iced tea," Kia said to the waiter.

All I could do was laugh.

"Ain't nothing funny, boy. I'm hungry as shit. This baby is greedy, too. All this shit is for her."

"Everything you eat is for her, huh? I didn't know that unborn babies preferred shrimp. That's a new one on me, but I'm always open to learning new things."

"Is that right?"

"Yeah, that's right. But let me ask you this, if the shrimp and lobster is for the baby, what are you gonna eat for you?" I asked Kia jokingly.

"What am I gonna eat? For me?"

"Yeah." I picked up my glass of water and took a swallow.

"The alfredo is for me. All I need for me is alfredo and dick."

I almost spit water all over the place. "What you say?"

Kia looked at me salaciously, licked her lips, and repeated herself. "Alfredo noodles and dick. That's all I need for me to be good. The alfredo, I'll eat now. The dick, I'll eat later."

"I tell you what, Diva. They still call you Kia the Diva, right?"

"Only when I'm putting on shows. When I'm horny, it's Kia Kitty. You do remember Kia Kitty, don't you?"

"Do I? That's why I suggest that you call the school and tell them that you're not coming back to work today. We can get our food to go, and I can holla at Kitty now instead of later."

Kia licked her glossy lips again and then slipped her foot out of her shoe. She lowered herself in the booth and then her foot found my crotch. Kia's toes rubbed forcefully all over my dick. "So basically, what you're saying is that you want me to eat dick now instead of later?"

"Something like that. Make the call. I'll get the food."

********

I don't know if it was the baby making Kia's breasts bigger, but they sat up on her chest looking like perky melons. My eyes found the spot right over her left breast that had my name inked over it. That tattoo turned me on so much. Kia was the perfect cross between Lauren London and Megan Goode, only shorter. At five-feet even, Kia's caramel brown skin and tattoos on both arms and a leg gave her a celebrity appeal. And every time I gazed at her long black hair, pretty teeth, and juicy lips, I felt like paparazzi, a fan amid the awaiting public that just couldn't get enough of her. I always wanted to drink of her essence and get drunk just being around her. And at the moment, I was definitely intoxicated. I watched the expression on Kia's face change from pain to ecstasy as she sat on top of me and rode my dick. Her hands massaged my chest and her feet dug into the sheets on the bed. Her moans were enticing. The sound of her body slapping my body as she took every inch of me inside her made her appear brave. "That's right, baby. Take that dick! Take that dick!"

"I'm taking it, Charles. Damn, boo, I'm taking it."

"You like that dick?"

"OOOOh . . . I love it! I love your dick!"

"Kia, I love you, baby. Your pussy good as shit."

Kia gyrated her hips and then lifted herself up to where only the head of my dick was inside her. She worked her leg and pussy muscles to stay where she was and worked me like that. It was a feeling that I couldn't describe. "Don't ride it like that, baby. You gon' make me cum. That shit feel too good!"

"Damn, I wanna suck your dick so bad," Kia exclaimed as she continued to ride me. "Charles, I wanna suck your dick, boo. Oooh . . . Oooh . . . damn boy, I'm about to cum . . . OOOOh . . . OOOh. OOOh!"

"Don't cum yet, baby. Your pussy already too wet."

"I can't help it!" Kia moaned and then sat all the way down on my dick. "Shit! It's too deep in there, Charles! I'm cumming! I can't stop it! I'm cumming!"

"Cum for me, then. Cum all over my dick."

Kia hollered out my name and did just that. "I wanna suck your dick."

With the alacrity of a cat, Kia rose up off my dick and put it in her mouth. All I could do was close my eyes and wiggle my toes. As bad as I wished I could prolong the sensation, I couldn't. A minute later I was coming.

********

"Charles? Charles, wake up."

I opened my eyes and saw Kia facing me. I glanced at the digital clock on the cable box. I'd been asleep almost three hours. I'm up. What's good, boo?"

"Are we doing the right thing, Charles?"

Shaking my head to get the dust out, I thought about what Kia had just said. "What kind of question is that? Why do you ask me that?"

Kia sat up in bed and gathered the sheets around her. "It's a valid question. I wanna make sure that you feel the same way as me."

"Of course, I feel the same way as you. Why would you think that I don't?"

"Because of what happened to your mother and sister."

I sat up in the bed and faced Kia. "But . . . what does that have to do with anything?"

Kia hesitated before answering. "I say that for three reasons. Number one, do you remember the day we left DC and we stopped in South Carolina at the south of the border stop?"

"How could I forget that?"

"That day you asked me did I have any idea what I'd given up for you?"

"You told me that you did know what you'd done and gave up, and if you could go back and change anything, you wouldn't." Kia nodded with her eyes closed as if she were reliving that moment.

"In my own way I was telling you that I was with you for better or worse, and no matter what, I'd never regret my decision that I made that day. Well, now it's your turn to answer that question. We've been in Norcross for about two and a half months. Things haven't always been great, but we've handled all obstacles that we faced. And now we're pregnant, so I wanna know if you regret anything? If we're doing the right thing?"

"No regrets, Kia. Never have and never will regret anything. I just . . ."

"Let me finish what I was saying before I lose my train of thought. The second reason I asked are we doing the right thing by bringing a baby into this world is especially because we both know how ugly this world can be. We've witnessed firsthand the harsh realities of a cruel, cruel world. How many tears have we both cried because of heartache and pain? How much have we endured? Again, look at what happened to Quette, to Samantha and Dave, your mother and baby sister, Charity? Is that what we want to expose a child to? Do we wanna give all of this devastation, hurt, heartache and pain to our child?"

"Kia, it's too late to be a pessimist. I understand everything you're saying, but I believe that we can give our daughter all the love and joy that this world can offer. We can't live in the past. We have to focus on the future. Our daughter's. Our future. So you ask are we doing the right thing? I believe so."

Suddenly, Kia laughed a maniacal laugh and said, "We can't live in the past. We have to focus on the future. That's what you just said, right? Your words, not mine. But they bring me to my last point. This dude . . . what's his name? Khadafi, right? Yeah, that's it. Well, can you find it inside of you to forget about your obsession with Khadafi and your thirst for vengeance? Huh? Can you abandon your mission to go back to DC and kill Khadafi?"

When I didn't respond, I guess that gave Kia my answer.

"Well, at least you didn't speak and lie to me to my face. I've been with you for almost four months and it seems like four years. I feel like I've known you my whole life. All the time we've spent together, Charles, I've learned to read you, read your moods. A good woman has to be able to live in sync with her man. So I know more about you than you think I do. I can see the way you walk around here with just your body present because your mind is back in DC. I can see the desire in your eyes to kill. I know when you are hurting and trying to hide your pain. I can see through your smiles, when you try to keep me from knowing that your mother, your sister, and your god brother, Church—their deaths weigh heavy on your mind…"

Before I knew what was happening, tears formed in my eyes and rolled down my cheeks as if a river were overrunning. And I was powerless to stop them. It was as if my tears had a mind of their own.

". . . and heart. Not only does your body ache, your soul cries too. I walk around with you, beside you, and behind you and your emotion is palpable. So tell me again if you can look me right in the eyes and tell me that we can't focus on the past and that we must live for the future. Then in the same breath, tell me that you won't go back to DC one day and try to kill Khadafi. Tell me that you will stay here with us, love us, and never leave us. Go ahead, tell me that." Kia looked at me with tears in her eyes and a questioning look on her face. I opened my mouth to speak, but no words would come out. I was speechless.

Kia swiped at the tears falling down her cheeks. "See, that's exactly what I thought. You're a hypocrite. You say with your mouth what's not in your heart. Let me put this question to you another way then. Does killing Khadafi mean more to you than me and your unborn child?"

Again, I couldn't respond. I just didn't know what to say. And I didn't want to lie to Kia, so I kept quiet.

"You bastard!" Kia cried out and smacked my face hard. "I hate you. I fuckin' hate you." Then she got out of the bed and ran toward the bathroom. But suddenly she stopped. She turned and looked at me with tears streaming down both cheeks and said, "If you go back to DC, he's gonna kill you. I saw it in my dreams."

I lay back down and thought about everything that Kia had said, especially the last part. And I questioned myself about a lot of things. But again, no answers came to me, and all I could do was lay there and listen to Kia cry.

# CHAPTER THIRTY-FIVE

## TJ

The death of a ten-year-old Prince George's County school girl after a planned fight with another student has been ruled a homicide, the PG County Coroner's office announced today. Blunt force trauma to the head killed Dejanae Parker, who collapsed at her Temple Hills home after Thursday's fight at Barnaby Manor Elementary.

"Another man has died and the body of a young woman was found in her car at the rear of the Carter Barron Amphi Theater. We'll be right back in a moment . . ."

I glanced down at the dreadlocks at my feet. I was doing the one thing that I thought I'd never do and that's cut my dreads. Standing in front of the mirror in my bedroom, I snipped each dread at the new growth. Changing my appearance was something that had been on my mind for months, but now was the time to do it. All of my latest murders were newsworthy, and I knew that the net the DC police would drag through the streets would net me eventually, so I needed to sever the last link to me and the crimes I committed. And that link was named Kemie.

"Four nights ago, DC police were called to the scene of a shooting in the 2600 block of Birney's Place in Southeast, DC. Police found two men suffering from gunshot wounds. One man, Nairu Jones was pronounced dead at the scene, while the

215

other man was transported to Howard University where he underwent surgery for hours. Well, CUS Fox news at noon has learned that that man, identified as thirty-three-year-old Roger Robinson has died. In other news, DC police have also identified the woman found inside her car shot to death as Dawn Duvall.

"The DC jail has been taken off lockdown. Prison officials have thirty-nine-year- old Michael Boone in custody. They say Mr. Boone is solely responsible for the gruesome murder of a parole violator, identified as Ronald 'Bubbles' Frazier. FBI documents that were thought to have been redacted, were mistakenly given to Mr. Boone, identifying the decedent as a confidential Informant."

Tuning out the rest of the news program, I continued to snip my dreads. The way I figured it, the new look was long overdue. My new look would be one that nobody could see coming and that nobody included Kemie's family. The room I was in had grown semi-dark, and I noticed the sun now hid behind several storm clouds as I looked out the window. Even though it was about fifteen minutes after noon, the darkness of the day caused me to wonder if the sudden gloom was an ominous sign of doom to come.

Finally, I was done. I stared at myself in the mirror and saw a seventeen-year-old dude about to turn eighteen, excited about life and on his way to Atlantic City. For the briefest of moments, I saw the young teenager who was forced by a dog-eat-dog world to become a man too fast. I ran my hand over the length of my hair and smiled. Grabbing the Andies clippers, I put the one and a half-inch blade all over my head and evened it out. Then I showered.

Minutes later, I extracted the uniform from inside a bag leaning against my dresser and put it on. Next, came some smiley face socks and a pair of sky blue crocs. They matched my light blue hospital scrubs and North Carolina Tar Heels baseball cap. I grabbed a book bag out of my closet and put clothes, shoes, and two handguns inside, one of which was equipped with a sound reducing attachment. Inserting my arms through both shoulder straps, I stopped in front of the mirror again. I looked gay. I looked like I worked at the hospital.

********

Dressed in the right clothes gave you the mobility to move as freely as possible, even in a hospital. No one paid me any mind as I roamed the halls of the hospital trying to map out possible escape routes in case things went bad fast. When I finally reached the fifth floor, I noticed the hallway outside of room 512 was basically empty, a big difference from three days ago. I walked slowly down the hall. First, I knocked on 512 to see what happened, but I received no reply. Pushing the door open, I found that the room was empty and so was the bed. Puzzled, I walked backward out of the room and wandered down the hall to the nurse's station. The nurse at the station was probably in her middle to late 50s, but she was gracefully attractive like Debbie Allen. I asked her about Kemie.

"You mean Rakemie Bryant, right? That young girl in 512?"

I nodded.

"You haven't heard then? Poor child. Everybody around here was praying for that girl. It's a damn shame that somebody shot that baby in her head like that. She went into cardiac arrest, and the doctor's couldn't revive her. She passed away yesterday at 9:37 p.m.

On the bottom floor of the hospital, I changed clothes in the men's room. I walked out of the hospital in a black Shooter's Sports sweat suit, gray 993 New Balance, and a North Face Elements gortex coat. On my head was a Shooter's Sports skullcap. With a smile on my face, I started the Roadmaster and pulled off.

# CHAPTER THIRTY-SIX

## Marnie

"Ms. Curry, you can go in now," the receptionist announced.

"Thank you," I replied and walked into the office of Bernard Grimes, attorney at law.

Bernard Grimes was a handsome older man with a low haircut and neatly trimmed beard, peppered with gray. He stood the moment he saw me and walked around his desk to meet me in the middle of his office. We shook hands.

"Have a seat, please, Ms. Curry. Our conversation on the phone was brief, so I'm going to need you to fill me in again on exactly what you need."

I waited until Mr. Grimes was also seated before starting. "This is not about me, Mr. Grimes. My boyfriend was arrested recently. He gave me your name and asked me to possibly retain you to fight for him."

"Your boyfriend, huh? And what is his name?"

"Kha—I mean—Luther Fuller. His name is Luther Antwan Fuller."

"Can't say that I remember that name. Have I represented him before in a matter?"

"I have no clue, Mr. Grimes. All I know is that he asked for you by name."

"Okay, that's neither here nor there. You say he was recently arrested? And please, call me Bernie."

"Yes. He's been at DC jail for about a week or two. Right now he has a public defender who has been representing him."

Bernard Grimes leaned his chair back and put both his hands behind his head. "And what charge or charges is he being held on?"

"Well, right now, it's some bullshit. Excuse my language. They got him on three misdemeanors, eluding the police, reckless endangerment, and destruction of government property. But the public defender told him that a gun charge and possible other charges were imminent. That's why he asked for you."

"Well, I'm game. With the charges you just named, they aren't hard to litigate at all. The gun charge is a little more serious. Does Mr. Fuller have any other pending charges?"

"Not that I know of. If he did, I'd know."

"What about—has he ever been convicted of a crime? How old is he?"

"Khadafi is—Luther is his government name but he hates it. Everybody calls him Khadafi. He's twenty-nine."

"Khadafi, huh? He's middle eastern?"

I laughed. "Not at all. That boy was born and raised in Capers projects. He converted to Islam in prison and changed his name. It's just not legal yet. So to answer your question, yes he has been convicted of another charge before. He did ten years for murder."

"So he's on parole?" Bernard Grimes asked.

"I'm not sure. If you decide to take his case or cases, he'd like to meet with you as soon as possible, anyway. You can ask him."

"Okay, Ms. Curry. I think I can take this case or cases. For the whole matter, the gun charge and the three misdemeanors,

I charge fifteen thousand. And if any other charges come later, that price will change. Quickly. So just to get started by petitioning the courts for a change of attorney and to enter any appearances on behalf of Mr. Fuller, I'm gonna need a ten thousand dollar retainer. Now if . . ."

"Done," I interrupted Bernie. Opening my purse, I pulled out a wad of money and counted out ten grand in one hundred dollar bills. I handed the money across the desk. "I could give you the whole fifteen if you'd like?"

Bernard Grimes pocketed the money and said, "This will do for now. You can let Mr. Fuller know that I will be to see him either today or tomorrow."

Standing up, I fixed my skirt. "Thank you, Bernie. It was nice meeting you."

"It was nice meeting you too, Ms. Curry. I'll be in touch."

********

Just as I stepped out of the building, I turned my cell phone back on. It rang as soon as I did. The caller was Reesie's little sister, Tera. "Hello?"

"Marnie . . . I know how you felt about my cousin Kemie, but I still figured that on the strength of your closeness to my family, that you'd want to know . . ."

I stopped walking as soon as I got to the Escalade. "Know what, Tera? What happened now?"

"Kemie . . . um . . . Kemie died, Marnie. She passed away on Saturday."

I couldn't believe what I just heard. "Tera, what happened?"

"All I know is that the doctor's tried to revive her after her machine that she was hooked up to went crazy and started beeping real loud. I was outside in the hallway with my mother. The doctor came out of the room shaking his head, and then he told my aunt that Kemie was gone. This was

221

Saturday evening. My aunt hasn't been outta her room for two days. Me, my mother, and my other two aunts are over here and everybody's hurting bad."

I didn't know whether I should feel bad or feel glad. At one point in my life, I wanted Kemie dead. I wished death on her every day. I prayed for it, but as time went on, I just wanted her to stay in a coma. All I wanted was Khadafi. That thought made me remember Khadafi and where I had just left. "I'm sorry to hear that, Tera. I swear to God I am. Even though Kemie and I weren't friends anymore, she didn't deserve to die like that. First Reesie and now Kemie. This shit is getting . . ."

"Don't forget about Esha," Tera added.

"Yeah, you right. Esha, too. Listen, please tell your family that I send my condolences and that whatever y'all need financially, I wanna help. You hear me, Tera?"

"I hear you. I'll tell 'em."

"And one last thing before I go. Have you or somebody in the family called up the jail and told Khadafi yet?"

"I don't think so, but I can—"

"No. Don't worry about it. I'll take care of it. I'll make sure that he calls y'all when he can, okay?"

"I'll let my aunt know. Bye, Marnie."

"Bye. And thanks for calling me. I love you."

"Love you, too, Marnie. Bye." Tera hung up.

Climbing into the truck, all I could do was shake my head. Kemie was gone. My prayers that I prayed months ago had been answered, and I didn't even feel good about it. Kemie and I had been friends for twenty years and enemies for about five. I hated her, but deep inside I still loved her cruddy ass. As I started the truck and pulled into traffic, I noticed that I was crying. "Damn, I can't believe it. I won. Kemie is out of our lives and I won. Khadafi is mine."

After the initial shock wore off as I drove, I thought about Khadafi and the pain he would be in. He loved Kemie more than anybody in his life. And now she was dead. He would be devastated. I picked up my phone and called DC jail. They connected me to the chaplain's office.

"Chaplain's office. Chaplain Green speaking. How may I help you?"

"I need to let an inmate there know about the death of a family member."

"Okay, ma'am. I'll need the name of the inmate, the name of the deceased, and the relationship to the inmate."

"Luther Fuller is the inmate. Rakemie Bryant is the person who died . . ."

# CHAPTER THIRTY-SEVEN
## Khadafi

D o you read a lot of them urban novels?" Ed Robertson, my celly asked me.
"I read a rack of them joints on my last bid. Them joints all right. They cool."

"The reason I ask is because my sister came to see me last week and told me that she mailed off some joints by some homies. A joint called Larceny 2 by Jason Poole and Lorton Legends by some dude from uptown named Eyone. I ain't wanna tell her that I don't read that shit because she had already sent 'em. I ain't tryna read them joints, though, slim. No bullshit."

"Why not?" I asked.

"Because them joints are all the same to me. And you got too many muthafuckas writing them joints. Everybody and their mother done wrote an urban novel. I wouldn't dare spend no more money on that bullshit. Back when Dutch came out, B-More Careful, Angel, them Thug joints and all that good shit, the game was good. That urban book shit was a good look because we could identify with the street shit. Real live street nigga shit. Killing, murder, rape, robbing, money, bitches, etcetera. But now you read them joints, everybody got ten to twelve-inch dicks, exotic half-breed bitches, futuristic cars and millions of dollars. Niggas come home from the joint on page one, by the time you get to page twenty, the nigga has a Colombian connect and a hundred bricks of coke. Get the fuck outta here. Niggas got houses in the hood with eyeball scanners to get in. Get the fuck outta here with that bullshit. I'ma stick to them Eric Jerome Dickey joints."

Laughing at what Ed said, I added, "Everything you said is a true bill, cuz. But I checked out a couple of them Eric Jerome Dickey joints and they be welling like shit, too."

Ed burst out laughing because he knew that I was right.

"He got a block nigga in the book . . . The nigga Gideon, he all over the world killing muthafuckas on some hitman shit. All that is some shit anything. I think that joint is called Waking with—"

The cell door buzzed and then opened. Ed got up and went to the door. He stepped outside the cell and threw up both of his arms.

"What's up? Who y'all need?" Ed asked the CO.

"Both of y'all. Robertson, you pack up. You're on the move sheet. Where's Fuller?" the CO asked.

"He right here," Ed replied. "What block I'm going to?"

"You're going to Southeast 3 around the corner. Tell Fuller he gotta go see the chaplain, they just called for him."

Ed turned to me to speak, but I said, "I heard him, cuz." I got up and brushed my teeth while Ed packed up his small amount of property. All the while, I couldn't shake the foreboding feeling that sat in the pit of my stomach.

It was the afternoon on a Monday and a summons from the chaplain could never be good news. Especially since I never attended church, and neither was I a Christian. It had to be bad news, and all I could think about was Kemie.

*Please, please, please Allah, don't let this call be about Kemie.*

"Ay, slim. I'ma holla at you when I see you again," Ed said. "You be cool and stay sucka free."

"A'ight, cuz." I stopped, turned around, and embraced Ed. "You do the same."

Slowly, I got dressed and ran water over my frizzy cornrow braids. They looked like any day now they were gonna lock up and dread. I walked up the tier and jogged down the stairs to the police bubble. They gave me a pass and opened the sally port grill. On the first floor, I walked into the chaplain's office.

"Somebody called for me?"

A lady who appeared to be in her early 50s was xeroxing papers. "And who are you?" She was sexy as shit to be old.

"Luther Fuller."

"Mr. Fuller. I'm sorry to inform you, but there's been a death in your family. A relative by the name of Monica Curry called and wanted you to know that Rakemie Bryant passed away Saturday, January 29 at approximately 9:37 at night. I called the coroner's office and confirmed the info."

I knew that the chaplain's mouth was moving, but I couldn't hear a word she said after 'Rakemie Bryant passed away'. I stood riveted to my spot by the desk and choked up. My breath got caught in my chest. I turned and left the chapel. Oblivious to every and anyone around me, I found myself back at the grill to Northwest 3. Getting back to my cell felt like I was walking the green mile on my way to the death chamber.

As soon as my cell door closed behind me, I lost control. I started by throwing punches at the wall. The pain in my knuckles reverberated all the way to my elbows, but I kept punching. My tears came in tidal waves. The bottomless pit inside my body where my heart used to be echoed a dark sound, an animalistic scream. I never knew how loud that sound was until the COs appeared at my cell.

"Fuller! Fuller! What the hell are you doing? Sarge, call a code. There's blood on the walls and the floor. Call a code!"

The idea of time meant nothing to me then. All I knew was that TJ was in front of me and I was hitting him, killing him with my hands. Spit flew out my mouth as my tears fell. My screams could be heard all over the block. Then several TJs appeared before my eyes and I charged them all and threw all kinds of punches. Then they tackled me. But I still didn't stop fighting. TJ killed Kemie, and I needed to kill him. I fought and fought and fought. That was all I could do. At some point, I blacked out.

When I came to, I was strapped down to a bed in a hospital room. There were correctional officers everywhere. My mouth was dry. I looked down and saw that both of my hands were by my side but were bandaged up.

"Fuller?" a white shirted lieutenant named Worthy spoke. "You are in the infirmary at CTF. We have you strapped down for your own safety. We know all about the death of your relative, Rakemie Bryant, so we didn't charge you with assault on staff. The doctor gave you some meds that should keep you calm for a few days. We're gonna leave you here until tomorrow and then you go back to DC jail. Per policy, we have to put you on suicide watch for twenty-four hours after. So you need to chill out, and we'll have to find another way to deal with your grief. Maybe . . ."

I was extremely tired and my eyelids were heavy. I went back to sleep.

"Kemie?"

"I'm here, baby. I'm here."

"They told me you were dead. I thought you were dead."

"Khadafi, baby, I will always love you. Don't forget that and I will always be with you."

"I love you with all my heart, Kemie. Don't ever leave me. I'ma change my life and it's gonna just be you and me. I swear.

# The Ultimate Sacrifice III: No Regrets

I swear by Allah. Wallahi, Kemie. Promise me that you won't leave me."

"I won't leave you, baby, I promise. I promise you that."

"Fuller! Fuller! Wake up! Fuller!"

Kemie disappeared and in her place was a pretty face that I'd never seen before. I closed my eyes and then opened them again. "Where'd Kemie go?"

"Kemie? Who's Kemie?" the CO asked, looking befuddled.

"She was just here. I just talked to her. You had to see her," I argued.

The female CO shook her head. "Fuller, I been here since eight o'clock this morning and ain't nobody else been here but me. I heard about your loss. I'm sorry. But you have to get yourself together. Your lawyer has been trying to see you for the last two days.

"The doctor says that physically, you're fine. You just have to heal mentally. You gotta pull yourself together. I know you don't know me from Adam, but I know what you're going through. My baby father got killed recently. I used to feel like I couldn't go on, but one of my girlfriends told me everything that I'm telling you now. Although our situations are different, in a way they're the same. This is just a job to me, and I hate to see y'all young brother's fucked up in here. But I gotta pay the bills, ya know. Anyway, you can survive this. These muthafuckas think that you are gonna kill yourself. That's why I'm here. To babysit you. Prove 'em wrong, baby. Prove 'em wrong. Your lawyer is here, and he wants to see you. So what's it gonna be? You gonna lay here and feel sorry for yourself or get up and go see your lawyer?"

I thought about everything the CO lady said and realized that Kemie was speaking to me still, but it was through her. It was time to pull myself up.

\*\*\*\*\*\*\*\*

My legal visit with Bernard Grimes was short but sweet. He'd gone over the case and decided that it was weak as hell. He said the gun charge would never even make it to court if the U.S. Attorney did decide to indict on that. And until the government made a move, he couldn't countermove or come up with a strategy. So everything was just a waiting game. He'd also heard about my loss and encouraged me to keep my head up.

Just as soon as I got back to the block from the legal visit, they called me for a social visit, and my instincts told me exactly who it was. When I walked into the visiting hall and saw Marnie, my heart swelled. Through it all, Marnie had turned out to be the one. The real ride or die chick. When she said she had my back, she meant it.

"What happened to your hands?" she asked as soon as she sat down and grabbed the receiver.

I glanced at the band aids that covered my knuckles and then looked at Marnie. My eyes must have told the story. "Thanks for having my back, boo. I know how you felt about Kemie and all that, and I never once told you that you were wrong for feeling like that. I killed two men over the same thing you and Kemie were beefing about.

"And Kemie was definitely a sheisty bitch, but I loved her, Marnie. I loved . . . I still love her ass more than you can ever imagine. She's been all I know since I learned all I know. Feel me? I believe that it's possible to love two women at one time. Whoever said that's impossible is a lying muthafucka. Because I love you, too, Marnie. But I can't lie to you and tell you that I'm not fucked up about Kemie. Because I am. That's all I can think about, and I wanna kill muthafuckas, boo. Bad! I wanna kill this nigga TJ so bad that I can taste it."

"Baby, you tripping. Remember these phones . . ."

"Fuck these phones, these people, and their bugs. If they listening, they can record me telling on myself 'cause by Allah, I'ma kill that nigga and every relative he got left. That's my life's work. I gotta do that so that Kemie can rest in peace.

"When them people called me down to the chapel and told me about Kemie, I lost it. That's what happened to my hands. For a few minutes, the wall in my cell was TJ and I was beating him to death. They had to sedate me. They had me on suicide watch.

"A CO bitch that I'd never seen before talked to me and told me to be strong. I could've sworn it was Kemie talkin' to me. I listened. Bernard Grimes came to see me today."

"He said he would when I paid him." Marnie told me all about her meeting with Bernard Grimes, her last prenatal visit, and everything else that was going on.

"They say the police have Capers under siege. They got roadblocks and shit. Remember how they did Trinidad a couple years ago? That's the way they got Capers. Keisha says that ain't nobody seen TJ yet. He didn't go to Devon's funeral or Esha's. Well, neither did I, but people noticed. Just like they noticed that Bay One didn't go to Esha's joint either."

"For real?" I was totally blown away by that fact.

"For real. She put everything together and paid for it, from what I heard, but she didn't show up at the wake, funeral, or repast. They say that she's disturbed like shit about Esha."

"Wouldn't you be? Did you call her and tell her what I told you to tell her?"

"I sure did. Has your secretary failed you yet?" Marnie asked.

"Naw. They told me that you were the one who called up here and told them to tell me about Kemie. That means a lot to me, cuz."

"Don't mention it. I'm just playing my position. You heard about Dawn, right?"

I nodded. "One of these dudes in here saw it on the news. You know slim did that, too, right?"

"Naw, I didn't. Keisha did say that he been messing with Dawn ever since Reesie died. So if anybody had the opportunity, I guess it would be him. But why would he kill Dawn?"

"That nigga out there on one and ain't nobody safe. He feeling himself out there like that nigga Achilles in that movie Troy, but even Achilles had a vulnerable spot. I'ma bake slim shit when I get outta here. That's on my mother. But that's already understood between us, so ain't no sense in keep talkin' 'bout that. How did you find out about Kemie?"

"After I went and paid your lawyer, Reesie's little sister, Tera called my cell phone and told me. She said that Kemie's mother had a breakdown, but that they wanted you to know." I ran my hand over my head.

"From now on, whenever you call me, call my cell phone because I haven't been staying in my apartment. Ever since the last time I came to see you and you said what you did about me being in danger. I been over my mother's house uptown. Way uptown by Walter Reed."

"That's good. Stay up there until I tell you it's safe to go home. Where you got all that shit at?" I asked, suddenly concerned about my stash of money and drugs.

"It's put up somewhere safe. Don't worry about it. I'm like Allstate, you in good hands," Marnie replied and smiled.

Her smile was contagious, and as if for the first time, I really looked at Marnie and recognized what a true gem I had in her. "How's my baby doing?"

"The baby's fine. Moving around a lot, but that's to be expected."

"You look good, still."

"Wait until I gain thirty pounds. Make sure you're still generous with the compliments then, because God knows I'm gonna need them. I miss you so much, Khadafi. I want you to come home, and I know this might not be a good time to bring this up, but you don't have any more excuses when it comes to us being a family. You can be a good father if you choose to be."

"We'll talk about it another time. My visit is almost over. What happened to my pictures I asked for?"

"So much been going on that I forgot. I got you though. Fat stomach and all."

"Keep your head up and your eyes open. You are the closest person in the world to me now, and TJ knows that. Plus, you are a witness to Kemie's shooting. He knows that, too. Be careful and stay away from down Capers."

"Yes, daddy. Anything else?" Marnie asked sarcastically.

"Yeah, is that pussy wet, and what color are those toes?"

Marnie leaned in close to the glass and said, "It's always wet, but it would be even wetter if I had your dick in my mouth. And my toenails are painted a hot pink color. My panties are a lacy boy shorts style that match my bra and as soon as I get home I'ma play with my pussy while imagining you there. So hurry up home, brotha."

With that said, Marnie got up and sashayed her sexy ass over to the elevator. All I could do was sit there with a wet, rock-hard dick and watch her leave.

# CHAPTER THIRTY-EIGHT

## TJ

I was really starting to think that Khadafi moved Marnie before he came at me. Either that or she worked the most odds hours because I couldn't catch her to save my life. For three days straight I looked for her to come home or to go to work. Nothing. Was I missing something? I turned down the music in my car and circled the block on Half Street again in search of Marnie's Chrysler 300. Did Khadafi buy her another car? Up and down the street I drove, scanning both sides of the street. Had Khadafi figured out that I would come after Marnie? Or was I just missing her? And exactly how much did Khadafi know about what I'd done? What had Devon told him, if he told him anything? There was a lot of shit that I didn't know. But the one thing I did know was that I was determined now to crush Marnie. Not because she might have seen me shoot Kemie. Simply because she's Khadafi's bitch, and she's having his baby.

Killing her would send Khadafi over the edge, and that's exactly how I needed him when he got out of jail, so I could smash his ass. The more I thought about it, the more I figured that Marnie was probably gone and I'd have to find another way to murder her. Driving down the street, I decided to leave the James Creek area and go up Capers. I didn't want muthafuckas to speculate too much and whisper too often. Esha's funeral had passed already and I hadn't attended. On second thought, that wasn't a good look. I should have gone, but I wouldn't make the same mistake with Dawn's funeral. Something my homie Wayne-Wayne said to me on the phone the other day came to mind.

"—all this shit down here geekin', slim. These muthafuckas out here talkin' bout Capers is cursed and all that dumb ass shit because people keep getting murked. They told me that it's the end of the world shit. It should've been the end of the world when them people first sentenced me to all that damn time. Niggas gon' wait until I get home and start talkin' that end of the world shit. I'ma be mad as shit if it is—"

I had to admit that Capers projects did have sort of a cursed feel to it now that everybody who lived there was witnessing the wrath of one man. To think that one incident and the betrayal by one man had sparked the deaths of so many was almost unfathomable. To some. But not me. Bean created an animal the day he decided to kill my family. I parked my car on Sixth Street and called Wayne-Wayne to see if he was in the house. He was, so that was my destination. I walked into Wayne's house and saw a few of the homies gathered there. "What's up with y'all?"

"Dawg, what's good?" Bowlegged Deon, who had just recently come home right before Wayne-Wayne said.

"Ain't shit, Deon. I'm chillin'."

Pee-Wee was totally ensconced in a video game, but he paused the game long enough to get up and embrace me. "Tee, where you been, slim? Muthafuckas been askin' 'bout you all week. We expected to see you at Esha's funeral, but you never showed."

"Slim, on some real live shit, I'm tired of going to funerals. After Reesie's joint, I told myself that, that was it for funerals. So I been on my laid back shit."

"What I wanna know is," Wayne said as he entered the living room rolling a blunt and then licking it shut, "when we gon' put some work in? This shit is crazy. All our muthafuckin' homies and home girls gettin' killed and ain't nobody doing nothin' about it What's up with that?"

"If y'all find out who been doing all the killin', sign me up. Y'all know how I do," I responded to Wayne-Wayne.

"I already know who doing it," Tubby said and walked over to the window by the couch.

"Who doin' it?" I asked.

"You is. C'mon, homie. I'ma say what these niggas ain't tryna say. Everybody talkin' behind a nigga's back. Me, I'ma keep it one hundred with you. You was the last person to see Reesie alive. You was the last person to be seen with Devon alive. You was the last person seen with Dawn alive. You was the last person to see Esha alive. Esha was on the phone with Bay One when you walked through the door. After Esha hung up the phone, Bay One called back thirty minutes later and Esha never answered the phone again. You started fuckin' Dawn after Reesie got killed. Everybody know that. Then shorty ends up dead. C'mon, Moe, keep it real with your men. What the fuck is up with you and everybody in the hood? What the fuck did niggas and bitches do to you?"

I was twelve-feet deep in my feelings at the way Tubby was addressing me, but I held my composure mostly because the shit was true. "Ay, Tub, you tryna see me about something, slim?"

"See you for what?"

"Fuck you mean, 'see you for what'? You right here talkin' 'bout I'm the last person this and last person that—what the fuck? Are you tryna see me? Better yet, you talkin' 'bout you gon' say what niggas in the room ain't tryna say—" I stood to address the whole room. "Somebody in here need to get something off their chest with me?"

"Slim, if I had something to say to you about any of that shit I would and you know that. I don't play that he say she say shit. I'ma coldblooded man and can't nobody speak for me," Wayne-Wayne stated.

"Man, we in this muthafucka about to start beefing with each other over a whole rack of bullshit," Pee-Wee stated but got interrupted.

"Y'all niggas on some bullshit!" Tubby exploded. "With the exception of Wayne-Wayne, y'all niggas been whispering what I just said. Be men and tell the nigga what's on y'all mind. Y'all niggas acting like whores right now."

"Dawg," Bowlegged Deon offered. "It is what it is, and the truth don't need no support. I don't know if TJ killed anybody, but it definitely ain't no good look."

"What ain't no good look, Deon?" I asked, about to get mad and start crushing shit.

"I'm just saying, dawg. Tub got a good point. That's all."

"How the fuck Tub got a good point and all that shit he sayin' some bullshit?"

"Khadafi killed Devon 'cause Devon jumped out there with him about his brother. Khadafi is the one that you niggas should be accusing of foul play," I said. "That nigga brought me a move before he did that goofy ass shit and drove his car off the bridge. As a matter of fact, I don't owe nay nigga in here no explanation about nothin'. I don't give a fuck about a nigga's feelings. Feelings are for bitches. So if ain't nobody in here tryna see me about nothin', then I'm about to go outside and chill."

"I think everybody in this muthafucka need to go outside and get some air," Wayne-Wayne said. "'Cause either we gon' talk it out or bang it out, but something has to be said to end this misunderstanding."

"It's already ended to me. I said all I'ma say about it," I said and headed for the door. "If somebody tryna see me, I'ma be outside."

# CHAPTER THIRTY-NINE
## Detective Tolliver

C aptain Dunlap, you gotta back me on this one. Two months ago, you called me in here and literally chewed me a new ass because I wasn't getting anywhere with my investigations."

"I know what I did and said, Tolliver," the Captain answered with a vexed expression.

"All I'm saying, Cap, is that I finally have a chance to bust this case wide open, and I need your help. You are the only person in the building that can get a judge to even listen to me."

Captain Dunlap leaned back in his seat and put his feet up on the desk. His gaze fell on the window in his office. "What do you have, Tolliver? Tell me exactly what you want from me."

"What I got is two men who are responsible for over forty murders in the city. And nobody, not Kevin Gray, Calvin Smith, Rodney Moore or Wayne Perry can compare to these two guys. They are a tandem, a team. The Canal Street murders, they did it. The Harbor Marina killing, they did it. The six murders at the Capers recreation center, they did it. The Omni Shoreham Hotel massacre, the triple homicide on 'V' Street, Sheree Tate, Nomeka Fisher, Ronesha Lake, Teresa Bryant. . . . Did you know that Rakemie Bryant passed away at PG hospital five days ago?"

"Rio Jefferson informed me the same day it happened."

238

"Somebody connected to my case shot Rakemie Bryant. Cap, I could go on and on with unsolved murder cases that these two pieces of shit are responsible for. I need the edge. I need a little help to get Fuller and Carter."

"Again, I ask you, what do you have? I need something concrete to work with, not just assumptions. You want me to call in a marker with one of the judges that's sympathetic to the department, right? Gimme something more concrete to give them."

"I got fingerprints, Cap. Luther Fuller is already over the jail on charges that won't keep him in prison long, so I can come back to him later. Right now I wanna get Tyrone Carter off the streets. I have Carter's fingerprints at three different crime scenes. We got his prints out of Teresa Bryant, Nomeka Fisher, and Ronesha Lake's apartments. We got a witness that worked at the beauty salon on South Capitol Street who recognized Carter. She says he came in for a dread treatment and left thirty minutes before two people were killed in the parking lot there. Two people who just happened to be connected to Mark Johnson and the Canal Street murders. We got a video surveillance tape that puts Carter at the scene of a fight that turned into the massacre at the Omni Shoreham Hotel.

"We got the murder weapons that have been connected to the Canal Street murders. Cap, it's only a matter of time before we can connect one of those weapons to Tyrone Carter. I gotta Springfield Armory Colt .45 handgun that we recovered from a vehicle belonging to Luther Fuller that has Carter's fingerprints on it. And I can connect that gun to at least one murder. It was the weapon used to kill Thomas 'Black Woozie' Fields. With Carter off the streets, Captain, I am willing to bet that people will come forward and testify against him. Help me to help us. Get me a sympathetic ear."

# THE ULTIMATE SACRIFICE III: NO REGRETS

For several minutes, Captain Dunlap stared out the window without saying much. Then after what seemed like an eternity of silence, he turned and looked me straight in the eyes. "You better make me look good, Tolliver. I'm going out on a limb here, and if I fall out of the tree and get laughed at, your career is over. Do I make myself clear?"

"Crystal clear, sir," I stated with conviction.

The Captain dropped his feet to the floor, sat up and grabbed his cell phone. After dialing a number, he said, "Marge? Hi . . . Greg Dunlap, do you have a minute? I need a favor."

********

I left the Carl H. Moultrie Courthouse on Indiana Avenue happier than a homosexual with a duffle bag full of dicks. I reread the arrest warrant for Tyrone Carter and wanted to break out dancing. I jogged back to my car and called the warrant into dispatch over the radio. I pulled TJ's file from under my front seat and searched for a last known address. The only one listed was the address for his father. It was the address to the house where his family had been killed.

That house was abandoned after the real estate company had been unable to sell the property because of the superstitions of all buyers. I searched for an alternative address, but found none. No fixed address. That's what was listed on the paperwork that freed TJ from a Maryland prison several months ago. Starting the car, I decided to hit the Capers neighborhood and see what I'd find.

I parked on the corner of Seventh Street. From inside my black Grand Marquise with the tinted windows, I could observe the comings and goings of everybody in the area. Sitting TJ's file in my lap, I read over every detail and piece of paper I had while periodically glancing up to look for TJ. He was rumored to drive a black Buick Roadmaster, and there was one parked on 'I' Street a few blocks back. I was hoping that it was his. My cell phone vibrating caught my attention.

"Yeah?"

"Detective Tolliver, Emily Perez. Gotta minute?"

I looked at my watch. It was 2:43 p.m. School would be letting out soon and then the block would be crawling with kids. "Got more than a minute, Emily. What's up?"

"I got some good news for you."

"I like good news, Emily, but do I get it today or next week?" I asked facetiously.

"Oh . . . yeah, I'm sorry. This morning I arrested a woman named Latasha Allison on Third and 'L' Streets. She was out there selling weed and e-pills. She has priors, and when I reminded her of that she decided that going to prison in Alderson, West Virginia, wasn't exactly in her best interest. She told me about a murder, well a double murder—"

"The one on Birney Place? Not my case. That case is—"

"No, not the Birney Place murders. How about Devon Harris and Gregory Strong?"

My interest suddenly piqued, and I perked up in my seat. "She witnessed them?"

"According to her, she did, and I'll give you one guess at who she named as the killer."

"Tyrone Carter? Please tell me that she saw TJ kill Strong and Harris."

"No, that's not it, but you're awfully close. She saw a red haired dude who drove a Cadillac Escalade commit the murder."

"Khadafi?"

"She called him by that name. Strong was her boyfriend."

I couldn't believe my sudden stroke of good luck. First an arrest warrant for TJ, and now a real, live, breathing witness that could testify against Khadafi in court. I wanted to yodel.

"Where is—"

"Latasha Allison."

"Latasha Allison. Where is she now?" I asked.

"Still in the holding cage downstairs. I purposely delayed her processing until I could reach you."

"Emily, I could kiss you," I said and meant it.

"I'm married, Tolliver, but if I wasn't . . ."

"Give me about twenty minutes and I'll meet you in the—" I looked up and saw a green Nissan Altima turn the corner. The driver's eyes were glued to a group of men that had appeared practically out of nowhere. I scanned the faces of the men. One of them caused my heart to stop for a minute. Something about the appearance was different, but the face was the same. It was unmistakable. It was TJ.

"Detective, are you still there?" Emily Perez asked.

Moving the file from my lap, I set it on my passenger seat. Then I grabbed my department issued Glock 19 from my hip.

"Yeah, I'm here. Hang up now and get dispatch to send me two back up cars and a transport vehicle to the 600 block of Seventh Street in Capers projects. Do it now. I'm out."

The green Altima turned the corner on 'J' Street and disappeared. Stepping out of my car, I kept my eyes glued to TJ as I approached the circle of men. What happened next seemed to happen in slow motion. It was like a movie in my head shown in 3D. A lone figure crept through the court and surprised the crowd of men. The dark clothed figure pointed a gun and fired it.

Once. Twice. Three times. The crowd scattered in seconds.

"Freeze! Police!" I yelled to the figure that now stood over top of one of the men.

The closer I got, I could now make out the fallen man as TJ. The lone figure stood frozen over him, but TJ was still alive and attempting to get up and crawl.

"Put the gun down!" I yelled, ten feet away now. "Drop it! Don't make me shoot you!"

The hooded figure turned slowly and looked at me. I recognized the face immediately. "Don't do it Bay One! He's not worth it. He's not worth you doing life in prison. Drop the gun, Bay One! Do it now, Bay One. Drop the gun and it's over."

Bayona 'Bay One' Lake's eyes bore into mine and time stood still. Tears fell down her cheek. Then she spoke. "He killed my daughter. I was on the phone with her when he came in the house. I don't know why, but he killed my baby. So I gotta make it right."

"Bay One, please . . . put the gun down! Let the courts do their jobs . . . Let . . ."

*Boom! Boom! Boom! Boom! Boom! Boom! Boom! Boom!*

And just like that, my arrest warrant became a worthless piece of paper.

Bayona Lake avenged the death of her daughter, Ronesha and countless others, and she didn't even know it. When her gun was empty, she dropped to her knees and put both hands on the back of her head. I walked up to her and looked her straight in the face.

"You just did the world a favor. Don't ever forget that."

Bayona Lake nodded. I grabbed her wrists and cuffed her.

# CHAPTER FORTY

## Ameen

I was sitting on my bunk reading the Quran, feeling like every word I read was referring to me. Am I the one with the disease in my heart? Am I a hypocrite? Every time I self-reflected on my life and the things I'd done and wanted to do, I asked myself did I really believe in Islam the way that I was supposed to. And every time I told myself that the answer to that question was yes, then my conscience reminded me that I wanted to kill Khadafi and the fact that he was a Muslim. One of the greatest sins that one Muslim can commit in his life is to kill another Muslim. The Quran says that there is no mercy for a man who kills another Muslim unjustly. Therein lied the enigma inside me. I felt completely justified in my quest to kill Khadafi. Because he violated all that I held sacred. A Muslim's property, family, wealth, and his life, all those things were sacred and should be treated as such by all Muslims. So I felt justified. If I was wrong, I prayed that one day Allah forgave me and let me out of the fire. Just as I opened the Quran to finish reading, a commotion outside my door caught my attention. Although I wanted to ignore it, I couldn't because something could happen in the block in seconds that could cost me my life. So I walked out of my cell and saw a crowd gathered two cells down from mine. About to turn on my heels, I spotted my celly, Trey, Tim-Tim and a few

244

other good men in the crowd, so I went down there. I walked
up to my celly and said, "What's up, slim? Y'all good?"

********

I looked down the tier at the telephones mounted to the
wall and wanted to go and get on one. The urge to call
Shawnay was getting stronger and stronger each day. I wanted
to talk to her and see her, but I stuck to my guns. When I went
on visits with my family and saw my daughters, it blew me
away how much Kenya and Asia looked like their mother.
Every time I asked them how Shawnay was doing, they'd both
just say that she was doing good and then skip the subject.
Inside I felt slighted a little, but I understood her attitude
toward me. I could definitely empathize with her anger, her
hurt, her pain. It wasn't everyday that a man comes to your
house and puts a gun to your face and then says that your baby
father sent him. And that's what Umar had done to her.
Because I sent him. So I could definitely understand her
discontent. But why couldn't she understand mine?

Not only did she betray me by fucking one of my friends,
but now they have a child together. I betrayed her by sending a
man to kill her. She betrayed me by crossing a line that
shouldn't have been crossed. Whose degree of betrayal was
worse? Mine or hers? The more I thought about Shawnay and
Khadafi, the more upset I became. Then suddenly a thought
hit me that exed out the plan I thought of earlier. My eyes
roamed all over the block searching for the one person that I
knew could help my cause. I didn't see him. "Ay, Fila, where
Champion-Bey at?"

Fila Rob looked up from his game of spades at a nearby
table and replied, "That nigga on his grand sheik shit down in
the space under the TV room. He tryna convert muthafuckas
to the Moorish Science Temple and shit. You want him?"

"Yeah," I said and leaned on the railing of the top tier.

Five minutes later, Dwayne Champion-Bey appeared from under the TV room.

He walked up to me. "What's up, Ameen?"

"You still work down by the chapel, right?"

"Yeah."

"Can't you call people out their blocks to the chapel?"

"Yeah. I'm on detail down there, so I see the whole roster. I make the list for church, Jumah, the Nation, and Moorish Science. I can put whoever I want on the list and take whoever off."

"I know that. What I need to know is can you go to work and call me and another dude to the chapel. Say for instance on a day when there ain't no service?"

Champion-Bey thought about it for a few minutes and then said, "I guess I could. I can get the chaplain to call the block for y'all. I just have to figure out a good lie to tell her. But I believe I can do it."

"I believe in you, ock. So here's exactly what I need you to do."

********

Two days later on a Sunday afternoon after church let out in the chapel, the CO in the block called my name.

"Felder! Antonio Felder! Come to the bubble!"

"They callin' you at the bubble, Ameen," Trey said as he popped his head into the cell.

"Thanks, slim. I heard 'em." I was already digging into the spot in our cell where I kept my and Trey's knives.

Trey came into the cell and slid the door shut. "You want me to go with you?"

"Naw, slim. I'm good. I told you a million times already that I need you to go home. Just in case these people shoot my appeal down and I don't make it out. I'ma need you in the streets. This is my mountain I gotta climb. My war that I gotta fight. And I'ma fight it. Just make sure that you give all my shit to the cop, so that I can have something down South One."

"Slim, listen, I know your mind made up, but think about your kids. Your daughters need you. If you kill that boy in that hallway, you gon' get washed up. Why don't you wait until you see whether or not the appeals court gon' give you some play? If they shoot you down, you ain't got nothing to lose. If they let you go, you can see that nigga on the bricks."

I thought for a moment about what Trey was saying, and then shook my head. "I gotta get him now while I can. What if he gets released tomorrow and I lose the appeal? Or what if I win and he loses in trial. See, there's too many what ifs. I gotta get him now. I'ma let Allah sort out the mess after I leave his blood on the walls."

"I respect you, slim, but you hardheaded," Trey added in defeat.

"Naw, slim. I'm just determined."

********

Walking down the hallway toward my destiny, my adrenaline picked up, and I could envision exactly what I wanted to do to Khadafi. The element of surprise is a muthafucka, and it should be used at all times during times of war. I took the escalator stairs two at a time. Right beside the escalator on the first floor is a small maintenance area. I peeped it a couple of Friday's ago after Jumah. The way it's made, there is just enough room for a single person to hide in a space by the door marked 'NO INMATES ALLOWED BEYOND THIS POINT'. I slid into the space, pulled out my knife and waited.

# CHAPTER FORTY-ONE

## Khadafi

I always figured myself to be homophobic to a degree, and no matter how much time I did in prison, I vowed to never let myself stoop so low as to stick my dick in another man, but the thought of what I'd done to Money's father years ago vividly came to mind. It was right after I raped his mother, William Smith had definitely looked me in the eyes and what I saw was hatred, rage, and despair. He spoke clearly when he said, "I pray that God kills you soon and that you die a slow and painful death."

I couldn't believe what I had just heard. "You said that you hope that God kills me?"

"Fuck you, muthafucka!" William spat before I could finish my sentence.

I laughed at the doomed man's words. But I respected his gangsta. He'd rather die a thousand deaths than betray his son.

"Fuck me, huh?" I repeated and became more enraged every second. "Die slow, huh? Fuck me and die a slow painful death, huh?" I cut the fabric of his pants all the way up to his boxers, and then split them open. "Fuck me, huh? Naw, nigga, I'ma fuck you!"

And I did just that. Rage and revenge had overtaken me and caused me to fuck my enemy's father. That homosexual act would forever haunt me. And it was doing so now as I sat on the bench attached to the table in the TV room and allowed a known homosexual to braid my hair. I was desperate for a better look and faggie Carlos was my only option. Carlos was on my sixth braid when the CO in the bubble called my name. "Did he say Fuller?" I asked the dude that had just entered the TV room.

"Yeah, dawg. He said Luther Fuller."

"Carlos, go 'head and do my last two cornrows, and then I'ma see what the cop wants."

Ten minutes later, I approached the bubble. "You calling me?"

"Fuller?" the CO asked.

"I'm Fuller."

"We been calling you for fifteen minutes. The chaplain wants you. Here's your pass."

"The chaplain?" I repeated back to the CO. "You sure it's the chaplain, cuz?"

"I'm positive."

A panic attack seized me as goose bumps rushed up my arms. Why was the chaplain calling me again? I moved toward the sally port slowly as if my shoes were laden with lead. All I could think about was Marnie. Somehow TJ had gotten to Marnie and killed her. Killed my unborn child. Killed my dreams, Kemie, and the rest of my life. Again, I said a silent prayer to Allah and begged him to spare Marnie and my baby. Marnie had a lot of good in her. She wasn't like Kemie. Kemie had taken a life before, but Marnie hadn't. If something had happened to Marnie, my life would be over. With Kemie's funeral coming up, depression had threatened to overwhelm me on a few occasions. If Marnie was dead, it would have me. All the way to the soul.

Although I was deep in thought as I descended the escalator, my uncanny ability to sense danger kicked in as I hit the first floor, and as usual it saved my life. The knife that had been intended for my jugular, embedded itself in my shoulder. "Aaarrgh!"

"Don't cry out now, nigga. Take this knife like a man!"

The look on Ameen's face was one of undistorted anger and unbridled fury. Just as he pulled his knife free, I shot out a jab with the power in my good shoulder behind it. The punch caught Ameen flush on the chin and backed him up. I reached for my knife in my sock, but Ameen lunged again.

"You gon' have to do better than that to stop me!" Ameen hissed.

All I could do was throw up my forearm to ward off the next blow. I felt the knife enter my arm and out of a pure will to live, I grabbed Ameen. I reached up and grabbed his knife hand with one hand and attempted to get to my knife with the other hand.

But Ameen was too strong. He ended up cutting me across the face, on my cheek. My left shoulder throbbed, and I felt blood causing my undershirt and jumpsuit to stick to my body. I ignored the pain in my forearm as I drew strength from somewhere deep inside me and pushed Ameen off me. It was either now or never. Ameen was thrown a few feet away and appeared to slip before catching himself. As I lifted my pants leg and grabbed my knife, it was then that I noticed all the blood on the floor. Ameen rushed me again, and I stood my ground. Even though I was getting lightheaded, I refused to go out without a fight. Ameen's knife was underhanded, turned downward, which meant that his thrusts had to be overhand.

I gripped my knife with the blade facing upward. So as he attempted to bury his knife in my neck, chest, or face, I automatically swung upward as we collided. I heard Ameen grunt and knew that I had hit him. His knife had found my same shoulder and the pain was excruciating, but I couldn't go down.

"Break it up! Code red! First floor, code red!"

I heard the voice before I saw who had hollered the code. In seconds, the first floor was flooded with correctional officers. I was immediately wrestled to the floor. Ameen was also on the floor with COs all over him. He looked me straight in the eyes and said, "I ain't finished with you yet."

"Where are you hit at?" a male officer asked me.

"Everywhere," was all I could mutter before I lost consciousness.

# Chapter Forty-Two

## Marnie

D C jail contacted Khadafi's lawyer, Bernard Grimes, and he called me. I pulled up to the parking lot at DC General Hospital still wiping away tears. Deep inside, I wondered when my heart would be able to smile some. Over the last year or so, I'd cried enough tears to provide water to a small nation in Africa. On the phone, Bernie never told me the condition Khadafi was in. All he said was that there had been a knife fight and that both men were taken across the street to DC General. Apparently, an inmate had manipulated the system and got both men called out of the block to go to the chaplain's office. Thus the knife fight. When would all the bloodshed end? Khadafi getting hurt was becoming like a record that had played too many times on repeat. I prayed that he was okay all the way to the room where he was. I guess the cops that guarded Khadafi had already been told about my visit because they let me right in. One female CO sat in a chair across from the bed. I nodded at her and she nodded back. Then went back to her book she was reading. At Khadafi's bedside, I stood and stared down at him. Tears welled up in my eyes again. I swiped at them and tried to put my lover's pallid complexion out of my mind. I tried to ignore the fact that he had a bandage taped across his left cheek and the bandages on his arms and shoulders. But what I did notice was that he was still handsome and his hair was neatly done. I also noticed that his leg was shackled to the metal bed pole. It took me a few minutes to stop crying. I wasn't used to seeing Khadafi look so helpless and so hurt. I was used to the strong and invincible version of Khadafi. The scarred thug, the pretty boy nigga with the shit bag on. I was used to the gun-toting giant amongst men. The cold-blooded killer. I remembered the day he showed up at my door with blood dripping on my floor fresh from a gunshot wound to his leg. He never winced or said a word as I cleaned his wound and then massaged his back where the slugs had hit his bulletproof vest directly. To me, Khadafi was like a machine. But the Khadafi that lay before me now looked human. He looked meek. I reached down and traced his lips with my finger. Then I leaned in and kissed him. Khadafi's eyes opened. Our eyes locked and then a smile spread across his face.

"You must be an angel," Khadafi whispered.

"And you must be the devil. You stay in some shit, baby. What happened?"

Khadafi slowly told me what happened at the jail. He told me who had stabbed him and why. As he mentioned the name Ameen, I remembered that Ameen was the dude Antonio Felder that Khadafi had me look up on the computer months ago. Then I remembered the story that Khadafi told me about why he and Ameen started beefing in the first place. Over a woman named Shawnay.

"I found out that Ameen was at the jail from Shawnay right after I sent her some money for my son. Right after New Years. He got back on appeal and his lawyer got him brought up from Beaumont to the jail. I knew that he was in the jail somewhere, but I didn't know where. I also knew that . . ." Khadafi paused for a minute as if he was winded or it hurt to talk.

"Are you okay?" I asked him.

"Yeah, I'm good. Just thirsty as hell."

I turned and faced the CO lady. "Miss, he says he's thirsty. Can I get him something to drink?"

"No, you can't. Just hit the call button. The nurse will answer. Tell her and she will bring in a pitcher of water."

I did as I was told. Five minutes later, Khadafi handed me his empty cup and I sat down on the bed table next to him.

"I knew that Ameen wanted to kill me. He was the one who tried to kill me in Texas. I didn't know when we'd see each other, but I knew that we would."

"But how did he know you were at the jail? In the intake block? From Shawnay?" I asked.

"I doubt it. They don't communicate. Ameen sent one of our friends to her house to kill her. He felt betrayed by both of us. Ameen must've heard through the grapevine that I was there. Niggas talk, and there's a rack of niggas at the jail that know me. Ameen put this together. He was waiting for me on the first floor. He knew I was coming."

"Another inmate orchestrated everything. He got the chaplain to call you and Ameen out of y'alls blocks."

Khadafi looked at me in disbelief.

"It's true. The people at DC jail told Bernie what happened and he told me."

"Ameen orchestrated it. I know it and I knew it was coming. That's why I kept my knife on me. Wait a minute, is Ameen here in the hospital?"

I saw the look of alarm on Khadafi's face. This dude Ameen really scared him. "Uh . . . I'm not sure. But I know he had to be hospitalized, too. I can find out."

"No. Leave it alone. But I know Ameen, and as long as he's breathing, he's gonna try to kill me. Marnie, I love you, cuz. You are all I have left in this world. You, our unborn child, and my son Kashon. When the CO in the block told me to go to the chaplain's office, I thought—I thought that some . . . I thought TJ had hurt you—killed you." Tears rolled down Khadafi's cheeks. "I was—I was about to . . ."

I put two fingers to Khadafi's lips and shushed him. "TJ is dead, Khadafi. He got killed down Capers a few days ago. The police arrested Bay One for killing him. She did it in front of everybody in broad day. So we don't have to worry about TJ anymore. The day I found out, I left my people's house uptown and went home."

Khadafi closed his eyes. He was speechless. Just as I was starting to believe that he'd fallen asleep, his eyes opened.

"I can't believe it. Karma's a muthafucka, huh?" he said.

I nodded. "That's why you gotta change your life, baby. I don't want to lose you. I need you. The baby needs you. It's over. Finally, it's over."

"It's not over, Marnie. Not until both Lil Cee and Ameen are dead."

"Lil Cee?"

"The dude I told you about. The one who tried to kill me down Capers. The one I tried to kill at the Omni Shoreham. I killed his family. He will never forgive or forget."

"Where is he? Do you know?" I asked.

"The last I heard he was in Georgia somewhere."

"Maybe he'll stay there then. Maybe he decided to leave it alone. Maybe he no longer wants to kill you. Maybe. . ."

"Maybe you're right, but then there still leaves Ameen."

"I have listened to every word you've ever said about that dude, and I understand everything. You just lay back and get yourself together and let me worry about everything else. A'ight?"

Khadafi gripped my hand with his. "Do what you do. I love you, Marnie."

"I love you, too."

# THE ULTIMATE SACRIFICE III: NO REGRETS

When I got home, I went straight to my drawer where I kept all my personal effects. I rummaged around in the drawer until I found exactly what I was looking for. The piece of paper that Khadafi had given me with his son's name on it and a phone number for his son's mother, Shawnay. I believed it was time for me and Shawnay to meet. I picked up my cell phone and dialed her cell phone. She answered on the fourth ring.

"Hello? Is this Shawnay?"

Shawnay invited me to her grandmother's house on Morris Road after I explained that we needed to talk face to face and why. I parked the Escalade on Pitts Place and walked up the street until I crossed Morris Road.

Opening the screen door, I knocked a few times. The door opened shortly, and a beautiful, caramel complexioned woman with a killer body and a Kodak smile told me to come in. Her hair was jet black and curly, falling in layers down her neck and back. She was stylishly dressed in designer clothing, and I could instantly understand why Khadafi had been tempted to partake of a forbidden fruit.

"Monica?"

I reached out and shook her hand. The handshake was genuine. After all, she was not into Khadafi anymore or so he said, so I didn't feel threatened and I needed her help. "Thank you for seeing me, Shawnay."

"Mommy! Mommy! Mommy!" a tiny voice said moments before a small blur appeared around the corner and leapt into Shawnay's arms.

"Hey, baby!" Shawnay cooed and kissed the lively bundle in her arms.

The little boy had to be about a year old, and he was the spitting image of his father. I was floored. Shawnay probably noticed me with my mouth hanging open because she said,

"Monica, this is my son Kashon. Khadafi's son, Kashon. Kashon say hello to the lady."

"Hello lady . . ." Kashon said with clarity.

I smiled and couldn't help cheesing so hard. "He's so cute, his hair, his freckles, he's . . . he's . . ."

"Khadafi," Shawnay interjected.

"Yeah, you took the words right out of my mouth."

"As soon as you saw him and your jaw dropped, I knew what it was. Believe it or not, I still do the same thing sometimes." Shawnay's eyes dropped to my stomach.

"So, Kashon is gonna have a little sister or brother, huh?"

I nodded. "And I want Khadafi to live to be able to be the best father he can possibly be. That's why I needed to talk to you. I need your help."

"Whatever I can do to help you and Khadafi, I will."

# CHAPTER FORTY-THREE
## Shawnay

T oday you had a visitor or should I say an old friend/but wait a minute, that's not where it ends/she said a real woman wouldn't do this over the phone/ and you never told her about me until after the baby was born . . ."

The lyrics to Mary J. Blige's song just wouldn't leave my head for some reason. The song popped in my head two days ago when Khadafi's newest baby mother arrived at my front door. Despite the irony, I had to laugh because life was funny that way. All stars are aligned in a way where this great cosmic force causes the right people to cross paths at the right time. I believe that wholeheartedly. I pulled my car into a parking spot outside of the DC jail. A place that I hadn't been to in years. A place that I thought I'd never see again. I stood beside my car and stared up at the behemoth rust colored cemented structure, built up my courage, and then headed for the visitor's entrance.

I had rehearsed my spiel that I wanted to say to Antonio, but the more I tried to memorize it, the more I forgot it. But however it came out, this would be a conversation that was way overdue.

"Ma'am, and who would you be visiting today?" the female CO asked from behind the control booth.

"Antonio Felder. DC number 254884."

The CO typed in Antonio's name and then said, "He's on the first floor now. In the Special Management Unit, South One, on twenty-three hour lockdown, but it says here that he is not on LOP, so you can see him."

"LOP?"

"Loss of privileges. The first floor visiting room is small and there's only three cages for inmates on lock up. So there may be a short wait for a cage. Do you mind the wait?"

This would be a conversation that was way overdue. "No, not at all."

"Please fill out all these forms."

Even though it had been years, my fingers seemed to glide over the form, filling in all the blanks. Seconds later, I was on the elevator headed to the first floor. To Antonio. I handed my visitor form to the male CO in the bubble in the visiting hall. To my right, I could see that one of the three cages was empty. Having been through the same shit with Antonio before, I knew then an officer in his block was probably notifying him that he had a visit.

Antonio would brush his teeth, wash his face, and put on a fresh orange jail issued jumpsuit. Then a white shirted lieutenant would have to go to South One to escort him to the visiting hall. I smiled to myself as I remembered all of that. Some things never change. Some people never change. My thoughts went again to Monica Curry. "Call me Marnie," she'd said. I thought about how much her face lit up when she spoke about Khadafi. I saw in her what I used to feel for Antonio. I saw in her exactly what Khadafi made her feel. The same things that he'd made me feel. A little, tiny piece of me was jealous. But only a tiny piece. The emotion shared between Khadafi and Marnie was what I once thought I felt for him. Although I lusted after Khadafi and enjoyed the sex that we had, at the end of the day I long ago admitted to myself it was just sex. I liked Khadafi a whole lot, but I didn't love him. Never had. Even though at one point I thought I did. In life we love who we love. And that's the gospel truth, and no matter how upset I'd been with Antonio, I couldn't deny the fact that I still loved him. I always did. Always will.

The solid steel door of the visiting hall opened and in walked Antonio. He looked just like he did in the dream that I had before Christmas. His waist was encircled with a belly chain that allowed his hands to be cuffed at the wrist and attached by his belly. He looked around the visiting room until his eyes settled on me. My heart pounded in my chest. Did he still hate me? Did he still want me dead? Would he refuse the visit? I waited to see an expression on his face. His expression would tell the story. For what seemed like an eternity, we held each other's stare. Then slowly, but surely, he smiled. My heartbeat slowed as I rose, smiling back. The white shirted guy put Antonio into the empty cage and locked it. Antonio's chains were loose enough for him to reach up and grab the phone receiver on his end. He did. I pulled up a chair, picked up the receiver on my end, and sat down.

"Hey," I said, breaking the silence.

One of Antonio's front teeth had a small chip at the corner that was new, but it was sexy and fit him in a fabulous sort of way. His moustache was trimmed real low and lined up, but his beard was thick and curly. His baldhead glistened.

Antonio's eyes pierced me and made me feel transparent. "What's up, bay?" 'Bay' was a term of endearment that Antonio always used when we talked. It was short for baby.

"You look good."

"But you look better."

I blushed like a little girl with a crush. "I heard that you are up for appeal. Congratulations."

"I haven't won yet, but Rudy says it looks good. Once we win you can congratulate me then. I'm fighting the fight of my life, and it's in the later rounds. Rudy is trying to get me—"

"Rudy?"

"Yeah, Rudy. Rudolph Sabino. The lawyer that you paid for my case."

"I'm sorry, so much has happened. I forgot."

"A lot has happened. Shawnay, I'm glad you finally decided to come and see me. I wanted to tell Asia and Kenya to drag you up here, but I couldn't bring myself to beg. I just prayed that one day you would forgive me for all the wrong I've done and love me again."

"I never stopped loving you, Antonio. Never. Just because—because I—"

"Fucked Khadafi? Is that what you want to say but can't?" Antonio asked.

I could read the hurt in his eyes. "That's why I came here today. To clear the air with you. For me, for you, for Khadafi. You stabbed him two days ago and almost killed him."

The look on Antonio's face went from hurt to rage. "You came here to defend that muthafucka? You're mad because I almost killed your boyfriend?" Antonio stood up and was about to hang up the receiver.

"No!" I shouted. "Listen to me! Please let me talk."

Antonio sat back down in his seat and put the receiver to his ear. "Talk."

"Khadafi is not my boyfriend, and no I didn't come here to defend or protect him. I came here to protect you. I came here for you. I've been wanting to come here and face you, but Antonio, I'm a coward. You know that I hate confrontation. I knew that I crossed the line when I started messing with Khadafi. I knew he was your friend and how close you two were. I made a mistake, Antonio. One that has caused so much unnecessary bloodshed. What can I say, other than I fucked up. I was lonely. I was weak, and I didn't have anyone. I had never been with any man sexually before Khadafi. I was always upset with you inside even though I never said it. I blamed you for breaking up our family. I blamed you for being a single parent. When you sent Khadafi to me with all the money, I lost focus. He came around at the time when I needed you the most. In my mind I was repaying you for all the pain you caused me. I never loved Khadafi. I have always loved you and only you. But again, I was vulnerable. I was smitten. I was easy. In the midst of my betrayal . . . That's what you call it, right? Betrayal? In the midst of my betrayal, I let lust overtake me, and I slept with Khadafi without any protection.

"And from that I got pregnant. I know how much that hurts you, Antonio. I can feel the pain that you feel inside of me. You committed a crime. I committed a crime when I betrayed you." I never noticed I was crying until I felt a tear hit my chin. "But was my crime so serious that you sent me a message and an executioner? Had I wronged you that much?"

"Yeah, you did. And at that time I was so hurt that I didn't know how to respond. Violence begets violence. It's all I know, Shawnay, but you didn't know that because I kept that side of me away from you. What I did in the street stayed in the street. When somebody hurts me I lash out. I strike out to harm, to hurt, to kill, to destroy. It's how I was raised. It's all I know. I was irrational.

"I was in pain. I called Umar and told him to kill you and Khadafi. I wanted you both dead, not just you. But later, I realized I was wrong. I prayed that it wasn't too late, and Allah answered that prayer, Shawnay. I was so relieved that you were okay. I would have killed myself if you would have died.

Please forgive me for what I did. I was out of control and I'm sorry. Can you forgive me for that?"

"Two days ago, I was at my grandmother's house when I got a call on my cell phone. A woman was calling me and asking to speak with me in person. Antonio, my first thought was that she was someone else that you were sending to finish what the dude with the beard didn't. I was afraid, but then she mentioned Khadafi and I became intrigued. I agreed to let her come and meet with me. We met that same day. Her name is Monica, and apparently, Khadafi is quite a lover. He was having his way with not only me, but her and his main girl, Kemie. I knew that Khadafi had a girlfriend. I just never asked about her. Anyway, she's . . . Monica. . . . Did you know that Khadafi's girlfriend Kemie got killed?"

"Naw, I didn't know."

"Well, she did. But Khadafi had Marnie, too, so he didn't miss a beat. Monica is now pregnant with his baby. She loves him, and according to her, he loves her, too. She came to me after visiting Khadafi in the hospital. She told me about y'alls knife fight. Were you stabbed, too?"

"I was. I got hit once in the side, but I'm cool," Antonio replied.

"Glad to hear that. Khadafi is in bad shape. He told Monica that he couldn't change his life and move on with her and their child until you were dead. Or something like that. You are the boogeyman that lurks over his shoulders, Antonio. Monica wants to protect Khadafi, and I want to protect you. She asked me to come here to beg you to let your desire for vengeance go. I came here to tell you that you shouldn't throw away what life you have. What life we have left by killing Khadafi and staying in prison forever. I love you, Antonio, like I said earlier. I never stopped. Even as I slept with Khadafi, my love for you never stopped. This latest situation with you has

THE ULTIMATE SACRIFICE III: NO REGRETS

opened my eyes. If you keep this super thug stuff up, eventually somebody is gonna kill you. And I need you to live. To love again. Your daughters need you. I need you. I came here to ask you to let it go. Let your will to kill Khadafi go. And I will let my fear and anger at you go. I forgive you. Hopefully, you'll forgive me as well along the way. I want to be a part of your life again, Antonio. No matter what happens with your appeal. I wanna love you and prove myself to you again. I promise to never betray you again.

"Promise me that you will abandon your quest to kill Khadafi, and we can start over. Can you do that?"

"I can do that. For you I can do anything. I promise you that from here on I will not try to kill Khadafi," Ameen said and smiled.

"Say Wallahi."

Ameen laughed at that. "You remembered. Wallahi. By Allah, I promise to leave Khadafi alone. But what about him coming at me? I can't let . . ."

"Monica should be having this same conversation with Khadafi as we speak."

"What about his son? How can we—"

"Antonio, Kashon doesn't know Khadafi. Khadafi has only seen my son one time and that was by accident. So Khadafi is not in the picture. You can grow to love my son, just like you love me, because he is a part of me. I know that it's a lot to ask from you, Antonio. To raise another man's son is a lot to ask of any man, but if you really love me, you can do it. I love my son, Antonio, and I regret sleeping with Khadafi. But I don't regret my son. So you decide right here, right now, whether or not that's too much to ask of you, and I will walk away and never look back. What's it gonna be, Antonio? It's all or nothing."

"Since you put it like that I'll take it all."

# CHAPTER FORTY-FOUR

## Ameen

I'll take it all."

"Are you sure that you can put the last three years behind us and focus on what we need to do to secure our future?"

"I need to be asking you that question."

"Antonio, just answer the question."

I looked into Shawnay's brown eyes and remembered the love and the pain. The scales of justice are sometimes unbalanced as are the scales of love and forgiveness. I decided right then before I said a word to put all the good times on the scale and weigh them against the last three years. It didn't take long for me to conclude that the good outweighed the bad. Everything that I hoped for since coming to prison was finally coming to fruition. But winning my appeal and living without Shawnay wouldn't be living at all. "Yeah, I'm sure."

"I can't believe that so much blood has been spilled all because I got weak and slept with Khadafi. I feel so bad inside because at the end of the day, I am the cause of it all."

"Didn't you just ask me whether I can put the past behind us and focus on what we need to do to secure our future?"

"Yeah, that's what I said, but—"

"But nothing. The blood that was shed was shed because Khadafi violated the sacrifice," I explained.

"The sacrifice?"

"Yeah. Khadafi killed a muthafucka in Texas, and I took the beef. I sacrificed myself so that him, Boo, and Umar could go home. That was the ultimate sacrifice that one man in the pen could make for another, and I made it with no questions asked. At the time I made that sacrifice, I had no regrets. Khadafi promised me that he'd take care of you."

"He told me all about it. Khadafi explained the whole situation to me, and he admitted that he was wrong for crossing the line. We were both wrong. I'ma be completely honest with you. In my mind, I actually told myself that you would rather I deal with somebody that you trusted, accepted as a friend. I guess that's how I allowed the situation to go on for so long. That's why I was so caught off guard by the dude with the beard showing up at the door. That's crazy, huh? I thought that I wasn't doing anything wrong, but at the same time I was doing everything I could to keep the relationship a secret from you. After I knew that you knew, I spent a lot of time hating you. But then over time, I tried to put myself in your shoes and understand how I must've made you feel. I wanted to talk to you to ask you why and to try and get some understanding, but trepidation and stubbornness kept me silent. And the fact that I believe you and I are connected so deeply lets me know that those same things kept you silent, too. For the last couple months, somebody has been calling my job and not saying anything when I pick up. That's been you, hasn't it?"

I felt like I'd been busted with my hand in the cookie jar by my mother. "Yeah."

"I knew it was you. I just never had the nerve to ask if it was you."

"I just wanted to hear your voice. Hearing your voice gave me hope that one day we'd be together again."

"Well, here we are and here we will be—together. I'm glad you held onto some hope. I never completely lost faith in us either, now. But that's neither here nor there. Hopefully, after today we can leave all that stuff behind us. With that said, what's going on with you now?"

"They still got me in the hole down Beaumont, even though I beat the murder beef in Texas. They wrote me a shot and that shot is gonna get me sent to ADX if I happen to lose this appeal—"

"You gon' win it," Shawnay said convincingly.

"Insha'Allah. It looks good though, according to Rudy." But anyway, Rudy explained to me how my trial attorney made several mistakes, and the fact that, that attorney was ineffective for not discovering sealed documents that would have helped me in courts is grounds for a reversal. The dude that testified against me—"

"Your friend, Eric Frazier?"

"Right. He was under investigation for his own charges, that's why he gave me up. To help himself on his charges. The government took the matter in front of the judge ex parte, and the judge placed it under seal. My attorney never knew about the ex parte meeting, but the document was in my jacket. She never discovered it. They violated my right to confront witnesses against me. So now, I'm just waiting for the appeals court to either reverse my conviction or gimme a new trial."

"I believe in my heart that things are gonna work out for you. I need them to, and your daughters need them to. We need you."

*******

"Lay back for me, Mr. Felder, and open your jumper. Better yet—" The pretty medical intern that resembled Brittany Spears went to the door and peeped outside. She called to the CO waiting in the hall. "I need you to uncuff him

267

so that I can get to this nasty wound on his side, please?" The CO looked over at me and I smiled.

"I'ma take these cuffs off, Felder. Don't start no shit and there won't be none. You feel me?"

"Ain't nobody gon' do nothing to your scared ass, Walker. You good. Go 'head and take 'em off so that I can get this wound cleaned."

The CO took off my cuffs and the intern cleaned me up. I winced in pain the whole time, but we got it done. Khadafi had caught me with a pretty good shot about two-inches away from my left kidney. Every time I looked down and saw the stitches, I got mad. Any other time I would have been plotting my revenge, but not now. Before leaving the visiting hall yesterday, I gave Shawnay my word that I would let the beef between me and Khadafi go. For now.

"There you go, Mr. Felder. You're as good as new. No more knife fights in the hallway, though, okay?"

"You got that, doc. No more knife fights."

Early the next morning, my cell door popped and in walked Lieutenant Worthy. He had a smile on his face like the cat that ate the canary. "What's up, Worthy?" I asked as I got up out the bunk.

Worthy pulled from behind his back a one page document and handed it to me.

I looked at it like it was a poisonous snake. "What's this?"

"Read it, nigga."

I read the document and goose bumps ran up and down my body. I couldn't believe it. Was I dreaming? In my hand was the document that I had dreamed of for almost twelve years. In my hand was my freedom. I wanted to cry. I wanted to sing. I wanted to dance.

"You did it, Tonio. You made it. You almost crashed out by knife fighting in the hall, but you did it. I knew I should've kept you down here in South One in the first place. But either way, you made it out. Immediate release. I'm happier than a muthafucka for you. Before you left and went to open pop', you and me was talkin' about pussy and all that, and now you get to get some with me. That's big. Get your shit—whatever you wanna take with you and come on. I'ma take you down R&D in a minute. But first, you can go and get on the phone and call your peoples."

I heard every word that Worthy said, but I didn't hear him because I was somewhere else. Suddenly, I was back in Beaumont, in my cell. It was the day that I got the letter from Rudy telling me that I was coming back to DC and that my appeal looked good. It was that day that I started to truly believe that I would be free one day. I thought about the K-Jon song that I sang that day and danced around the cell. The day that I felt like Puffy dancing in the rain on that "Missing You" video. That day was the first day that I allowed myself to dance since I'd come to prison. I was somewhere out there on the ocean and my ship had finally come. In the office upstairs, I sat at the desk with my heart pounding. I needed to make one call before I offered my prayer and thanked Allah for letting me go free. I dialed Shawnay at work.

"Virginia Hospital Center. This is Shawnay Dickerson speaking . . ."

"Shawnay, it's official, baby. I just got the paperwork today."

"Okay, so they're giving you a new trial, right?"

"Naw, the witness that told on me in the first trial is dead, so the government decided that they don't wanna retry me. I'm coming home—"

"When?" Shawnay asked, unable to contain her happiness.

"Right now. I'm about to walk out the door in a few minutes."

"Stay right there. I'm coming to get you."

# Chapter Forty-five

## Lil Cee

*February 2012*

O ne year later . . .
DC MAN TO START TRIAL TOMORROW FOR A
DOUBLE MURDER
A local man believed by authorities to be responsible for over thirty-six murders in and around the greater Washington, DC area will begin trial tomorrow morning at the DC Superior Courthouse. Thirty-five-year-old Luther Antwan Fuller of Southeast DC, is charged with the January 2011 murders of Devon Harris and Gregory Lamont Strong. Strong and Harris's murders were the second and third murders of the New Year in 2011. Well known defense attorney Bernard Grimes calls the upcoming trial 'alarming and teeming with insufficient evidence.' "This is 2012, an election year and not just for Barack Obama, but also for key members of Congress who rely on local support from the City Council and Mayor of DC. Living in Washington, DC makes an arrest and trial like this seem political. The thinking is, How can we be the epicenter of global politics, when we can't control crime in our own backyard? This thinking has created a widespread paranoia and has resulted in the public lynching of my client."

Law enforcement officials disagree. "Luther Fuller is directly associated with and responsible for over thirty-six

271

murders that we know of. Due to our interagency collaborative efforts, we were able to find a witness courageous enough to come forward and identify Mr. Fuller as the gunman responsible for two homicides in 2011. Homicide and the violent crimes branch in conjunction with the Metropolitan Police Department are still actively investigating Luther Fuller as a suspect in the Canal Street murders of 2010, the Capers Recreation massacre of 2010, and the Omni Shoreham Hotel parking lot killings. We are dedicated to bringing Luther Fuller and all of his accomplices to justice," Police Captain Greg Dunlap said.

"Luther Fuller, who will wear an electric shock belt as a security precaution to trial, has pleaded not guilty to all charges and denied all unindicted allegations."

Closing the Metro Section of the Washington Post newspaper, I threw the paper across the room. I didn't want Khadafi in prison. I needed him in the streets. It was bad enough that I couldn't catch Ameen because he was in prison. If Khadafi lost in trial, I would lose my last shot to kill him.

I stood up and walked up the hall to my bedroom. I cracked the door and looked in on Kia as she slept, and the baby, Charity, named after my dead sister, lying next to her in our bed. They were both sleeping peacefully. After the birth of my daughter, now six months old, I thought that I had exorcized my demons and got Khadafi and my thirst for retribution out of my system. But that didn't happen. Playing with my daughter only made me think more and more about my mother, who would never see her, and my little sister, who would never play with her. I knew that Kia recognized my errant mood swings and knew exactly what was bothering me. But after that night we argued about my desire to go back to DC to kill Khadafi, she never again mentioned a word to me about the subject. And neither did I, although I never forgot her words to me: "If you go back to DC he's gonna kill you. I saw it in my dreams." I quietly closed the bedroom door and walked back to the living room. I pulled the envelope containing all my personal bank info, a last will and testament, and a letter inside of it and placed it on the table where I knew Kia would be sure to find it. I was sneaking out of the apartment in the middle of the night like a petty thief in the dark, but it was the best way to avoid the dramatic scene that was sure to happen if I left in any other way. I planned to go to DC and look for the best opportunity to avenge the deaths of my mother and sister. Vengeance consumed me. And that would never change. Kia couldn't and wouldn't understand my situation. Well, one day she would. When I got back, it would be a better life for us all. I checked my pocket for my money and plane ticket. They were both there. I picked up my overnight bag and walked over to the door. I stopped and whispered, "I love you, Kia. I love you, Charity." Then without looking back, I left the apartment. Destination: Washington, DC.

# CHAPTER FORTY-SIX
## Khadafi

I t's four a.m. and my lover won't answer/he's probably somewhere with a dancer/sipping champagne while I'm in his bed/it's four a.m. and I think I might lose it/ . . ."

"That new Melanie Fiona joint like that, ain't it, slim?"

I snapped out of my reverie and looked to my right at the dude sitting beside me on the court bus. His name was Mark 'Blue Black' Harris, and he was supposed to start trial on a murder charge today, too. "Four a.m., huh? Yeah, that joint a bad muthafucka. I been trippin' off the fact that they be playing the curse word part on the radio."

"Slim, that ain't shit. They play all kinds of goofy shit on the radio now. But slim, I'm on that bitch."

"Who?" I asked.

"Melanie Fiona. That bitch bad as shit. Long hair, golden brown complexion, pretty toes. I love her. " Blue Black suddenly slapped his forehead with his hand. Then he exhaled loudly. "This trial got me stressed out. All them muthafuckin' rats tellin' on a muthafucka."

"I know what you mean, cuz. I been like that for months now. The government indicted me on a double joint and never even revealed who my witness is. I been tryna figure out who it could possibly be."

"But ain't that against the law? They gotta disclose certain shit in the discovery and under Brady."

274

"They got some new laws on the books then, because I gotta witness against me and don't know who it is."

********

In the holding cage behind the courtroom, I was just slipping my other shoe on when Bernie came in.

"Today is the big day, kiddo. You sure you wanna make this ready call to start trial?" he asked.

"Did they tell you who their witness is yet?"

"They have until the day before that person testifies to reveal an identity and the grand jury testimony. The decision is yours. We can prolong the trial until my investigators find out who it is and what they are saying, or we can go ahead with the trial. Your call."

"I been waiting a year to go to trial. I'm tired of waiting. If your investigators didn't find out who it is yet, chances are they won't. Let's go to trial."

"You're the boss, kiddo. I work for you. I'm ready to rumble. Are you?"

"Always."

********

"Your honor, I'd first like to say that the defense would like to concede to counts seven, eight, and nine, the misdemeanor counts. But we'd ask that this court defer the sentencing until after the trial," Bernard Grimes announced to the court.

"Motion granted," the judge, a slim, white, middle aged man replied. "We can move on to your other pretrial matter, counselor."

"Thank you, your honor. I submitted a motion to the court to vacate the CPWL count that pertains to the SUV in 2010. The government has not, nor can they prove that Luther Fuller ever possessed that handgun."

"Your honor," Anne Sullivan addressed the court as she stood, "a partial print that belonged to Luther Fuller was extracted from the butt of the .45 Sig Sauer handgun. So what we do know is that he possessed that handgun. We just don't know when."

The argument went back and forth between my lawyer and the prosecutor, until finally the judge decided that he'd heard enough. The prosecutor mentioned the $184 thousand that was found in cereal boxes inside the Infiniti. They wanted to produce Alex Tarif, the owner of Auto Source, who gave them sworn statements that I paid cash for two Range Rovers and the Infiniti. The judge ruled that the evidence was insufficient. A partial print was not enough to convict me of possessing a handgun found in an empty SUV full of bullet holes. He dismissed the CPWL count of the indictment pertaining to the truck. That left only the two murder charges left to take to trial.

With all the pretrial issues out the way, it was time to pick the jury. After seating a jury, opening arguments began early the next morning. Then the government put on cops, crime scene investigators, the medical examiner, and a ballistics expert. Finally, the day arrived for the government to produce their star witness.

"Your honor, we'd like to ask for a continuance until tomorrow," the prosecutor said to the judge.

"A continuance for what reason, counselor?"

"Apparently, our witness is AWOL, your honor. We need to locate her. As we speak, officers are out and about trying to locate our witness. So we'd like to recess until tomorrow so that we can find the witness."

"Would you like for me to issue an arrest warrant for the witness, Ms. Sullivan?"

"If we cannot locate her by tomorrow, your honor. Yes, I would ask that you issue an arrest warrant. First, we'd like to locate the witness and find out why she isn't present. But I would like to mention for the record that our witness is very afraid of the defendant and fears for her safety."

"Your request for a recess until tomorrow is granted. Court will be adjourned until tomorrow at 9 a.m.," the judge said.

# CHAPTER FORTY-SEVEN
## Lil Cee

Talk about being in the right place at the right time. I just happened to be sitting at a table in the courthouse cafeteria when the prosecutor in Khadafi's trial and two other women entered and sat down across from me. The prosecutor, Anne Sullivan, was a short, white woman with no visible shape, dressed in a navy blue pinstriped pants suit and a pink shirt. Her hair was pulled into a bun, but it wasn't hard to see all the visible gray hairs peppered into the black. Frown lines creased her forehead and encircled her lips when she was irate, and at the moment she seemed to be irate.

"Emily, you promised me that you would have Latasha here every day and on time," the prosecutor bellowed as soon as they were seated next to a Hispanic looking woman dressed in pants, a thick cashmere sweater, and stylish black boots with a nice sized heel.

"It wasn't my fault, Anne. Latasha is a grown woman . . ."

"Don't give me that grown woman shit, Emily. We went over this one hundred times. We don't wanna look bad in front of this judge. Nobody pisses Lucan Posen off and stands a chance at winning in his courtroom. We promised the judge that we'd produce our key witness against Fuller yesterday. Do you know how humiliating that was to stand there and try to explain her absence to him?"

"Well, since you two are gonna talk about me as if I ain't even here, I might as well leave," the other lady said and rose. "Excuse me."

"And where are you going, Latasha?" Anne Sullivan queried. "That deal that we made with you can easily be taken back. If you've decided that you can't help us put Luther Fuller away forever, well, we can let him go and put your ass away. With all your priors, I'm certain that Judge Gilliam will see to it that you do hard time in a high security federal prison for women. Don't fuck with me, Latasha. I am the wrong cracka bitch to be trifled with. Now, sit your ass down and listen to me."

The woman I now knew to be the key government witness against Khadafi, stood where she was for a minute, as if locked into a mental struggle with herself. Then finally, she retook her seat.

"Now, you listen and you listen good . . ."

I pretended to be rifling through papers in my briefcase as I strained my ears to hear every word said. "Don't play games with me, Latasha. You knew that you were supposed to be here yesterday and Friday of last week," the prosecutor said. "We went—"

"I know what we went over, and yeah, I knew about the two days that I missed, but some shit is unavoidable. I'm a mother with two kids—" Latasha stated, but was cut off.

"I'm well aware of the fact that you are a mother. I was fully aware of that fact the day I agreed to not prosecute you in exchange for your testimony against Fuller. I am a mother, too, goddammit, and I know all about responsibility. You are the only living, breathing, witness against that goddamn monster we're trying to convict. I am—we are trying to make these streets a lot safer for your children and my children to walk on, play on, live on. Getting Fuller convicted for the murders of your boyfriend—"

"Baby's father. Greg was my youngest son's father." Latasha corrected her.

"Well, child's father. We need to get him convicted for Greg's murder and the murder of Devon Harris. We also have information that Luther Fuller killed Devon Harris's brother, Omar Harris a few years ago. This man is a killer that kills with no regard for life or limb. He has to be stopped. Now, do I have to put Emily Perez outside your house on a twenty-four hour basis to ensure that you uphold your part of our agreement?"

Latasha shook her head no.

"Good, now let's go over your testimony again. I'm putting you on the stand the first thing in the morning, right after the 911 dispatcher that talked to you after the murders that night."

Sitting at my table, now sipping on a Dr. Pepper soda and occasionally taking a bite of my turkey club sandwich, I listened to the woman's testimony. And it was incriminating. According to her, her baby's father, Greg Strong got a call from Khadafi on his cellphone about 7 p.m. that day. Khadafi told Strong that he would be by his house on Third Street later to drop off six pounds of weed, in which Strong was supposed to pay fifty-five hundred dollars. Sometime before 10 p.m., Khadafi called Strong again to say that he was on his way to see him. No more than fifteen minutes later, a horn blew and a call came in on Strong's cell phone. The caller was Khadafi. Before Strong could leave the house, gunshots erupted outside. Greg Strong ran upstairs to get his gun after screaming that somebody was robbing his man. Latasha begged Strong not to go outside, but he went anyway with her on his heels.

She stopped by the curb, but Strong proceeded out into the street and around the black Cadillac SUV. From her position, she could see Strong and another dude. The one she described as Khadafi. He raised a gun and shot Strong, and then he casually hopped into his truck and pulled off. "How did you know who Khadafi was?" the prosecutor asked. Khadafi had been to their house on Third Street before. Khadafi and Greg Strong were friends, and she even had pictures of them together to prove it. That was all I needed to hear. Periodically, I saw the Hispanic woman glance in my direction. Just from her posture and what I deduced from their conversation, I concluded that Emily Perez was a cop. I smiled to myself and finished my sandwich while thinking about my daughter and how much I missed her. I wasn't worried about the lady cop recognizing me from anywhere because I had gone through somewhat of a metamorphosis. All my hair was gone, replaced by a low cut Caesar. Light green contact lenses overshadowed my brown eyes. My eyebrows were trimmed down and barely noticeable. All my facial hair was gone, moustache and all. I rocked a pair of gold and wooden framed Armani glasses, and a mean all black Armani suit, white shirt, and a black silk tie. Armani loafers complemented my outfit. I looked like a prominent investment banker on Wall Street or a corporate lawyer. I looked like anything but a scorned vigilante murderer. Nobody would notice me.

I eavesdropped on a little more of the prosecutor's conversation with her star witness before finally gathering my trash, dropping it in a trash receptacle, and leaving.

Having already been at the court building for days, I went back to the courtroom of Judge Lucan Posen and lounged outside as if talking on my cell phone. It didn't take long for the trio of women to appear. As I stared in their direction, my mind was already figuring out how I could do what I needed to do.

After changing into another set of clothes, street clothes that were less conspicuous, I stood outside and waited for the government's star witness to emerge from the court building. At some point she did, accompanied by the lady cop, Emily Perez. The good thing about downtown DC where the courthouses were located was the congestion of parked cars. So a lot of the streets surrounding the area were no parking zones. Therefore, people had to park at least three to four blocks away from the courts or use public transportation. I needed to see which method Latasha had used. My options were limited. I only had two that I could use to pull off my mission.

If Latasha used mass transportation, I could follow her somewhere, but if she got a ride to court from the lady cop, then I had to improvise. The closest train stations were Judiciary Square and Gallery Place. The direction that they walked led me to believe that either they were going to the Judiciary Square metro station, or they were headed to the parking lot area adjacent to the Mitch Snyder homeless shelter on Second and D Streets. Patiently, I walked with the throngs of people, lurking here and there, waiting to see what option I had to take. Silently, I cursed when both women walked right past the subway station. I was hoping the lady cop would walk the woman to the station and then turn around and leave. No such luck.

"Shit!" I muttered as the realization of my second option came quickly to mind. I didn't wanna do it but I had to. I couldn't let the woman testify against Khadafi. That was totally out of the question. At the corner of D Street, they turned the corner and just like I thought, headed for the parking lot on Second Street.

It was a little before 5 p.m. and already starting to get dark outside. The two women were so caught up in their conversation that they never looked back and saw me closing the gap between us. By the time they reached a dark blue Chevy Traverse crossover SUV, I was five feet behind them. The lady cop was the 'it' factor. I had to concentrate on her. As soon as both women were in the car, I ran up on the driver's side and opened fire on the lady cop. The window shattered as her blood and brain matter splattered on the passenger, Latasha. Quickly, with not a second to spare, I raced around the car and pulled the door open. The frightened woman screamed and tried to climb backward over the dead lady cop.

"You are the victim of circumstance, boo. You should've stayed outta this," I said before shooting the woman in the chest and face. By the time I left, she was a bloody mess. I ran back the way that I came and entered the subway. The city would be in an uproar, and the winter of 2012 was about to get as hot as July.

Anytime a cop gets killed in the city, it pisses off the entire law enforcement community, but to kill a cop two blocks from the police chief's office and the mayor's building, the entire city was about to be sick.

# CHAPTER FORTY-EIGHT
## Detective Tolliver

The mutilated, bullet riddled bodies of officer Emily Perez and Latasha Allison spoke to me. "This is all your fault," they said subliminally. And they were right. Their deaths were my fault. I was the one who personally involved Emily Perez and made my fight hers. She was just a patrolwoman with two years on the force. One who believed wholeheartedly in the notion of 'to protect and serve'. Now she was dead. Her and the woman that she talked into becoming a witness against Khadafi. I couldn't help but feel like an abject failure. I failed to protect them. Somehow, Khadafi reached out from behind the walls of DC jail and had his witness killed and a police officer with her. Muthafuckin' son of a bitch. The desire to keep Khadafi locked up faded, and the desire to kill him took a hold of me. But if I did that, I'd be no better than him.

I thought about Emily Perez's husband, Rueben, and instantly dreaded being the one who broke the news to him that his wife was dead. They had only been married for two years. They'd met in college and then pledged to love one another until death did they part. Well, that time was here and now. And then I thought about Latasha Allison's two kids, a beautiful, six-year-old girl and a bright eyed, precocious five-year-old son. Their mother was gone forever. It was sad. Suddenly, I couldn't breathe. I was starting to feel like a little boy trapped in a dark closet. I felt claustrophobic. I had to get away. Someone called my name, and I ignored him as I walked up the block to the corner of First and 'D' Streets.

"Shit! Muthafucka! Bitch! Fuck! Fuck! Fuck!" Stuffing both hands in my pants pockets I fought back tears. Emily Perez's death was hitting me hard, and there wasn't a damn thing I could do about it. No one had seen the killings. They'd only heard the gunshots. My cell phone vibrated on my hip. It was my office. "Hello?"

"Tolliver?" The caller was Captain Dunlap.

"Yeah, Cap, it's me," I replied.

"Get your ass over here to the triple nickel! Right now!"

The 'triple nickel' was police slang for the U.S. Attorney's office address, 555 Fourth Street, I was about two blocks away from the triple nickel, so I simply walked there. When I finally reached the conference room on the 4th floor of 555, I saw an assembly of powerful people already there. The mayor included.

"Nice of you to join us, Tolliver," Captain Dunlap announced as soon as I stepped through the door.

Both the chief and deputy chief of the DC police department were there, looking as if they were both constipated. "Is this the detective that we've been waiting for?" the deputy chief asked.

Dunlap nodded. "Tolliver, tell us how this was able to happen."

"Sir, with all due respect, I am not Speedy Gonzales. This tragedy just happened. I haven't had time to investigate."

"Isn't this—the Luther Fuller case. Your case?"

"Yeah, but there's no evidence to suggest that Luther Fuller . . ."

"No evidence to suggest?" This condescending question had come from District Attorney Don Silva. "Isn't Luther Fuller on trial?"

"He is."

"And wasn't Latasha Allison the only witness that the government had to testify against Luther Fuller?"

"She was."

"So don't give me that no evidence to suggest shit, detective." He turned and addressed a white man dressed in khakis and a button down. "This is Hue Christian, and he's the FBI liaison to the department. Mr. Christian, I need a list of all the people that have visited Luther Fuller at the jail in the last thirteen months. I also want DC jail's phone recordings in Fuller's unit. Go all the way back to when he first entered the jail, and lastly I need the good ole Federal Bureau of Investigation to go into Luther Fuller's cell tonight and get all of his mail. I need something that connects Luther Fuller to the murder of a government witness and police officer. Can you do that for me?"

"I can," Hue Christian responded, and then he got up and left the room.

"Mr. Tolliver." Dan Silva turned back to me. "What else do you have on Luther Fuller? What other crimes can we hit him with and attempt to prove?"

"We have a bag of guns that we fished out of the Potomac that we believe Khadafi—Luther Fuller used at the Canal Street—"

"Can we connect him to them?"

"Not really."

"That means no, right? Okay, what else do you have?"

"Nothing," I mumbled.

"Speak up please, Mr. . . . . Detective Tolliver."

"Nothing. I said nothing," I answered irritably.

"Has anyone notified the next of kin for the slain police woman?" the chief of police asked.

"I was on my way to do it when the captain called."

"Detective, please leave now and do so. Then contact the family of the witness."

"Latasha Allison."

"Huh?"

"Latasha Allison, sir. The witness's name was Latasha Allison. Mother of two."

"Well, since you investigated Luther Fuller and still don't have anything else to aid in his conviction, then I guess your talents would be better served notifying both victims' families. Get the fuck out," the chief ordered.

I picked up on the insult, but kept it moving anyway. I was always told to never argue with fools because people looking from a distance couldn't tell who was who.

********

"Baby, what's wrong?" Dollicia asked as she stood behind my chair and massaged my shoulders.

"Work. Work is wrong, Doll."

"I thought you enjoyed being a detective, Moe."

"This shit is starting to break through my tough veneer. Today, a friend of mine got killed. She was escorting a government witness on her own time. Can you believe that shit? Getting killed in the line of duty, but not even being on duty. Today was her off day, Doll. But she believed in the system and wanted to do her part in ensuring that a piece of shit named Luther Fuller went to prison. She went out and found a missing witness, then made sure that the witness appeared in court. Well, today somebody killed her. Her and the witness. And I feel fucked up about it. Doll, I'm fucked up because Emily Perez was only twenty-five years old and married only two fuckin' years. Tonight, I had to break the bad news to her husband, Reuben. Then I went to the witness's house, her name was Latasha. And guess what? A neighbor had her kids, and I found out that she had no family. Now her kids have no one.

"I asked Emily to get involved with my case. She talked Latasha into being a witness against Khadafi. When she got cold feet over the last year, I talked to her and told her that everything was gonna be okay. I promised her that nothing would happen, and she would be a hero. She believed me. And guess what? I couldn't keep my word. Everything didn't turn out right, and she never got to be a hero. She died a witness that never got the chance to become the woman who put away a monster. I couldn't protect her, and I lied to her. I got them both killed. I fucked up, Doll, and I feel fucked up."

Dollicia came around my chair to face me. "Baby, don't do this to yourself. You can't wallow in self pity and fault yourself. You have to pick yourself up off the ground, brush yourself off, and keep pushing. "You make a difference out in them streets. Don't let this one case break your resolve to make a difference." Then she kissed me.

I stood up and faced Dollicia. Looking straight into her eyes, I said, "It already has."

********

Two days later, I walked into courtroom 213 and took a seat in the gallery.

"Your honor," prosecutor Anne Sullivan proffered, "my office asked for the recess yesterday to regroup. Luther Fuller reached out from his jail cell and had the witness against him killed."

"Your honor." Bernard Grimes stood. "I object to what's being inferred here. For the record, I'd like to say that my client had nothing to do with the vicious and brutal attack on a DC police officer and a government witness. Need I remind this court that Mr. Fuller is and has been incarcerated at the DC jail since January of 2011. And may I also remind this court that the identity of the key government witness was withheld from the defense at the behest of the government. At no time was that identity revealed to myself or my client. So it is preposterous to infer that my client had anything to do with this tragedy. And your honor, I would also like to say for the record that the government and the FBI raided my client's cell yesterday without a proper warrant and extracted certain personal effects from him. I humbly ask for a declaration of mistrial. Or I would ask that you dismiss all charges against my client with prejudice with the understanding that if the government does procure some future evidence against my client that then the charges can be reintroduced. Thank you, your honor."

"Ms. Sullivan," Judge Lucas Posen leaned forward, "does the government plan to produce an eyewitness on this trial? Or does the government have any other egregious evidence that it plans to put before a jury in this case?"

"Your honor, if it pleases the court, can I please have a moment to confer with my office?"

"You may. I'll take a fifteen minute recess and then return here to proceed."

I sat in the gallery and watched the U.S. Marshal take Khadafi in the back of the courtroom to the holding cage. Several people in the gallery got up and left the courtroom, but not me. I stayed riveted to my seat. Didn't want to miss a thing.

"Your honor, I conferred with my office, and at this time we don't have anymore."

"Thank you, Ms. Sullivan. At this time I have no other choice but to dismiss the jury and declare a mistrial. So the verbal motion put forth to the court by defense counsel is granted. I hereby sentence Luther Fuller to 180 days in prison for the three misdemeanor counts on the indictment that was conceded to by the defense, pretrial. Mr. Fuller has been detained since January of 2011. That gives him thirteen months in custody. He will be credited for time already served. So it is hereby ordered that Luther Fuller be released from custody forthwith. Are there any other concerns that need to be addressed before this court?"

"No, your honor," said Anne Sullivan.

"No, your honor," answered Bernard Grimes.

"Well, this court is adjourned. Luther Fuller can be released from DC jail at some point today."

And just like that, the Luther Fuller saga ended, and he'd be a free man again, soon. It was time to go. I got up and walked through the courtroom. I saw everything from a different eye. The world seemed new to me. My rose colored glasses were gone, replaced now by real life contact lenses. Outside, I thought about all the victims in this case. I thought about Teresa Bryant, Black Woozie, David Carlton, Samantha, Sheree, and countless others. I thought about Ronesha Lake, Bayona Lake, and Devon Harris. There would be no justice for anyone. As I walked to my car, something dawned on me that I never realized before. I needed to add my name to that list, because I, too, was a victim.

********

I drove back to the precinct and climbed the stairs to my boss's office. Knocking before I entered, I stood in front of Captain Greg Dunlap. I reached in my pocket, extracted a piece of paper, and handed it to Smiley.

"What the hell is this, Tolliver? I hope it's something new in the Fuller case."

"It is something new, sir. It's my resignation. I quit."

# CHAPTER FORTY-NINE
## THE NEWS

C US FOX News, I am Maria Wilson reporting to you live from the DC Superior Courthouse. Any moment now we expect lawyers for the man that DC authorities believe is responsible for over thirty murders in the city, to come out of one of these doors behind us here. The trial that some Washingtonians have dubbed 'the trial of the decade' has come to an end. Sources close to the scene has told Fox News that Judge Lucas Rosen has dropped all charges against Luther Fuller and declared the trial a mistrial. On yesterday evening as most of you know, two women were brutally gunned down not three blocks from this very courthouse.

One of those women, Emily Perez, was a decorated patrolwoman with the Metropolitan Police Department, and the other was Latasha Allison, a thirty-three-year-old mother of two and the lone witness in the case against Luther Fuller. This situation is reminiscent of the early trials of the notorious late Mafioso, John Gotti. When authorities in New York tried to take him to trial, the witnesses would be killed or they'd simply disappear. And with no witnesses, there's no case. Nothing has been substantiated as of yet, but authorities here are vigorously investigating whether or not Luther Fuller was able to reach out from his cell at the DC jail and order the deaths of a DC cop and the witness against him. So folks, without a witness—eyewitness, that is—against Luther Fuller, the judge in this case ordered that all charges be dismissed and that Luther Fuller be freed.

"The trial—wait a minute—I'm receiving news that lawyers for the defense are coming out now, and we need to get a word with—Mr. Grimes. Attorney Grimes, can we have a word with you? The viewers would love to hear from you about this well publicized trial and how it all came to an end."

"Good afternoon, Maria . . . Today, an innocent man was vindicated. The US Attorney's Office overreached in this case. They never had a case against my client. The public outcry for—"

"Mr. Grimes, how do you respond to the allegations that your client ordered the death of the witness from the DC jail?"

"Those allegations are egregious and libel. They are baseless and false. They are indicative of the government's case—farfetched. The judge signed off on a written agreement with the government that allowed the identities of all witnesses to be kept secret until trial. As I understand, there were some security concerns.

"My client could not have ordered carryout food from DC jail, let alone the deaths of two people. The allegations are preposterous. Better suited for an urban novel of some kind."

"Mr. Grimes, Luther Fuller has been incarcerated at the jail for over a year now. When do you expect him to be released from custody?"

"I've been told that my client will be processed out of the DC jail and released by no later than 12 midnight tonight."

"Thank you for your time, Mr. Grimes. For those of you who are just tuning in, the top story of the day is the mistrial—"

# CHAPTER FIFTY
## Khadafi

The CO banged on my cell door. "I need to see in there." "I'm takin' a shit," I hollered back while staring at the white sheet tied to my bars to cover the door. The CO walked on by, but then he backtracked.

"Fuller, as soon as the count clears, I'ma pop your door. So get ready to bounce."

"A'ight, cuz."

After washing my hands and pulling up my jumper, I hit the wall to get the attention of my partner next door. "Young boy Tay? Young boy, you up over there?"

A few minutes later, Tay answered, "I'm up, slim. I had my walkman on. Damn, 102.3 crankin' like shit. What's up?"

"That faggie ass nigga, Miles just told me that I'm gone after the count clear. So I'ma pass you this phone and shit now before that geekin' ass nigga get to tryna shake my bags down. I'ma drop the bags off when they pop my door. You ready?"

"C'mon with it, slim."

I put my cell phone and charger in a pair of socks and passed it through the bars to Tay. Put that up first and then come back."

"I'm back, slim. My arm already out there."

"Yeah, I bet it is. Geekin' ass nigga," I joked. I passed Tay a wrapped up plastic sandwich bag filled with drugs, two

293

street knives, cigarettes, and my iPod Shuffle. "You gon' have to suitcase that plastic bag, cuz. You know how them K9s be all on a nigga's line."

"I got this, big boy."

"This is what I need you to do. Get them twenty grams to Pat across the hall. Tell him I said to give KD ten of them joints. Tell them I said to call the number in a few days. You got that?"

"Sure 'nough."

"The pills go to Lil Kamau, so he can take 'em back out the Feds with him. Send the weed to black Jontay."

"Jontay?"

"Yeah, black Jontay from 18th and M. He's around the corner in SE. One. You got the phone, cigarettes, iPod, and all the food and cosmetics. My number is already programmed into the phone, so call me in a few days. I'll be ready to hit y'all again then. I'ma go through our regular man."

"Who? The cat eyed dude?"

"Yeah. Other than that, you be cool, cuz, and get ready to rumble them people in June. They ain't got shit, so don't give 'em shit by running your mouth to these potential rat ass niggas about your case."

"No need for a sermon, preacher man. I know better. Ain't none of these niggas about to go home off a me."

Before I could say another word, my cell door opened.

"Bring your sheets and blankets with you, Fuller!" the CO shouted from the bubble. I dropped two trash bags full of food, cosmetics, and clothes in front of Tay's cell. I stripped my bunk bed and stood looking around the cell. I was finally getting out of the never ending nightmare known as the DC jail. Twelve months, thirteen days and some hours, that's about as long as I've ever stayed here. A year and some change. And I'd lost a lot in the last year. Losing Kemie had been the most devastating thing that ever happened to me since my mother and uncle died. I didn't think that I would get up from that knock down, but I did. Saved by the bell. Marnie and my children. I lost my father too. Luther Fuller Senior had died sitting in a chair in his backyard. He'd had a massive heart attack. I didn't shed a tear for him.

But I did shed a tear for Esha and Dawn. They were my home girls and didn't deserve what happened to them. Word was out that TJ killed them both. The cops connected TJ to Dawn's murder because of the gun he had on his waist the day Bay One killed him. They also connected TJ to a rack of other unsolved murders because he had a rack of guns in his apartment that had bodies on them. LaLa's body had finally been found, bloated and decomposed somewhere near the Chesapeake Bay. I'd also lost contact with Shawnay, but it was expected after Ameen won his appeal and went home.

It didn't take a rocket scientist to figure out that they would get back together. I knew that the day Marnie told me that Shawnay was going to visit Ameen. So other than my link to my son, all I'd really lost was Kemie and some blood. And this too shall pass, was something that Marnie always told me to keep me strong. And it did just that. In conjunction with my faith in Allah, I knew I'd make it. I knew I'd survive.

Although I had always felt like that. I could remember a time when I didn't expect to live long. "I'ma outlaw, boo . . . I live by the gun . . . I'll never marry and I'll never have kids . . ."

I stood in the middle of my cell and smiled. Somebody had killed the only witness that the government had against me. She turned out to be Strong's girlfriend named Latasha Allison. Maybe she had told on another muthafucka, that's why somebody crushed her hot ass.

I still had money saved up so I could start a new life and I still had my kids. Thoughts of my daughter, Khadaja always gave me a renewed sense of being. For the first time in my life, I wanted to live, to grow and to be a father. Marnie had given me a beautiful little girl who looked just like her daddy, and I loved her more than life.

"Fuller! Let's go! Before I lock you in that cell. Let's go!" the CO shouted.

Dudes on the tier called my name and I said my goodbyes. Then I walked down the tier to the sally port and to freedom.

\*\*\*\*\*\*\*\*

"Drop them sheets and shit in that orange basket over by the wall. Then come back." I did as I was told. The CO asked for my name and DC number.

"Luther Fuller. 283751."

The R&D door buzzed open. "Go on through. Stop at the window and pick up your release clothes."

Thirty minutes later, I was processed out and dressed in black Yves Saint Laurent high top tennis shoes and a matching belt. A Dungeons & Dragons skull imprinted hoodie, a North Face ski vest, and a Solbiato pull down skull cap.

"When you get out that door," another CO explained, "walk over to the big gate that the court bus comes through. The officer in the tower will open the gate, ask you for your name, DC number, birthdate, and social security number. That's to verify that you are in fact you. After that, he'll open the second gate and you're home free. Good luck."

I stepped out into the brisk February night air, and the wind took my breath away. Zipping my vest up further to my neck, I walked to the first gate. A minute later it opened.

"Full name, DC number, date of birth, and social," the CO shouted down from the tower.

From inside the gate, I could see the officers' parking lot, the cemetery directly across the street, and a black Cadillac Escalade with the hazard lights on and the engine running. I smiled. "Luther Antwan Fuller. 283751, 7-16-83 and my social is 577-87-3377."

A few minutes later, the second gate opened. Before I could get five feet, Marnie jumped out of the truck, ran, and leapt into my arms. She showered me with kisses.

"Baby, I love you! I love you! I love you!" Marnie repeated as she held me tight.

"I already know. And I love you back, back, back, back. Where's the baby?"

"At my mother's. Ms. Tawana knows that we need to be alone tonight. You can spend all day tomorrow with her, but tonight you belong to me."

We walked back to the Escalade arm in arm until Marnie hopped into the driver's seat. I walked around to the passenger side and grabbed the door handle. Looking at Marnie through the rolled down window, I saw the look on her face go from joy to confusion to fright.

Then the barrel of a gun kissed the back of my head and I knew that it was over. I had done too much wrong in my life to just walk away like that. Knowing that my time had come, all I could do was close my eyes and shake my head. Being on the business end of a loaded gun wasn't fun at all.

"Did you really think I was gonna just go away and never come back for you? Did you think that you were gonna just walk away from here and never look back? Never pay the piper? I've been waiting for this day for almost four years. It's been a long time coming, but it's finally here. This—"

I recognized the voice immediately. How could I ever forget it. Although I never really counted Lil Cee out, I never expected him to be outside the jail waiting for me. All I could think about was the book Caught 'Em Slippin', because Lil Cee had done just that, caught me slippin'. Tears formed in Marnie's eyes as she sat in the truck in disbelief, slowly shaking her head no. As bad as I wanted to live, I refused to beg for mercy. After all the lives I'd taken, I had no right to be spared. My pride would never let me give anybody the satisfaction of hearing me beg, or see me cry. Instead of going out like a bitch, I embraced the moment. I mouthed the words 'I love you' to Marnie and then said aloud, "What's taking you so long? Go 'head and kill me."

Then I heard a sound no louder than a cough. I expected some type of pain but felt none. I heard a soft thump and the sound of metal hitting concrete. I expected the world to go dark to me, but as I opened my eyes, the bright lights installed on the walls surrounding DC jail's parking lot shone bright in my eyes. Slowly, I turned and saw Lil Cee's body sprawled out on the ground. His hat had been knocked off his head by the bullet that splattered his brains all over the side of the Escalade. I noticed his hair and facial hair were gone, but his identity was unmistakable. It was Lil Cee. But who—? How? Out of the shadows of the brick wall that surrounded the Congressional Cemetery, stepped Ameen. Dressed in all black, he held a big ass handgun with a perforated cylinder sound suppressor attached to it. I remembered the last time I'd seen Ameen, the day of our knife fight.

"What's up, ock? Surprised to see me, huh?"

*To be continued ...*

# ANTHONY FIELDS

# STUDY GROUP QUESTIONS

1. Were you expecting a confrontation between Ameen and Khadafi in the beginning of the book?

2. Were you disappointed to find out that Shawnay was dreaming that Ameen was home?

3. Who was the character that you most identified with?

4. Did you hate TJ the entire story?

5. Did Ameen's character get too many good breaks?

6. Should Lil Cee have moved on with his life and forgot about Khadafi?

7. Did Khadafi escape death too many times?

8. Was Marnie stupid for loving Khadafi so much?

9. Were you surprised to learn that Marnie didn't shoot Kemie?

10. Were you surprised to learn that Bean was behind the deaths of TJ's family?

11. Should TJ have killed Esha? What about Dawn?

12. Were you sad to learn that Kemie died? Should she have lived and ended up with Khadafi at the end?

13. Was Bay One wrong for killing TJ?

14. Did the story end how you expected it to? Was it predictable?

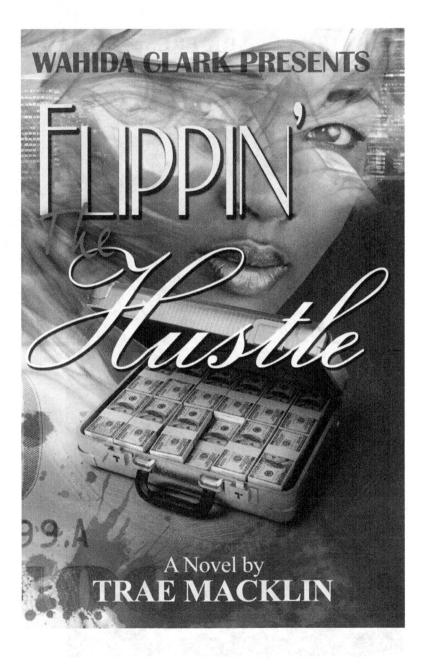

WAHIDA CLARK PRESENTS

# FLIPPIN'
## *Hustle*

A Novel by
## TRAE MACKLIN

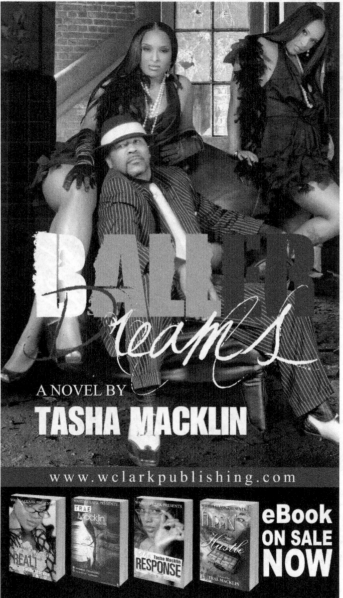

New York Times Bestselling Author of *Justify My Thug*

CASH MONEY CONTENT

# HONOR Thy THUG

## WAHIDA CLARK

WAHIDA CLARK PRESENTS

*The Devil's* GAME

A NOVEL

SHAWN 'JIHAD' TRUMP

got art?

f NUANCEART    @NUANCE_ART    NUANCEART@GMAIL.COM

www.acreativenuance.com

got art?

f NUANCEART    @NUANCE_ART    NUANCEART@GMAIL.COM